TRAFFIC

Featuring Amelia Barton of the National Crime Agency

Book 1

Nicky Downes

Traffic
© 2019, **Nicky Downes**
Self-published
nicjaydownes@gmail.com

Other works by the same author:

Bat Girl

Available on Amazon.

Prologue

Slung against the wall of the truck lay the body of a woman with crimson hair - hair that was naturally blonde, but was now a deep, bloody red where her head had ricocheted against the metal side bars. Her PVC jacket hung off one shoulder revealing a rose tattoo and the discoloured strap of a vest top. Her black jeans were ripped and stained. She wore no bra. Jake recognised Elena. He slammed his fist into the side of the van.

Could this be down to him?

Chapter 1

The Van

It was bad enough having to drive on the motorway, something DI Amelia Barton had avoided as much as possible since Joe died, but only being able to see the blurred tail-light from the vehicle in front made her heart race.

Jake pointed to the hard shoulder. 'It's just up ahead. The black van.'

She wished he'd pointed this out earlier. The last thing she wanted to do was skid across two lines of traffic. She indicated and went for it, ignoring the horn from the vehicle in the lane next to her, just managing to pull up successfully behind the van.

'I'm sorry, we're about to close a lane.' A uniformed police officer had obviously seen her reckless driving. Amelia tried not to blush. The officer continued to shout over the sound of the passing traffic. 'The van was involved in a collision. The driver's run off. We heard some voices from the back. Women's voices, which is why we've contacted you. They said they were being held against their will. We can't get into the back of the van until the motorway lane's closed. It's too dangerous.'

They'd been walking towards the van as he spoke. Rainwater had pooled all along the hard shoulder and every passing lorry sent out another huge spray. Amelia shook her foot, regretting wearing court shoes.

Before reaching the van, she introduced herself to the traffic cop. 'I'm DI Amelia Barton. This is DS Jake Faris.' She pointed to Jake, who was holding his jacket above his head to protect his hair. 'Haven't you even opened the back door? They must be terrified. Do you even know the extent of their injuries?'

'That's the thing, they say they're fine. There's large boxes all around them, which must have protected them. They're lucky.'

Lucky was not the word she would use. She knew what happened to women trafficked in stuffy, windowless vans.

She needed to free them as quickly as possible.

Finally, she saw the blurry, blue lights and heard the sirens of three approaching police cars. They were slowing each line of traffic until they could come to a stop, block every car behind them and lay out the cones to close the lanes. Amelia didn't wait to be told they were ready. She took a crowbar from a young PC and forced open the back doors of the van.

She couldn't see the women at first, just the large, brown boxes. One of the boxes flew from the van next to her shoulder. She heard the splash behind her as it hit a puddle. A tall, blonde woman stared down at her. 'You going to get us out, or what?' she screeched.

Ten women were removed from the van. They mostly followed the police without complaint, looking at the floor, oblivious to the rain, silent, all except for the tall, blonde woman, who later gave her name as Elena Tereshkova. She had fought the police as they had helped her from the van, kicking, screaming, scratching and biting. 'Let me go, you bastards!' she shrieked.

It was only when Elena moved towards Amelia that she stood still and stopped wailing. Then she spat at her, splattering her cheek with warm, sticky mucus. 'And you, you bitch. You can go fuck yourself.'

The banshee laughed. Amelia wiped her face with the sleeve of her jacket, refusing to show any outward emotion. This was the one thing Amelia hated. She could be slapped, punched, anything – but spit in her face was the absolute worst. It was such an intimate, repulsive act that it made her sick to the stomach.

'The driver's long gone. There's blood in the front of the van. They're getting the dogs out.' Jake was squinting, the rain dripping from his chin.

Amelia's main concern was the women. They would be driven to the hostel, Poppy's Place, where they would be interviewed in the morning when they'd had the chance to get warm and dry.

'Get some basic details and I'll meet you back at the office,' Amelia said, dismissing Jake. 'Siobhan will get them settled and they'll be more talkative tomorrow.'

Amelia had often been criticised for her tactics. Even Jake sometimes questioned the lack of speed with which she approached the task of gathering evidence, but Amelia had worked with abused women in the sex crimes unit. She knew that, if they were rushed, didn't trust you or were uncomfortable in any way, they would clam up.

An hour later, Amelia was back at her desk. She had received from Jake and the local force a photograph of each woman with some scant background details about them. Glancing at the photographs, it was hard to move past the women's same dead eyes. Their stories reflected back at her. Each had experienced horror, adding to the bottomless pool of despair.

Amelia stopped herself thinking about the trafficked women for a moment, picked up her phone and called her mother. 'I'm going to be late. You may as well put the girls to bed. Can I just say goodnight to them?'

Her mother tutted and said, 'The girls you pick up at work mean more to you than your own two.'

Amelia ran her hand through her auburn hair, pulling out imagined knots as she did so. She'd lost count of how many bedtimes she'd missed, but the girls meant everything to her. She began to tell her mother just how unfair she was being when Caitlyn, her youngest came to the phone and said, 'Hi, Mummy. Becky just called me an idiot.'

'You're not an idiot.'

'I don't know my six times table and we've got a test tomorrow.'

'Do you know your threes?'

''Course I do, we did the threes two weeks ago,'

'Can you double?'

'Up to 100. I'm good at doubling.'

'Double your threes and you'll get your sixes.'

'Really? Are you sure?'

'Yes. Try it.'

'Ok, 'night, Mummy. Love you to the moon and back.'

Then it was Becky's turn.

''Night, Mum.'

'Have you done your homework?'

'Yes.'

'All of it?'

'Yes.'

''Night, then. Love you.' Her eldest daughter had already put down the phone. Every parent must get to the point when their teenage kids detest them, but it was killing her.

Straight back to the photographs. The tall blonde, Elena Tereshkova… what was her story? The interviews would have to wait until the morning. At least the majority of the questions were planned. Another hour or two and she could drive home.

She woke early the next day, finding herself right at the edge of the king-sized bed. Caitlyn was lying diagonally with her feet pressed against Amelia's pyjama-covered thighs. She could hear her daughter's soft breathing. Amelia daren't move her. She'd rather lie here uncomfortable for a few moments. She used to love the weekends when Joe, her husband, had been alive. Both girls were much younger then and would race into the bedroom at the crack of dawn for an early morning cuddle. In fact, they had bought this king size bed to accommodate them.

She covered her head with the pillow and moaned. Why did she still wake thinking of Joe? On the night of his death, she wasn't even supposed to be on car patrol, but a probationer needed road experience and so, as usual, she offered. An hour later, they received a call to attend a road traffic accident. It was a two-car collision. A lad in a souped-up racer had jumped a red light and ploughed straight into the side of another car. She walked right up to the carnage and saw the license plate, realising immediately that it was their estate. One day, maybe she would see her husband's face without the blood or his broken body crushed against the steering wheel.

Chapter 2

Poppy's Place

Siobhan Grady had opened the refuge, Poppy's Place, two years ago. Her daughter, Poppy, had been murdered by her pimp in 2010. Amelia considered Siobhan to be more than a colleague: her iron will to succeed brought admiration and, more importantly, trusted friendship.

Siobhan had begged and borrowed enough money to set up and staff the refuge for the first five years. It was open to any woman who wanted to leave prostitution. It had taken months for Amelia to convince Siobhan that this should be extended to trafficked women. Siobhan had received so many death threats in the first year of opening that she had a full-time bodyguard, whom she married months later. Ellie, Siobhan's wife, was now the security guard at the refuge. It was bad enough having pimps after her blood; she didn't want human traffickers too.

The second battle Amelia had with Siobhan concerned interviewing protocol. Amelia had wanted to use the Rape and Sexual Violence Suite at a local police station, but it had been vetoed by her misogynistic ex-DCI. He didn't want rape victims at the Blue Sky Centre having to share facilities with prostitutes. Amelia was saddened by this response. So was Siobhan – saddened and furious. Siobhan had even screamed abuse at DCI Martin when she had met him at a charity event. He'd just been even more adamant that the trafficked women couldn't use the suite. Siobhan had then reluctantly agreed that any interviews could take place in the lounge at the refuge.

Jake and Amelia arrived at Poppy's Place before the dew dried on its expansive lawn. Amelia got out of the car and announced their arrival into the intercom. Ellie asked to see Amelia's ID card despite the fact that she had been here hundreds of times. Amelia held it up to the camera and Ellie opened the heavy, cast iron gates that added extra security to the former children's home. It was ironic that the home had been run by a vile group of paedophiles who had recently been convicted. It was impressive though, in a dilapidated, stately home kind of way.

When Amelia and Jake entered the house by the kitchen door, they found Elena smoking at the large oak table that dominated the room. She looked up and sneered at Amelia. 'Look who it is,' she said between puffs.

'You're still here, then,' Amelia said, surprised that Elena hadn't walked out by now. The women could leave at any time. Neither Siobhan nor Amelia were the women's jailers.

Elena carried on smoking, flicking ash into a saucer. No one was allowed to smoke inside the refuge, but you could see why she was given dispensation. Not even Ellie would want to cross this woman.

'Anyway,' Elena added. 'I like the food. The company – not so much.'

Amelia agreed that the food was worth staying for. It was lovingly baked by a resident cook who went out of her way to provide for the cultural needs of the residents.

Amelia knew that this group of women were from Eastern Europe, mostly Poland and Slovakia. The interpreter, Kesia Trent, had arrived and was drinking coffee on the other side of the expansive kitchen, as far away from Elena as she could be. The girls spoke English reasonably well, which probably meant that they had been in the UK a while, being passed around, bought and sold by UK traffickers.

'I'd love a coffee, Jake,' Amelia said and sat down directly opposite Elena. Reaching into her bag, she took out a packet of menthol cigarettes and a lighter, then lit up, suppressing the urge to cough. She was one of those rare smokers who could have the odd one and then stop. It had come in handy over the years. Some of her best friends hated her for it, particularly those who'd taken years trying to give up. She always laughed at them smoking those ridiculous vape things.

'I don't how you can smoke that shit,' Elena said, offering Amelia one of her cigarettes. Amelia declined. If she smoked one of Elena's strong nicotine sticks, then she really would cough.

Jake put the coffee down next to Amelia, gave her a disapproving look and went to sit with Kesia.

'You fucking him?' Elena asked, pulling down her vest top and revealing more cleavage and the hint of a tattoo above her right breast. 'I would.'

Amelia hoped she wasn't blushing. Pleasant as it was, fucking Jake was probably all it could be described as. They certainly weren't in a real relationship.

Elena got up without warning, walked around the table and emptied the entire saucer of nub ends into Amelia's lap. 'You might want to clear that up. We're not allowed to smoke in here.'

Jake stood up, weaving through the chairs to ward off imaginary punches. Amelia raised her hand to stop him. She could handle it. The kitchen door slammed as Elena left the room. Amelia brushed off her trousers, silently relieved it hadn't been the hot cup of coffee.

Twenty minutes later at the kitchen table, Jake and Amelia held a group briefing for all the women, explaining the interview process, their rights and the national referral mechanism. The clock was running for Amelia to produce a report on each of their cases, which would be sent to the Human Trafficking Reporting Centre. She guessed that, despite them originating from Europe, they'd entered the country illegally – a ridiculous anomaly that Amelia had raged about to anyone that would listen. Why weren't they just given leave to remain? If they'd come by plane with a valid passport then there'd be no issue. Instead, they were being punished for being trafficked, but her job was to prove that they had been illegally trafficked and convince them to help with police enquiries, even if that meant putting them at risk – a dilemma that had often kept her awake at night.

One woman sat apart from the others, running her hands through her long, black hair, separating strands and loosening knots. She was listening, but clearly getting more distressed as the briefing went on. While Jake spoke, Amelia saw that this woman was now pulling lumps out of her hair, winding her finger around each before violently wrenching them from her scalp. Siobhan had recently entered the room, so she tried to attract her attention, nodding towards the distressed woman. Siobhan noticed and pulled up a chair next to the woman, calmly taking the woman's hand in her own and starting to gently stroke it. Some of the trafficked women could not stomach any kind of physical touch, but they didn't feel intimidated by Siobhan. It was a gift she had. She could cut through all the shit to comfort these women. Amelia decided to interview this woman first, who she came to learn was called Jola, before getting her an emergency counselling referral.

In the living room, Amelia sat in one of the armchairs and Jake took the other, using the rickety, pine table next to him to support his notebook. Jola and Kesia were on the settee, Jola perched on the edge as though preparing to bolt. She looked uncomfortable, but at least she was no longer pulling out her hair.

'Do you mind if DS Faris stays in the room, Jola? He's only here to take notes,' Amelia asked. She had been advised on many occasions that it would be good practice to exclude Jake, as a male officer, from any contact with the women, but every time Amelia asked women that question they never seemed to mind. This was a relief as there weren't any female detective sergeants in her unit.

Jola didn't appear concerned. She now sat pressed against the back of the sofa, shivering. 'No,' she muttered.

'Tell me a little about yourself,' Amelia urged, leaning forward.

Jola didn't talk about her life before being trafficked at all. Her story was typical of many that Amelia had heard. She spoke in a mixture of English and Polish, which Kesia translated without missing a beat: 'My mother sold me for three hundred Euros. Three hundred Euros. That's all I'm worth to my mother. They came to the house. Three men. They offered my mother money. Who wouldn't think that this is odd? Only my stupid mother would think she was doing her daughter a favour.'

Amelia didn't speak. She sat not showing any emotion and

waited for Jola to continue.

'The first man raped me within five minutes from my home. He pinned me down in the back of the van. Then the second man. That's how they break you. My legs and arms were tied with plastic cable ties and the van stopped four more times to pick up women, but now I only had to watch. Each time we set off again, there was another woman sobbing. Until they stopped and went silent.'

Another pause. Jola was pulling her hair again. Kesia reached over and took her hand just like Siobhan had done earlier. 'It took us three days to get to the UK from Poland. I counted them. We changed vans many times – twelve times. Each driver took a turn with each of us. Maybe that's how they were being paid… and it was worse at night. They would drink and became more brutal.'

She looked straight at Amelia. 'I don't know how long I've been here in the UK. I've been moved many times. Always different nasty, cramped houses with one or two rooms with beds in. The men ring a number when they arrive, they choose which of us they want and take us to one of the rooms. As soon as it's done, we have to go back to the waiting room. It's just a grubby living room with a television in. We spend most of our time there. They gave us small bags of food to cook with. Natalia did all the cooking. She would sometimes ask for certain things like vegetables and get hit for it.' Then Jola stopped. 'I can't… I don't know what else to tell you.'

Amelia spoke for the first time. 'It's okay. We can stop here and take a break. There's no rush, Jola. Siobhan will speak to you this afternoon about medical help. Is that ok?'

Jola hoarsely whispered, 'Yes,' before leaving the room.

Kesia got up and paced the floor for a few minutes. 'Bastards.'

Kesia had worked with the National Crime Agency as a casual interpreter for a year. She spoke Polish, Czech and Slovakian. Her parents were Roma. Her mother was Polish Roma and her father Czech Roma. She'd recently married a police officer, which was unusual within her community. Even working for the police was unusual. Clearly, each woman got under her skin, just like Amelia.

There was a knock on the living room door. Jola opened the door and walked back in. 'I forgot to say. You've got Elena all wrong. She protected us. The men, our owners, beat us regularly. She stood up for us, so they beat her more. They tried to break her spirit. They never could. She kept saying – don't let the bastards get in your head.' Jola aggressively pointed to her forehead.

Jake and Kesia returned to the kitchen to eat lunch. Amelia let them go ahead. She needed time to collect her thoughts, particularly regarding Elena. If only they could get her onside. All the signs were that she was a leader, but there was still a sliver of vulnerability about her. Amelia brushed her hair to one side with her fingers before returning to her thoughts.

When she re-joined her team, Ellie was already eating at the table. She smiled when Amelia came in. There were various open sandwiches and a huge pan of soup on the sideboard. Amelia helped herself to some sandwiches and a bowl of soup, and sat down.

'Have all the women eaten?' she asked.

'Yes, except Elena. She's still outside. I saw her smoking by the lake earlier. No doubt she'll come back in when she's run out of fags.' Ellie replied. 'The doctor's arrived. Siobhan set up a room for her.'

Amelia looked across at Jake. He wasn't eating much, just picking the tomatoes and basil off the top of the bread. 'I'm wondering if we should halt our interviews until the doctor's finished?' she said.

His phone started buzzing on the table before he got the chance to answer. He stood up and left the room.

'He's quiet today,' Ellie said. Ellie was usually the quiet one. She would choose to eat away from the refuge residents. She always had one eye on the security cameras, which were relayed to a small room next to the kitchen. Despite having a large muscular frame, she had a soft, cheery face when she relaxed. If anyone tried to intimidate her, that would immediately change. Then everything about her – her voice, features, stance – became far more menacing and authoritative.

'Family stuff, I think,' Amelia replied, looking down at her food.

Jake had asked his estranged wife for a divorce the night before. He'd left her a few months ago, which had been hard enough, but this was a further step away from his son. With a vision of the child in her mind, Amelia twisted a length of her hair around a finger while dipping a spoon into the cooling soup. They had agreed certain rules in their relationship, the main ones being that their relationship would be kept secret and that they weren't having an actual relationship – just a physical one.

Jake returned a couple of minutes later. 'They've found a wallet in the van. They've got a name. Marcus Wright. They're going to pick him up now.'

Stupid idiot must have dropped it when he was trying to get away, thought Amelia. Hopefully, they would find him at home nursing his injuries. It was a miracle not more of the occupants of the van had been hurt yesterday. The driver had been showered with glass from the broken windscreen as a result of the van nudging the side of an articulated lorry. In the back of the vehicle, the boxes had largely protected the women, but nothing had protected the driver.

Amelia glanced at her phone on the table. No missed calls.

'They must've thought you were interviewing,' Jake said, noticing.

They often bypassed Amelia and went to Jake. They seemed to think she had the soft job — interviewing and working with the women, while they were all men together —gathering evidence and chasing suspects. It wouldn't be long before Jake joined that team, no doubt with a promotion, while his replacement would be a female DS with no experience of sex crimes. That's if they could get anyone, the recruitment to the NCA being at an all-time low.

'Let's carry on with the interviews,' Amelia said. She'd rather do that than go and join the circus chasing the low-end van driver.

After lunch, they interviewed Natalia, the youngest of the women.

Within an hour of arriving at the hostel, most of the women had discarded their clothes and accepted fresh clothes from the clothing bank that Siobhan made sure was regularly stocked. Natalia had chosen a pair of black jogging bottoms, a baggy red T-shirt and an enormous black cardigan that would have wrapped around her slender frame at least three times. She was clutching her knees, sitting as far back on the sofa as she could and biting the sleeves of the cardigan.

She looked much younger than she did yesterday. Now her face was clean, her smooth freckled, skin was evident. She had told the officers who found her that she was eighteen. Amelia wondered if this was true. It was odd that this young woman had taken on the role of cook. Odd, until she told her story.

'I lived with my granddad in Poland. I moved there when I

was thirteen. My mother was into drugs. Most of the time, she didn't know I was there. It started on the day I arrived at his house. The only time he wasn't hurting me was when I cooked for him. He liked sex, but he liked food more. I used to make huge pans of soup. I couldn't eat anything else.'

There was a woman Amelia had rescued three months ago... she could only eat soup and ice cream because the damage to her throat had been so extensive.

Natalia continued. 'He died on my seventeenth birthday. They said it was a heart attack. I didn't kill him... I could have... then my uncle took over. He hurt me more. But he decided he'd prefer the money. So, he sold me for five hundred euros.

'I've been bought and sold many times since.' She paused. 'I just switch myself off... except when I'm cooking. I like to cook.' Her eyes sparkled, and she smiled for the first time.

It was always a surprise how women who had survived the most awful circumstances would often just tell you what happened in a completely flat, monotone manner. They had no concept of the effect this had on those around them. Amelia showed no outward emotion, but inside she wanted to wrap this girl in her arms and take her home. Jake simply wrote down what she said, his pen shaking. Kesia was clearly fighting back the tears.

Natalia stopped talking. She yawned and ran her fingers through her short, blonde hair. 'Can I go now?' she asked.

'Yes. We can talk again tomorrow,' Amelia said.

When Natalia left the room, Amelia turned to Jake and said, 'We may as well call it a day. Leave them to their evening meal. We can start again in the morning.'

'Sure,' Jake said and closed his notebook, not looking directly at his boss.

There would be more to learn in later interviews. Amelia knew she wouldn't sleep tonight. She'd relive every one of these stories. They would play like a movie in her head in black and white, too vivid for colour. She thought about staying over with Jake. Maybe some physical comfort would help. It seemed to her that, the more women they saved, the less they discovered about the traffickers. The traffickers bought and sold so quickly. Their trails went cold before the force even tried to sniff them out. As Amelia left the living room, she shivered.

Kesia must have noticed, as she squeezed her shoulder. 'They're safe for now,' she said.

Leaving the house, Jake muttered, 'I want to speak to Elena.'

He didn't give Amelia the chance to reply. Instead, he left her on the terrace and went over to Elena, who was sitting on a bench facing the lake.

'Not sure that's a good idea,' Siobhan said, glancing towards the lake. Amelia jumped, not noticing Siobhan approach.

'The doctor's coming back tomorrow. She wants to admit Jola as a voluntary patient at Caludon Clinic. Jola won't agree. She wants to stay with the others. Can't say I blame her. All the women are in a terrible state, physically as well as mentally. There are the usual concerns about hepatitis and HIV, too. The results of their tests will be fast-tracked,' Siobhan added.

Amelia then turned to Siobhan, attempting to block out her anger with Jake. 'Thanks, Siobhan. We'll be back tomorrow, too.'

'Perhaps you need to keep him on a lead,' Siobhan suggested nodding towards her partner.

Jake had his arm across the back of the bench, not quite touching Elena's shoulder. Amelia could sense the anger rising from the pit of her stomach. She forced it down, swallowing hard and tried to hide the annoyance on her face as she turned back to Siobhan. 'Let's wait and see if he gets through to her.'

Siobhan smiled. 'Others may find you hard to read, Amelia, but not me.' She stroked Amelia's arm before returning to the house.

Am I that obvious? Amelia wondered.

Lighting a cigarette to calm herself, she sat on the topmost of the paved steps leading to the lawn. Jake knew he should never interview women alone. *What was he playing at?*

Ten minutes later, she was contemplating lighting another cigarette when Jake started walking back to the terrace. She stood up, not hiding her anger from him.

'Are you mad?' she demanded.

'She wasn't going to speak to you. I just used some of my charm,' he said.

'You spoke to her alone. Whatever she said won't be admissible. You know the score, Jake. You're a fucking idiot.' She felt like punching him, not clear where the source of her anger originated from. Was it his lack of respect for procedure or some deep-seated betrayal?

'I was just getting her onside. She said she's going to stick around and will be interviewed tomorrow.'

'She's probably playing you for the fool you are.'

'At least she didn't throw anything over me.'

She couldn't believe his arrogance. 'Take me home.'

The drive back was tense. Neither of them spoke for the vast majority of it. Then Jake's phone rang. He pressed a button on his dash and answered.

'What's up? Did you manage to arrest him?'

DS Will Maltby replied, 'Yes, he's in custody now. Your usual class of lowlife. Reckons one of his mates gave him fifty quid to drive from Birmingham to Coventry. He had no idea what was in the van and he says he was waiting for an address in Coventry to be texted to him when he arrived at the Ring Road. He reckoned he was just doing a mate a favour.'

Nothing new there and no doubt if they picked the mate up, the story would be similar.

'Do we have an address in Brum?' she asked.

'Yeah, but it's just a warehouse. No signs that the girls were there on initial inspection.'

Dead ends. But the investigation team would, no doubt, keep digging. Hopefully, they would find a link to the traffickers.

'Thanks, Will.' Jake hung up.

They were less than a mile away from Amelia's home. 'Do you fancy a drink?' she asked. She needed one and she didn't want to end the day angry.

This was a first, though. They'd never dated, never had a meal together that wasn't work, never seen a film or a play together. The only 'together' time was in bed. Colleagues did sometimes drink together, but Jake was no doubt aware that wasn't what she meant.

He glanced at her and smiled, the tension melting in a cool breeze. 'Sure.'

Amelia directed Jake to her local, unconcerned that they would be recognised or gossiped about as she rarely went there. They found a table by the window with a view of the canal, and Jake went to get her a gin and tonic. It was just after five and Amelia texted her mother to say she would be home in an hour. For once, hopefully, they could all have a meal together. Amelia smiled at the thought.

'Here.' Jake passed her the gin. She noticed he had a pint of a dark ale. Hopefully, he'd stick to one. The last thing she wanted was for him to be pulled over and have to explain that he'd taken his boss for a drink.

'This is nice,' Jake said. He stroked her thigh with one hand and supped his pint with the other.

Amelia moved away so they were no longer touching. 'What did Elena have to say?'

Jake screwed up his brow. 'Actually, we talked a lot about you.'

'What do you mean — me?'

'She asked if we were fucking. I told her to mind her own. She laughed and said she'd take that as a yes, then.'

'Are you completely mad?'

Jake laughed. 'You should see your face. Of course, that's not what happened. I just explained to her why we needed to know her story. I told her she could leave at any time. I even said I'd drive her wherever she needed to go if she did an interview first. She said she would. Happy now?'

'Okay, but you still shouldn't have done it. She could easily have compromised you.'

'I'm more concerned about your lack of trust. What the fuck's going on with you?'

Amelia drank some more gin, welcoming the warmth, before she changed the subject. 'The divorce, Jake. Why now? I mean it's not like we're a proper couple, is it?'

'Do you want us to be?'

Amelia blushed and wondered for a split second if she did. 'No' she said. 'I'm happy as we are.' No one else involved, particularly her children. She could box off the relationship without feeling or emotion. At least that's what she told herself.

Jake raised his eyebrows. 'I'm not doing it for us. I'm doing it for Charlotte. She needs to move on.'

They both sipped their drinks. Every time Amelia looked at Jake, he grinned back at her. He could be so infuriating. She wished she hadn't said she would go home. She didn't know what to think and wasn't sure why she was suddenly so unsure of Jake's motives, or her own for that matter. As soon as she finished her gin, she said, 'I can walk from here if you like.'

Jake stood up. 'Don't be daft. I'll give you a lift.'

He didn't take her straight home. There was a side road where they often pulled up. He did this without asking and kissed her before she could say anything. She returned the kiss enthusiastically. She stroked the side of his face as he sought the button on her trousers. She could feel herself getting more aroused.

She removed his hand with her own. 'We don't have time,' she sighed.

They stopped kissing then and withdrew to their seats, like boxers separating to their corners. Amelia flipped down the sunscreen and checked her make up. She spent the time covering her flushed cheeks, like masking bruises.

Jake waited until she had finished, then drove her the rest of the way home in silence. 'See you tomorrow at seven,' she said as she left the car.

She watched him drive away until she could no longer see the dim light from his car then went in. Caitlyn bounded up to her in the hall and grabbed her legs. Becky didn't look up from her homework.

Her mum said, 'I've made fish pie. It's almost ready.'

All thoughts of Jake were forgotten.

Chapter 3

Mariana and Lucia

The next day, Amelia and Jake drove back to Poppy's Place in silence, Amelia lost in her own thoughts. She'd had a difficult night with her nightmares consuming her.

'Come in, we're all in the kitchen,' Ellie answered as soon as Amelia pushed the button on the gate's intercom. No pleasantries, no asking for identification. This wasn't usual. Something had happened overnight.

Entering the kitchen with some trepidation, it was obvious that there were noticeable absences from the day before. 'We had visitors last night. A van drove up to the front gate and a group of the women decided to leave.' Siobhan shuffled, head down.

'Why didn't you ring the police?' Jake was looking at Ellie, accusing her of not carrying out her job properly.

Siobhan, without missing a beat answered, 'And what would she say? There's a van outside and the women want to leave? We're not their jailers, Jake, as you well know. They chose to leave. There was no evidence of coercion. They must have contacted the men for them to know they were here.'

'I can give you a recording of the van from the front gate camera. The men inside didn't hide their faces,' Ellie said.

Amelia nodded. Ellie got up and went to her office. Amelia turned to Siobhan. 'Which women have left?'

'Jola, Christina and Elena. They said that the men were Christina's brother and his friends. Before you ask, Jake, I didn't believe them, but I equally had no evidence they weren't who the women said they were,' answered Siobhan.

It was hard to believe, but it happened. Amelia had seen it many times with abused women. They often chose to stay with their abuser. It didn't matter that they had been regularly raped or abused. Elena was a shock, though. If Jola was to be believed, Elena had fought these men. Her confidence and spirit had not been completely destroyed. Why would she choose to leave with them? Was she still playing the role of protector?

'I need to speak to you alone in the office,' Siobhan said, looking directly at Amelia. This was an order. Amelia felt like she was back at school and had been caught smoking behind the science block again.

Siobhan's office was at the top of the house, in the eaves away from the hustle and bustle of the women's living space. Siobhan had clearly chosen it for the view. You could see for miles across the Warwickshire countryside at the perfect green squares of arable land punctuated by white, fluffy sheep. This was the back of the house. The view from the front was the edge of a Coventry housing estate, all concrete and pebbledash walls.

Siobhan had clearly slept on the sofa in here on occasion. A duvet was rolled up in the corner of the leather sofa. This was something that Amelia could empathise with. She regularly slept on the sofa at home so as not to disturb the rest of the house. She constantly wrestled with her demons as she had the most vivid nightmares that left her in a cold, anxious sweat. Her doctor had given her sleeping pills that she wouldn't take, scared she wouldn't wake if she was called to work. Her mother had offered to keep Amelia's phone with her at night, so she could wake her if necessary, but Amelia had got it into her head that this would be admitting defeat. It was also the only time she saw Joe's face, even if it was in horrific circumstances. She couldn't lose that.

Siobhan asked her to sit down. Amelia removed a pile of bills before sitting on a chair and did as she was told.

'I want you to know that this is a really difficult decision for us.' Amelia knew the 'us' meant Siobhan and Ellie. 'You and Jake, particularly Jake, are on borrowed time. I don't know why I ever agreed to let you work here. It's upsetting the other women, many of whom haven't had the best relationships with the police, as you know. We also want Poppy's Place to become women-only over the coming months –'

'I understand,' Amelia interrupted, and she did. She was surprised it hadn't been women-only from the start, like many other refuges for abused women. 'Do you want me to find another venue for the interviews?'

'Not yet. Complete these first.' Siobhan wasn't looking at Amelia, she was looking out of the window, biting her lip, clearly unsure if she should say what she wanted to.

Amelia said, 'I'll ask the local force to drive past as often as they can in case you have other visitors.'

Siobhan turned back to her. 'Amelia, I'm worried about you. Jake's not good for you. Maybe you need another partner.' There. She'd said it. She looked relieved.

'I don't see how that's any of your business.' Amelia stood up to leave, not wanting to hear anymore. Siobhan could have been referring to Jake as her colleague rather than her lover, but she wasn't going to listen to someone criticise her decisions in either case. She was an adult.

A scream broke the tension. 'You fucking bitch, you don't belong here!'

Something was kicking off downstairs. Amelia and Siobhan rushed down to the kitchen to find two women who had clearly been fighting being split up and dragged to opposite sides of the kitchen by Ellie and Jake. Kesia was standing by the sink looking horrified.

'She was looking at me like I'm scum!' The first woman to speak was one of Siobhan's regulars whom Amelia had met on a number of occasions. She came here every time her pimp chucked her out. He'd regularly tell her to go and live on the streets if she couldn't perform properly. Then he'd pick her up the next day, all apologetic.

Siobhan raised her hand. 'You know the rules, Hol. Any two incidences of fighting and you're banned. Consider yourself warned.'

Holly looked at the floor. 'She started it.'

The 'she' in question was Mariana, one of the newly arrived trafficked women, who now stood against the wall, checking her hair. One of her plaits had come loose in the fight. She didn't say anything to defend herself.

Amelia placed her hand close to Mariana's shoulders, directing her without touching. 'We'll be in the living room,' she said.

Mariana sat down, hunched in the corner of the sofa. Around her neck, she wore a small cross pendant, which she chewed.

'She's a whore. I'm not.' Marianna started to cry. 'She has a choice. Why would she do that? To herself? Her body?'

There was a box of tissues on the side table. Amelia passed her one. She wiped her eyes with it and held it tightly.

There was a knock at the door and Jake and Kesia entered the room.

'Mariana, do you mind if we do your first interview now?' Amelia asked as Jake and Kesia sat down.

'I know his name,' Mariana said, sniffing.

'Whose name?' asked Amelia.

'The boss. The main man. The one who caged us all,' Mariana screeched. 'I heard them talk about him – he's called The Devil.' She paused. 'I'm not joking. That's what they called him as they beat us. "We're doing this for The Devil." *D'ábel*, that's what they called him. *D'ábel.*'

Kesia confirmed that this was Czech for 'devil'.

'Mariana, let's be clear. Are you saying that the men who held you were Czech?' Amelia asked.

'No, some of them were Czech. When we were in Prague, they were Czech. I was homeless. They said they could get me a job as a cook or cleaner in a home for old people. They offered to take me for nothing, said I could pay them back when I'd earned some money. They said everyone gets paid well in England. It was easy money. I had nothing. I hadn't been able to find a job for months and my friends were getting fed up of me sleeping on their floors. So, I went with them. I was stupid… so stupid.'

She was biting her cross now. 'They took everything from me. I'd never had… a man. Never. I wanted to be married first. I wanted to have children. I… I had a child. The Devil took him.'

Mariana started sobbing, retching as if she couldn't breathe. Amelia stopped the interview and asked Jake to fetch Siobhan and the doctor, if she had arrived.

An hour later, Mariana had been seen by the doctor and been given a sedative. She was asleep in Siobhan's office so that Siobhan could keep an eye on her.

Amelia went into the garden for a cigarette. *A missing child. A baby.* Mariana could have been referring to an abortion. Amelia needed to speak to the doctor as soon as she was free.

Jake had followed Amelia on to the patio,

'Do you believe Mariana?' he asked.

'Yes, we've got no reason not to. Why, don't you?'

'I believe she's had her child stolen. I just meant the stuff about this devil. That's just, well, odd, and she's clearly religious. It could be in her head.'

'Jake, just leave me alone for a while. I need to think. Why don't you get on to Will and see if we or Europol have any intelligence about a trafficker known as The Devil or something similar? He might want to run it through ECRIS to see if anyone has a criminal record with that alias or similar sounding name.'

'Yes, boss.'

Amelia wasn't sure if he was being sarcastic. He was supposed to call her 'ma'am' but she'd vetoed that from the start. *I'm Amelia or DI Barton. I'm not the bloody queen.* She was going to say what she needed to, though.

'And, Jake – I've been thinking about how you were with Elena and the way you've been behaving lately. You can't charm your way into these women's lives. It's plain wrong. I'm going to ask that you're transferred. Siobhan doesn't want you at Poppy's Place, either. She wants it to be a women-only refuge.'

Amelia turned away from Jake and lit her cigarette. He was standing next to her and she waited for him to explode. Instead, she heard him walk away. She wasn't sure if that was worse.

When Amelia returned to the living room, Jake and Kesia were drinking coffee and laughing at something. When she saw Amelia, Kesia stopped laughing and blushed.

Amelia said, 'I think it might be an idea to interview one of the other Czech women. See if they can tell us more about the traffickers. Who do we have?'

Jake checked his notes. 'Lucia... no wait, she's Slovakian.'

Kesia said, '*Diabol*.'

'What?' said Amelia.

'*Diabol* is Slovak for "devil". It's very similar. A lot of Czech and Slovak words are similar.'

'What is it in Polish?' asked Amelia.

'*Diabel*. Again – it's similar.'

'So, he could be from any of these countries.'

'If he exists,' said Jake.

'Or Romanian… and Russian. The word's similar.' Kesia shivered visibly. 'If you're going to scare women of different nationalities, calling yourself The Devil would do it.'

'So, the actual name might not get us any nearer to finding the traffickers,' said Amelia. 'I want to pin down what nationality the majority of them were though. I'll fetch Lucia. Let's see what she can tell us.'

Lucia was a young woman with long, straight, black hair. She was stick-thin and hollow-cheeked. She talked so quickly that even Kesia could barely keep up. 'Have you found my sister? They took her. Have you found my sister? Her name is Nikola. You must know her. Where is she?'

'Your sister? I'm sorry…' Amelia said.

'My sister, Nikola. They took her, too. I haven't seen her in weeks. You must know… you must know where she is. Take me there… please.'

'Lucia, listen. My colleague, DS Faris, is going to phone our office. He will find out if we have found Nikola for you. What is her family name? Is it the same as yours?'

Kesia translated what Amelia said and Lucia's shoulders visibly drooped. 'It's Markova. Nikola Markova. You must have her. Maybe she's gone back to Slovakia. Maybe she's with my mother and five brothers.' Nikola then started speaking even more quickly to Kesia in, what seemed to Amelia, a completely different language. Kesia raised her hand to her own lips to get Lucia to stop speaking.

'Lucia is Roma. She has family here in England, in Peterborough, as well as in Slovakia. She couldn't say anything to them. The traffickers threatened to kill all of them if she ever spoke to them. Her sister was taken one night from the house they were last kept in. They never brought her back.'

Lucia spoke for the first time in English. 'Please… please, please find her.'

'Jake, ring Will, get him to check if we have a record for Nikola Markova. Oh, and get us some tea while you're there.'

Jake stood, shot a glance at Kesia and left the room.

Lucia looked more relaxed. She laid her head on Kesia's shoulder as if they'd known each other for years. She spoke to Kesia in what Amelia later learned was Romani. Amelia knew that finding this woman's sister was unlikely. She could be anywhere. She could be dead.

Jake returned with a tray of tea. 'One of our team of detectives is looking for a record of your sister. They will ring me back later, Lucia.'

'Thank you. Thank you so much,' Lucia lowered her head.

They sat and drank some of the tea. Amelia knew breaks were important; rushing could cause the women to clam up. It gave Lucia the time to compose herself ready to answer the next questions without feeling pressured. Jake fidgeted in his chair. Amelia shot him a glance.

'Lucia. Did any of the men who held you mention someone called The Devil?'

'The Devil?' Lucia stiffened.

Kesia whispered, '*Diabol*'.

Lucia was shaking. '*Diabol*… yes, yes they said the *Diabol* would kill my family.' Then she moaned. 'No… he's got Nikola, hasn't he… no…'

Kesia held her as she sobbed.

Amelia was close to stopping the interview, then Jake spoke: 'Who were these men – Czech, Slovak, Polish?'

'In Slovakia they were Czech. Here… they were English. All of them. They all had English names – Steve, Jason, Mike. They were all English and they hurt us. All the time. They hit us, punched us – but never on the face. Only Elena got punched in the face. They wanted the men to pay their money first – for the beautiful European women. They didn't want us ugly.'

Kesia still held Lucia like a child being comforted by her mother.

'I think we should stop now,' Amelia said. 'Kesia, take Lucia out to the kitchen and make sure Siobhan takes care of her.'

The door shut, leaving Jake and Amelia alone.

'Have they any record of Nikola?'

'No. None.'

'You shouldn't have kept that from her. That's bang out of order. We need to protect her family in the UK, too. Find their address and sort that for me. I'm going to tell Lucia.'

Fuming, Amelia left the room and went in search of Lucia. When she told her that they had not located Nikola, Lucia held back the tears. She thanked Amelia and whispered, 'Keep looking.'

Chapter 4

Family Life

Amelia woke early. She sat in her home office reviewing the interview notes that Jake had sent over in the early hours. She planned to speak to Dr. Kaminski as soon as the sun came up. All the women had given permission for the doctor to share their medical notes with the police and Amelia was desperate to know whether Mariana had given birth to a child.

Amelia looked up at the clock. It was 5:30 am. Her phone buzzed beside her. Will had sent her a report from Europol. There were no reports of convictions with reference to The Devil held by ECRIS. She was having second thoughts about Will; he could work hard when it mattered. Sighing, she opened the document on her laptop. Three hits.

Bosnia 2001. Reports of a trafficker, known as Davo, working between Mostar and Sarajevo.

London, UK 2011. A group of rescued trafficked women from Eastern Europe reported that the devil would kill them if they spoke to the police.

Paris, France 2015. A woman of Polish origin was discovered badly beaten in a Paris suburb. She reported that the devil had beaten her.

Amelia poured herself a coffee, sat in an armchair with the laptop on her knees and read each report in detail.

Two hours later, she stopped reading and rubbed her eyes. Maybe he was real, but it wasn't definitive proof.

A door slammed. Amelia jumped. Someone was up and about. She ran her hand through her tangled, auburn hair. Another coffee wouldn't hurt.

When she went into the kitchen, her mother was making herself some breakfast.

'You look pale, Amelia,' Jane said. No good morning proffered.

'I was blessed with the ginger gene, Mum. I'm always pale, remember?'

'For God's sake, Amelia, you know what I mean. You've not slept again, have you?'

'I'm okay.'

'No, Amelia. You're not okay. You were crying again last night. I know you… this isn't just work.'

Amelia decided that she'd heard enough and turned to leave the kitchen.

'We're going to have a picnic in the park this afternoon. It's Saturday. Join us, please,' her mother demanded in her wake.

Maybe that would be a good idea. A few hours off. She couldn't go to the refuge. Siobhan had banned any visits at weekends. She returned to her office, knowing that her daughters wouldn't disturb her there, not wanting them to see her in this state. Besides, there was plenty of work to finish.

She sat back on the armchair with her laptop. Her phone buzzed. It was a text from Jake: *I missed you last night. Why don't we meet later? X*

Amelia catapulted her phone across the office. It landed with a soft thud on the carpeted floor. She got up to retrieve it, relieved it wasn't smashed, as she remembered that she needed to phone Dr. Kaminski,.

Dr. Janis Kaminski answered the phone on the third ring.

'It's DI Barton.'

'Hi, Amelia. How can I help?'

Amelia didn't bother with any pleasantries, eager for the information. 'Mariana disclosed to us that she had a child taken from her. I need to know if she's given birth.'

'Wait a second while I check the waivers.'

Janis put Amelia on hold, presumably checking that she had permission to share that information and finding her medical file. The wait was interminable.

Janis returned to the call. 'There was no sign that she's given birth. She could have had an early abortion or miscarriage.'

'Thank you, Janis. I'm relieved.'

'How is Mariana? Have you heard?' Amelia added.

'They've admitted her to the Caludon. If you give my name, they may give you up-to-date information on her current condition.'

I doubt it, Amelia thought. It was also likely that they wouldn't get the chance to re-interview Mariana for many weeks. She was in the right place, though, and that mattered more.

Hours passed. The urge to text Jake back was driving Amelia mad. He'd been wonderful when Joe died. Always there, helping out, making arrangements when no one else would. They'd even, as a family, spent time with his wife and young son. There were clues, even then, that his marriage wasn't going well. A tension in the air. Snappy comments. The relationship with Jake had crept up on her. He'd been so attentive. It had started with the odd glance, the odd accidental touch that had shot sparks of electricity through her. When they finally got together, the sex had been loving, passionate and satisfying. But it was only sex, she reminded herself. She texted him: I'M BUSY TODAY. I CAN MEET YOU TONIGHT AT YOURS. LATE.

He wasn't bad, just hot-headed.

Sitting in the park in the sun, they looked like any ordinary family having a summer picnic, not one that had experienced so much trauma. Her mother was reading a book on her Kindle, no doubt some bodice-ripper. Caitlyn was making a daisy chain. She kept holding it up to show Amelia her progress. Becky was on her phone, reading messages on Facebook and smiling. *Is that all they ever do these days?*

Amelia picked up the football. 'Who's for a game?' she said.

'Me!' Caitlyn, ever sporty, jumped to her feet.

'Later…' Becky was still engrossed with something on her phone. Amelia just caught Becky smile again as she and Caitlyn ran to find a space on the field.

Amelia arrived at Jake's after midnight. She'd waited until the girls and her mother were asleep and had snuck out.

They'd undressed. Amelia lay on her back on the bed and turned her head to Jake, who lay down beside her. Their eyes locked. Gaze held. Without warning, Jake lunged at Amelia, grabbed both her wrists and forced them over her head, his eyes boring into her. Aggressively, he kissed her, smothered her mouth with his, gagging her. She couldn't speak. She couldn't move her hands. She wasn't ready. He didn't care. He kept one of his hands clamped on her wrists and the other hand cupped under her knee and slammed it up to her waist. He forced himself inside her. She closed her eyes against the pain, biting down on her lip. She moved with it, trying, but failing, to relax. It was never-ending.

Satiated, Jake withdrew and turned to the wall. Amelia lay staring at the ceiling, fighting back tears, then turned and gently stroked Jake's back. 'I'm sorry,' she whispered.

Jake didn't respond. He didn't turn. He didn't speak. Amelia decided to leave. It was her fault. She shouldn't have crossed him. She recognised his need for control and sensed that she had hurt him.

As she left the house in pouring rain, she ran to her car, driving away fast. A few miles up the road she pulled over. The tears came – hot, persistent, violent sobs. She slammed her hands into the steering wheel over and over and over until her palms were as red as her wrists.

Chapter 5

New Partner

Amelia arrived home and headed for the utility room. She
stripped off her jeans, T-shirt, pants and bra and stuffed them
straight into the washing machine. Instead of using the shower in the
en-suite upstairs, which would disturb the household, she scrubbed
herself clean at the sink using washing up liquid and water. She
scrubbed until she could no longer smell him on her skin. She would
have scrubbed herself inside, too, if she wasn't already so sore. There
were many women she knew that couldn't even complete the simple
act of washing away the stench after each rape. Dwelling on the
thought, she brushed away a tear.

Then she dried herself using a towel she found in a washing
basket. She covered her body with her softest pyjamas, which had
been folded by her mother with the rest of the washing and left on
the worktop ready to put away. She pulled the sleeves down as far as
they would go, covering her wrists as though binding them with
bandages. Only then did she go upstairs, relieved that her bed was
empty, Caitlyn not yet having taken her nightly walk. Despite
everything, she slept. Her tears had exhausted her.

The bedroom was filled with screaming – persistent, piercing screaming. Amelia's mother rushed in, clattering the door against the dressing table in her haste. Caitlyn woke, sat up, bottom lip quivering and started crying. Amelia's mother shook Amelia awake, trying to comfort Caitlyn at the same time. Amelia woke, shocked, realising her screams had been real. She immediately held her sobbing daughter. 'I'm sorry, I'm so sorry, baby. Mummy had a silly nightmare. I'm sorry… I'm fine now.'

Three generations held onto each other. The room fell silent until Amelia's mother got up off the bed. 'I'll make us some tea,' she said, leaving Caitlyn lying in her mother's arms.

'Thank you,' Amelia mouthed.

It had been a while since she'd had such violent, vocal nightmares. She'd had them most nights in the first year following Joe's death. Caitlyn had been a baby then, so they'd moved her cot into a bedroom on her own.

Although it was Sunday, Amelia went to her office at the West Midlands Regional Organised Crime Unit. She felt nauseous this morning, unsettled and anxious.

Will walked in a few moments later.

'Did you manage to read the reports I sent?' he asked. 'Oh, and by the way, Jake said to remind you that he wouldn't be in today. He's seeing his son.'

Amelia shuddered. 'Yes… Yes. They were helpful. What do you think? Do you believe there's a trafficker who calls himself The Devil?' Amelia asked.

DS Maltby sat back in the chair he'd taken opposite Amelia. 'Umm.' He clasped his hands behind his head. 'Do I believe in the *devvilll*?' He leaned forward. 'Seriously, I think whoever's leading this particular group is a vicious bastard. It's bad enough these women are being sexually abused – but they seem intent on emotionally abusing them with this monster, too.'

'So you think it's just being used to keep them in line.'

'Not necessarily. This is a group that employs nationals from many of the countries it operates in. There's some overarching figure leading them. He's the one we've got to catch. Without him, they'll just keep reappearing with new operatives in each country.'

Amelia knew he was right. She would have to be patient. They would all have to be patient and wait for the women to disclose as much as they knew about their captors.

'Did you get a look at the CCTV from Poppy's Place?' Amelia asked.

'It was grainy. I've got IT tidying it up a bit. Then I'll stick one of the lads on it looking for a match with some of our knowns. We might get a hit.' He added, 'We probably won't find those women, Amelia. I think you're going to have to give up on them.'

'I never give up, Will.' The thought of giving up on Elena, Jola and Christina was unthinkable.

Amelia felt nauseous and decided to go to the bathroom, ending the conversation.

The female toilets at the WMROCU were usually empty, but when Amelia entered there was a young woman with short, spiky black hair at the sink. Amelia turned on the tap and splashed water on to her face.

'Heavy night?' the young woman asked.

'No. I think I've got a bug or something,' Amelia muttered, relieved that the nausea was subsiding. She dried her hands with some tissue then pulled the sleeves of her green linen shirt down over her wrists.

'I'm DS Smith. Chloe.' The young woman held out her hand. Amelia shook it.

'I'm surprised I haven't seen you before,' Amelia said.

'I don't get to leave the dungeon often. I work in CEOP, downstairs.' Working for the Child Exploitation Onlinc Protection unit was one job Amelia couldn't do. She knew the nature of some of the videos they had to watch.

'DI Amelia Barton. I'm with the Human Trafficking Division. I'm not in the office much.'

'It must be good to have direct contact with people,' Chloe said and left the bathroom.

Amelia watched her go. If Jake was transferred, she thought, this woman would be an ideal replacement. Amelia had heard on the office grapevine that there was a promising recruit in CEOP, someone who handled herself in the field well and was able to work in the most extreme circumstances. She just needed the guts to put the request in. Last night had made her mind up. She needed to protect herself and all the women at the hostel.

Monday morning arrived. Amelia was awake at 3 am, then 4 am and finally got up at 5 am. There was no point in tossing and turning any longer. Caitlyn was curled in a ball on the edge of Amelia's bed. Amelia kissed her daughter on the top of her head, careful not to wake her.

Amelia had been running over the conversation she was going to have with her boss, Superintendent Rodgers. Keep it simple, she decided, but she was still going over all the possibilities as she drove to the office three hours later.

Superintendent Kevin Rodgers was a career copper. He had a degree in Criminology and started his career on a leadership programme with the police as soon as he left university. His main aim seemed to be to get the best statistical results compared to other regions. Every meeting with him was the same. He would quote statistics at you for hours, but he was supportive of Amelia's methods – up to a point.

Amelia entered Kevin's office and sat down. She took a deep breath and said, 'Siobhan Grady is planning to only allow women into Poppy's Place. She's not happy for any police to be there but, I think if it was two women, she might change her mind. I want a change of partner. I want Chloe Smith from CEOP, if she agrees. Then we won't have to recruit.'

'I'm not losing Jake from Trafficking, Amelia. We're short-staffed and there's a cap on recruitment at the moment.' Kevin was playing with his pen. Amelia wondered why he was nervous.

'If I can have Chloe,' Amelia paused, deciding what would appeal as an argument, 'we'd save money on transporting the women, hiring rooms, etc. It'd be an economy in the long run.'

Kevin's eyes lit up. 'I'll see what I can do. Jake's staying, though. He can work with Will in Intelligence. I'm not losing a good officer.'

Amelia knew this wasn't enough, but she'd at least remove Jake from having access to the women at Poppy's. She could never trust him around women again; she didn't believe that the other night was the first time he had abused a woman. *How had she not noticed this?* As she stepped out of Kevin's office, she bumped into Jake. He'd obviously been waiting to enter the office himself.

'I'm sorry if I was off the other night. I was tired,' he said. 'I'll make it up to you.'

'I –'

'Have you already seen Kevin then? It's probably for the best. We wouldn't want to live in each other's pockets, now, would we?' His mouth was smiling, but his eyes weren't.

'No, we wouldn't.' Amelia braced herself and attempted to dodge past Jake without looking at him.

He grabbed her right wrist as she passed him. Pain shot up her arm. 'I care about you Amelia, but you're not well. You need to make better decisions.'

Amelia pulled her wrist away. She wasn't going to respond. She wouldn't let him know how much he had hurt her.

Chapter 6

Brothel

Life was improving for Amelia. Since Jake was transferred three weeks ago, work had been much easier. The interviews had been concluded at Poppy's Place and the case files sent to the National Trafficking Centre for review. Amelia was hopeful that all of the women would get a year's residency in the UK while they continued to help the police investigation. Chloe had turned out to be professional and considerate of the needs of the women. Siobhan had agreed to continue their relationship with the hostel.

Amelia had even started her counselling sessions again. Her mum had insisted, threatening to leave the house and buy herself a bungalow if she didn't. The sessions were – kind of – helping. There was so much left unsaid. She only talked to her counsellor about Joe... how much she missed him. The counselling service was provided by West Midlands Police. There was only so much she felt she could say in the circumstances.

Arriving at work two hours later, Amelia found Chloe at her desk.

'You're in early,' Amelia said.

'I've been in the dungeon, speaking to the lads. There was a case I wanted to look at.' Chloe's face glowed and she could barely stop smiling.

Amelia yawned. 'Sorry?'

'A case when I was with CEOP. A nine-year-old boy. He constantly referred to the devil in his emails, only he didn't call him The Devil. He called him Davo. Here, look.' Chloe passed Amelia the thick file. Amelia opened it and found it hard to get past the case photo of a fair-haired boy in an Aston Villa T-shirt.

Chloe continued. 'I was reading the ECRIS documents again last night and I spotted the reference to Davo. The thing is, we caught it in time. This Davo guy was grooming him, getting the boy to send him photos. Just normal ones at first of him playing football in the park or eating ice cream at the beach. Davo was claiming he was a talent scout for the Aston Villa youth team and he'd seen him play. He'd got his email off his football coach, that kind of thing. He hadn't, of course. He'd found the email address on Facebook. All the details he needed were in the poor lad's profile.'

Amelia instantly wished she could get Becky to close her social media accounts. She mentally reminded herself to talk to her later.

Chloe was still talking. 'Then he started asking for other photos. It started with just shirtless ones: "We need to check you have the right physique to be a footballer." Then it was, "Use the camera on your laptop. I want to see all of you."'

Chloe went on to describe in graphic detail exactly what that entailed. She got to the part where Davo coaxed the boy to masturbate in front of him and stopped. She sensed, rather than saw, Amelia's discomfort. 'I'm sorry. We're used to dealing with this kind of thing every day in CEOP. We have to be graphic and precise.'

The kids always got to Amelia. Always. She showed no outward emotion on the occasions that they'd rescued trafficked children, but it was hard.

'We stopped it. The boy's mother found him standing naked in front of his laptop. She did the right thing and contacted the police. You'd be surprised how many ignore it. Too shocked and embarrassed, I guess. Davo was very computer savvy. Practically untraceable. He knew all the tricks. But we were lucky, we got a lead to an address in Birmingham. Unfortunately, he'd long gone.'

'Have you still got the address?'

'Yes, it's here somewhere.' Chloe took the file back from Amelia and turned to one of the pages. 'Here.'

She handed the file back to Amelia. 97 Hampton Road, South Yardley, Birmingham.

'Contact the landlord. We'll call round later today,' Amelia said, passing the file back to Chloe. Then she added, 'We might need to talk to the boy. Contact Social Services for me. We'd better go through them.'

The landlord tried to argue that they couldn't enter the property as he had new tenants that he didn't want to upset. He was being as unhelpful as possible, trying various keys to the terraced house and claiming none of them worked.

'I can break the door down if you like,' Amelia said. Miraculously, the landlord then found the right key.

It was quite clear why the landlord had been evasive when they got in. The place was a tip. Every room was the same, covered in dirty, filthy mattresses. Discarded condoms littered the floor. It was deserted. No doubt the bastard landlord had tipped them off, Amelia thought. She wanted to grab the slimeball by the neck and throw him against a wall. Instead, she read him his rights. He was still claiming he knew nothing about the house being used as a brothel as they took him away in the police van. Amelia contacted the Scene of Crimes team and waited on the doorstep with Chloe for them to arrive.

'Was it like this before?' Amelia asked.

'God, no,' Chloe answered. 'We'd have reported it to you if it had been. It was a mess, but not like this.'

Amelia was angry with herself. They should have got a warrant, not gone through the landlord. He wouldn't have been able to tip them off, then. Her phone buzzed. It was Jake. She'd avoided him as much as possible at work. Fortunately, he always seemed to be out in the field recently.

'What the fuck does he want?' she muttered. 'DI Barton,' she answered the phone.

'Amelia.' He used his softest voice. Amelia shivered. 'I hear you're at an address in Yardley. I might have some information on it. Shall I come over?'

She wanted to say no. 'Yeah, we should be here a while.' She cut off the call.

Jake arrived ten minutes later. He got out of his car and walked casually over to Amelia and Chloe. He smiled at Chloe. Amelia noted that she didn't smile back. A short burst of the theme tune to 24 blasted from Chloe's mobile and she walked away up the street to answer it in private.

'What information have you got for me, Jake?' Amelia needed this to be over as quick as possible.

'We had a tip off a couple of weeks ago, and we've had this place under surveillance.'

'What!? Why the fuck didn't you tell me? We're still on the same team!' Amelia couldn't believe she hadn't been told.

'Thing is... Elena and your girls were here. We didn't want to tell you because we knew you'd go bowling in to rescue them –'

Amelia slammed her fist into the brick wall of the house, instantly regretting it. It was either that or punch Jake just as hard in the face.

'We had a lead on The Devil, but you've ruined that,' Jake hissed, just out of Chloe's hearing. He took hold of the battle scars on her knuckle and squeezed. Amelia didn't even wince.

Fortunately, the SOCOs arrived at that very moment. Amelia nursed her hand, which was starting to throb. Chloe moved closer to Amelia, sensing there was something off.

Jake said, 'I can't stop and chat. I've got an informant from another case to meet.'

Amelia watched him leave, her eyes boring into his back. She and Chloe stayed at the house while the SOCOs collected samples, hoping that some would belong to the missing women.

Later that evening, Amelia returned to the office. Chloe had a date with a young detective from CEOP. 'We've both seen the monsters. It won't come between us,' Chloe had said. Amelia told her not to cancel. She'd done well today.

Will was working, incessantly clicking on something at the computer. He looked up when Amelia walked in. 'I wanted to tell you.'

So, Jake had spoken to him.

Will continued, 'Elena's been working as an informant. Jake

set it up. He'll probably meet up with her again. Don't worry.'

Amelia stared at him. 'When did he set her up, Will? When? And what about the other women, Jola and Christina? Were they just collateral damage?'

'Amelia, I'm sorry. I nearly didn't go along with it but if we catch the traffickers, more women – countless women – will be saved.'

Amelia moved close to Will, so she was right in his face. 'You're all fucking bastards and I hope you can live with yourself.'

Will flinched. 'I know… you're right.' He paused. 'I'm sorry.' He moved to touch Amelia's shoulder.

She pushed him away, returning to her corner of the room. 'You've killed them.'

'No. I'm sure they'll be okay. Elena will contact Jake soon.'

'He started this at the hostel. Didn't he, Will? He set her up right in front of my fucking eyes.'

'Yeah. I guess.'

'He's –' Amelia stopped herself from speaking. She couldn't say it. If she told Will what had happened between them… she just couldn't. She was so ashamed.

Will, without looking up, said, 'I'm as much to blame. I'll try to contact Elena, get her to meet with you. Maybe you can talk her into coming back to Poppy's to be with the other girls.'

'Wait,' Amelia said. 'Elena can come and go as she pleases?'

'Yes. It seems so,' Will said.

How could this be? Surely the traffickers would keep her permanently enslaved. Why would they let her out?

'Please, Will. Do that for me. Arrange it so I can speak to Elena.' She needed to speak to her. She had to warn her.

Chapter 7

Rounders

Every few minutes over the next couple of days, Amelia checked her phone. No call from Will. She considered phoning Jake and reasoning with him, pleading with him to let her meet Elena, but she didn't. She knew it wouldn't do any good. By Friday evening, Amelia was starting to feel desperate.

It didn't help that she couldn't convince Becky to shut down her social media accounts. Amelia had even considered bringing home the file that Chloe had given her and showing it to Becky. She hadn't, of course. It would have been completely unprofessional. In the end, she made Becky agree to set all her settings to private – friends only. Amelia still wasn't happy, though.

'I'm assuming you've met every one of your Facebook and Instagram friends. You know they're real?' Amelia said.

Becky didn't answer. She just swiped and smiled.

'Becky, I'm talking to you.' Amelia was angry. 'Would you rather I reported you to the social media providers? You're only thirteen.'

Becky finally put down her phone. 'Go ahead, Mum. Then I'll be the only one not on Instagram and Snapchat at school, and you'll be responsible for getting me bullied. But go ahead, if you must. You ruin everything anyway.'

Perhaps she did, Amelia thought. She hadn't been much of a mum. She was never there for her girls, particularly since Joe's death. She was never there in person or emotionally. But then, Amelia's mother had not been there for Amelia, either. She was too busy drinking. The freedom Amelia had enjoyed while growing up nearly killed her.

There was little left to say. Amelia knew that she might have to be more surreptitious to protect her daughter... maybe send her a made-up friend request and see what happened. If she accepted, she would have access to Becky's posts, although this was the equivalent of her mother reading her diary as a child. She knew how that had stung.

She tried one last time. 'I'm saying this for your own good, Becky. You don't know what I've seen.'

Becky got up. 'It's always about you, Mum. Always.'

Becky left the room as Amelia's mother walked in. She had finished the washing up. 'What was that all about?'

'Just me being a shitty mum. Don't worry about it,' Amelia said.

'Don't swear, Amelia. You're not at work now,' her mother insisted.

Amelia's phone buzzed. It was a text from Siobhan: *CAN U COME OVER TOMORROW? IT'D BE GOOD TO SEE U. SHIV.*

That was a first, Siobhan inviting her to Poppy's Place on a weekend.

The next morning, Amelia dressed in her usual grey trouser suit and pale green blouse and headed over to the hostel. She had considered inviting Chloe until she remembered that Chloe was staying at Dion's flat that weekend. Amelia was pleased that their relationship was progressing so well. Some couples should be having normal, healthy, happy times together.

When Amelia arrived at the hostel, she was met by an excited Natalia. 'Siobhan's given me a job in the kitchen. I'm going to be staying here.' She hugged Amelia.

'That's fabulous! I'm really pleased for you!' Amelia stood with her arms by her side, not sure what to do.

Natalia let Amelia go, scanning her up and down and laughing. 'You're not exactly dressed for it.'

'Dressed for what?' Amelia asked, but Natalia had run off outside.

Ellie walked into the kitchen carrying some cones and a rounders bat. 'Ah. Shiv forgot to tell you.'

'Tell me what?' asked Amelia.

Siobhan entered the kitchen and laughed. 'I may have

forgotten something important.'

'Is someone going to tell me what's going on?' Amelia asked.

'We're having a rounders match. We thought you might enjoy it.' Siobhan was still laughing.

Amelia looked down at what she was wearing.

'There's probably some sportswear in the clothes cupboard. Why don't you go and take a look?'

Amelia had never been in this part of the house. The rooms upstairs were pretty sparse. Each held three or four single beds and a couple of wardrobes. Someone had made an attempt to make them look homely. There were cut flowers in small, glass vases in each of the rooms. The beds were all covered with brightly, covered duvets in various patterns and all were freshly made.

The donated clothes, piles upon piles of them, randomly organised, were kept in a large airing cupboard. Amelia found a pair of jogging bottoms and a T-shirt she thought might fit. There were pairs of shoes and trainers at the bottom of the cupboard. Amelia looked at her flat court shoes and the trainers, deciding that she could run in her own shoes. The thought of sticking her feet in someone's castoffs held no appeal.

Amelia entered one of the bedrooms, hoping to get changed in there. There was a woman curled up on the bed, her face buried in the pillow.

'I'm sorry,' Amelia said. 'I thought the room was empty.'

The woman rolled over. It was Lucia. 'Found her?'

'I'm so sorry, Lucia. No, we haven't found her yet.' Amelia would keep looking. She would always keep looking. 'Why don't you join us? We're about to play rounders.'

'Not today.' Lucia turned her face back to the pillow.

Amelia left the bedroom and went in search of an empty one.

When she had changed, Amelia went outside. The hostel was blessed with a couple of acres of land. The match had already started on one of the flatter areas of the garden. Siobhan saw Amelia and pointed to the team that was fielding. 'You're on their side,' she said.

Amelia hadn't played rounders since she was in secondary school. She could run, though, so she placed herself as far away from those batting as she could. During the first half of the game,

Amelia managed to catch one woman out and helped the fielding side to keep the other team's score down to seven runs. It was great to see everyone enjoying themselves. It was then that Amelia spotted Mariana. She was standing by one of the posts, laughing as she missed a catch. It was soon time to swap. Siobhan called for a break and the women went to sit in groups while Ellie passed round glasses of orange juice.

Siobhan sat down next to Amelia.

'Mariana's here, I see,' Amelia smiled.

'Yes. She's been discharged. If you give it a couple of days, you can interview her.'

'That wasn't what I meant.'

'I know.' Siobhan touched Amelia's leg.

Amelia wiped her face with the sleeve of her T-shirt. She was sweating.

'I'm glad Jake's gone, Amelia. He was bad for you.' Siobhan didn't mince her words.

'He's still working with the division.'

'But you're not sleeping together. That's good.'

Amelia stared at Siobhan, who was looking across the field at the lake.

'How did you know?'

Siobhan looked back at Amelia. 'You're smiling.'

Amelia was tempted to tell Siobhan everything, but she couldn't. She couldn't tell anyone. What would Siobhan think of her as a professional woman who had allowed herself to be abused and hadn't fought back?

Ellie stood up and shouted, 'Second half!'

Amelia was relieved.

The innings passed without incident. Mariana stood in the line waiting to bat and chatted with Holly, who was back at the hostel again. Amelia smiled. When it was her turn to bat, she almost scored a rounder but she was outwitted by Ellie's fierce bowling. She'd obviously saved the fast ball just for Amelia and laughed when her hit had height but very little depth.

Chapter 8

A Body

A body was found on Monday morning – the body of a woman with light brown skin and jet black hair. A woman that matched Nikola Markova's description.

She'd been found on waste ground next to a disused pub on the edge of a council estate in Birmingham. Amelia and Chloe drove directly to the site.

A DI Branfield from the local force walked them to the white tent after they'd put on white Microgard suits and slip-on boots. He held open the tent flap for them. 'She was found this morning at 6 am by a guy walking his dog. She's been here a while. We thought she might be one of your girls. She was definitely a prostitute.'

Your girls. Definitely a prostitute. Amelia would have spent an hour putting him straight, but she was more interested in the dead woman who lay sprawled in the mud. Amelia desperately wanted to pull the hem of the woman's skirt down so the men in the tent would no longer be able to see her skinny, black thongs. She'd been degraded enough. Her face had taken the worst of the battering. It was blackened and swollen, her nose broken and squashed. Her mouth was open, revealing that the front teeth on her lower and upper jaws were missing. The gums had healed. Amelia had seen this before when she had worked in the Sex Crime Division but, mercifully, not often.

Amelia knew that she would need to support Lucia through an identification later. This thought filled her with dread. She left the tent and rang Kesia Trent. As she spoke to Kesia, she turned back to the tent and spotted Chloe throwing up outside the crime scene cordon.

Amelia finished her call, knowing that Kesia would join them at Poppy's Place ready to take Lucia to the mortuary. She got a tissue out of her bag and took it over to Chloe.

'Here. Don't worry, we've all been there at some point,' Amelia said. She wasn't surprised that Chloe had reacted in this way. Chloe, no doubt, had seen the vilest horrors online – but you never forget your first body. The smell alone stays with you. Amelia held her own stomach. The thought of it was making her nauseous, too.

'Thanks,' Chloe said, taking the tissue and wiping her mouth with it. 'Do you think it's Nikola?'

'Now comes the hard part. We need Lucia to identify her,' Amelia answered.

It was early evening by the time the body was ready to view. Lucia was remarkably calm. Amelia knew this wouldn't last. They entered one of the bereavement rooms in the hospital mortuary and she waited for Lucia to implode.

'Can I see her shoulder?' Lucia turned to Kesia, who looked as though she was about to faint. Kesia translated what Lucia said and the mortuary assistant turned down the white cloth covering the dead woman's body. Lucia took a step back. 'It's not her. It's not my sister.'

'Are you certain, Lucia?' Amelia asked. Lucia pulled down her top to reveal her shoulder. There was a large, red rose tattooed there. 'We all have them. This isn't Nikola. This isn't my sister.'

The women had been branded like cattle.

Amelia looked down at the woman on the mortuary slab. She was someone's sister, maybe even mother, too. Amelia nodded to the mortuary assistant to cover her up again.

The drive back to Poppy's Place was tense. Kesia tried chatting to Lucia in Slovakian and, when that didn't work, in Romani. Amelia hoped they could find her sister, preferably alive but with the knowledge that, even if she was dead, it might bring her some relief.

Siobhan greeted them when they got back to the hostel. She made hot drinks for everyone. Kesia went with Lucia to her bedroom.

'It wasn't her, then, I take it,' Siobhan said.

'No. We don't know who it is.'

Siobhan looked worn out. She ran her hand through her tight, curly hair. 'I hate that place.'

Amelia guessed she meant the mortuary at Heartlands Hospital. It was the same one Poppy had been taken to.

Siobhan drank some of her hot chocolate. 'Nothing prepares you for it, seeing your family member laid out like that.'

Amelia squirmed in her chair.

'Oh, God. I'm sorry. I forgot about Joe.' Siobhan reached out, not quite touching Amelia.

But Amelia wasn't thinking about the identification. For some reason, her mind led her back to a different hospital and a far happier occasion. She saw Joe's face – beautiful and whole – smiling down at her and Caitlyn, a tiny baby wrapped in a blanket. It must have been straight after the birth because she had left the hospital within three hours of delivery. Amelia hated hospitals. She wanted to touch Joe, smell him, hold on to him.

Then the tears came.

When Amelia looked up. Siobhan was weeping, too. The two women hugged each other. By the time Kesia came down to the kitchen, they were both tidying and washing up as though nothing had happened.

Arriving home, Amelia found her mother still up, knitting. She looked worried. 'Is everything okay?' Amelia asked.

Her mum looked up. 'No, not really. Becky didn't come home until past nine o'clock. I didn't know where she was. This is the second night in the last week that she's done that.'

'For fuck's sake!'

'Amelia –'

'I know. Don't swear. Did she tell you where she'd been?'

'She just said she was hanging around with friends. I asked her where. She said town.'

The thought of her thirteen-year-old hanging around in Coventry City Centre until late filled Amelia with dread. 'Did she say what friends?'

'She mentioned some names I've never heard of. She's probably just having a minor rebellion. You were the same. No, actually, Amelia, you were worse.'

Her mum was probably right about that. At thirteen, Amelia was smoking, drinking heavily and had lost her virginity to one of the local bad boys. So, yes, Amelia hoped that what she had done was far worse than anything her daughter would do. Nothing took away from the fact that Becky was testing the boundaries and she wasn't there, as her mother, to enforce them. Granted, Jane was far more strict and certainly kinder with her two granddaughters than she had been with her own daughter.

'I'll speak to her in the morning.' Amelia was exhausted and hoped she could sleep.

'I've had a chat with Caitlyn, too. I've set up a reward system. I think it's time she stayed in her own bed.' Jane pointed to the sticker chart on the table.

Amelia had woken the previous night to find her seven-year-old daughter stroking her hand in just the same manner that Amelia used to stroke Caitlyn's hand when she was trying to get her to sleep. She would miss having her snuggled up beside her, but her mother was right. Caitlyn shouldn't witness her mother's horrors anymore. It couldn't be healthy for her.

'That sounds like a great idea. Thanks,' Amelia yawned. 'I'm going to try and sleep.'

When Amelia woke the next day, she felt nauseous and rushed off to vomit into the toilet. She was aware then just how much her breasts ached and of that metallic, bitter taste in her mouth.

'No, no, no!' Amelia rested her head on the cool white porcelain tiles. She went back into the bedroom and sat on the bed, grabbing her phone from the bedside cabinet. She swiped until she found her calendar, then tried to work out the dates since her last period.

It had been eight weeks and she hadn't even noticed.

On the way to work, she stopped off at the 24-hour supermarket and bought a pregnancy testing kit. She sat in the toilet cubicle at work for minutes with her eyes tightly shut, not wanting to see the result.

It was positive.

Amelia already had a counselling session booked for that afternoon. Her counsellor sat taking notes. She'd done the pleasantries and the routine, 'Now, tell me how you've been since we last met.'

Amelia came right out and said it. 'I'm pregnant.'

Her counsellor looked up and didn't comment.

'Don't ask me who the father is. It isn't important.'

Not important? Who was Amelia trying to kid? Perhaps she should say it. ''He's a rapist and a fellow police officer.'' But she couldn't say it. Who would believe her? You went over to his house at night? Tick. You took off all of your clothes? Tick. You wanted to have sex with him? Tick. *So how was this rape?*

She'd done everything women in these circumstances shouldn't do: washed her clothes, washed herself, not reported it. She had to live with that and all the consequences.

Her counsellor still hadn't said anything. They both sat for minutes without speaking. Finally, Amelia said, 'I don't know what to do.'

Her counsellor still hadn't spoken. Eventually, she said, 'You're only allowed six sessions and this is your sixth. I'm going to extend your sessions, Amelia, in these special circumstances.'

Special circumstances. She'd got that right.

Amelia decided to return to work after her counselling appointment. Will was the only one in. He was typing up notes at his computer.

Amelia strode up to him. 'Have you heard from Elena?'

Will looked up. He didn't look at Amelia. He stared at the

space behind her.

Jake must have walked in. Amelia bit the bullet. 'Well, have you heard from Elena or has she returned to the shadows?'

'Yes.' Jake sneered. 'No thanks to you. Elena's fine. The traffickers thought she'd dobbed them in and she took quite a beating.'

Will interjected. 'I don't think it was all Amelia's fault… to be fair.'

Not all Amelia's fault? She was outnumbered. She left the room and went to the Ladies' restroom. The nausea was back with a vengeance. At least she knew that Elena was alive – for now.

As she splashed her face with water, she heard the door open and the scrape of metal dragging across the floor. Amelia assumed it was one of the cleaners. Then she felt a tight pressure on her breasts. She bolted upright. She saw in the mirror that it was Jake. He clamped one of his hands over her mouth and carried on stroking one of her breasts. She hated the fact that she was becoming aroused. Despised it.

'Don't speak, Amelia. I just wanted to say… I've missed you so much.' He twisted her nipple hard. 'I remember how much you love this.'

Amelia relaxed, knowing he would feel her slacken beneath him. Then she reared up, sending her head backwards. It connected hard with Jake's face, as she hoped it would. He fell backwards, clutching his nose. Amelia was pleased to see it gushing with crimson blood.

'Bitch!' he spluttered as he grabbed tissues from one of the cubicles.

Amelia stared at Jake, repulsed.

He went across to the exit door and kicked aside the metal bin that he'd put in the way. 'I was only trying to make you feel better.'

Amelia turned, clutched the side of the sink with both hands and vomited.

When she returned to her desk, Jake had left and Will had stuck a post-it note on Amelia's computer screen.

Elena will meet you tomorrow at 11 am at St Martin's Church.

Chapter 9

Elena

Waking in a sweat, Amelia touched her stomach and groaned. She dragged herself out of bed, pulled on a dressing gown and went downstairs. Caitlyn was sitting at the kitchen table, eating cornflakes.

'I did it, Mummy. I stayed in my bed and Nanny said I can have a present on Saturday.'

'Only if you keep it up for the rest of the week, Caitlyn.' Amelia's mother was buttering the toast. 'Becky isn't up yet. I think you should wake her and speak to her.'

Amelia, following her mother's instructions, went upstairs and knocked on her eldest daughter's bedroom door. She didn't wait to be invited; she turned the door handle and entered. Her daughter was lying on her front, her laptop open in front of her. Amelia closed the lid. Becky sat up and looked at her mother, sensing she meant business.

'Your nan tells me you've been staying out late without permission.'

'Only a few minutes late. It's no big deal.' Becky looked at the floor.

'That's not true. Who've you been seeing?'

'No one you know.'

'It can't carry on.' Amelia folded her arms. 'You're grounded until I've met these friends.'

'And how would you know if I stayed in? You're not here anyway.'

Amelia moved closer. 'If you go out, I'll get one of the local police to hunt you down, pick you up off the streets in front of your mates and bring you home.'

Becky laughed, then realised her mum was serious. 'You're kidding, right?'

'Try me,' Amelia got off the bed. 'You need to get dressed or you'll be late for school.'

And don't try any tricks. I've done them all.

St Martin's Church was on a main road not far from the city centre. Amelia arrived early. The church seemed out of place, an old, brick building complete with spire and a churchyard speckled with graves, smack bang in the middle of a city. The last time Amelia had entered a church, it was for Joe's funeral. Her mum sometimes took her girls to visit Joe's grave. They laid flowers on his birthday. Amelia never went with them. *Joe's dead. Who are the flowers for? He can't even smell them.* Amelia had said that out loud, once. Her mother didn't answer her question, just gave her a look of complete horror and disgust.

The large, wooden doors to the church stood open, inviting anyone and everyone in. Amelia entered and was surprised to see that Elena was already there, sitting in a pew near the front. Amelia sat down next to her.

'Amelia. I'd say it's nice to see you, but it really isn't.' Elena turned towards her so she could see her bruised, swollen cheek. 'Jake told me you've had a little falling out. He said you were a dried-out prune.' Elena laughed. One of her teeth was missing. 'Don't worry, he has me now.'

Elena continued. 'Do you want to know my story, Amelia? How I came to be in this evil place? Do you want to know how old I was when I became a sex slave?'

Amelia stared, unblinkingly, at a marble statue. She said nothing, just let Elena speak.

'I was two. Two years old. My mother handed me over willingly. Amelia,' Elena whispered in her ear, 'hell is all I've known. Men aren't the problem. They just follow their pricks. They can fuck you over and over. Rip you to shreds. Beat you. But they can't get in your head. It's women that hurt you. That – that's what kills you inside.'

Amelia shut her eyes and opened them, still staring at the same spot.

'Jake's a good fuck, Amelia. You must miss him.' Elena stood up.

'I'm not your enemy, Elena.'

'You're not my friend either, and you can't save me, so don't bother.' Elena started to leave.

Amelia asked, 'Why do the traffickers give you freedom, Elena? Why don't you leave them?'

She sat back down. She turned and stared deep into Amelia's light green eyes. 'Maybe I'm The Devil, Amelia. Did you think of that?' Then she laughed. 'They know I'll return. Every time, I go back to them.'

'But why?'

Elena got up and left. Amelia forced herself to stand. She would have gone after her, but the nave was spinning. She held on tightly to the back of the pew, then sat back down and put her head between her knees.

By the time Amelia left the church, Elena was long gone. Amelia knew she had messed up. She'd barely spoken, let alone convinced Elena to leave or tell her where the women were. Elena's story had chilled her. The damage that had been done. There was plenty of evidence against Jake now, though. She knew she had to speak to Superintendent Rodgers to tell him just how rogue Jake had gone.

When she got back to her car, Jake was leaning on the bonnet.

'Don't mess up our operation, Amelia.' His arms were folded. He wasn't moving anytime soon.

'You're using – no, you're *abusing* – trafficked women. And you expect me to go along with it?' Amelia stood her ground.

'You *are* going to go along with it. We're close, Amelia, near to finding the real bastard – the head of the trafficking ring.'

'Well, if Elena's as close to him as you all seem to think she is, why don't you just go in and arrest him? Please, Jake, get those women out.'

'She doesn't know exactly where he is. Not yet.'

'Elena's incredibly damaged, Jake. Surely even you can see that?' Amelia didn't know why she was bothering to appeal to his better side. She wasn't sure who was the most evil – The Devil or this upholder of the law.

Jake got up off the car and walked over to Amelia. He gently brushed Amelia's hair away from her face. 'There's no need to be jealous. We can carry on if you want. I've missed you.' He went to kiss her, but she shoved him away. 'Of course, if you said anything, anything at all about Elena and me, I'd just say you made it up to try and get me back because everyone knows we were fucking, you and me. Everyone.'

As Amelia moved towards her car, Jake continued. 'And I wouldn't bother going to Kevin. He knows everything, too. Who do you think authorised the op?'

He doesn't know everything, Amelia thought as she started her car.

Amelia didn't go straight to the office. She went home instead. She knew her mum would be at her knitting circle and the girls would be at school. She made herself a coffee and went to sit in the garden.

Her phone buzzed. It was Chloe: *ARE YOU COMING IN TODAY? I'VE GOT SOME NEWS.*

Amelia texted back: *I'LL BE THERE IN AN HOUR OR SO.*

The garden was strewn with bikes and toys belonging to Caitlyn. Someone had tidied the borders. They were resplendent with flowers and shrubs. Amelia had decisions to make. No time to be distracted. She placed her hands on her belly. So many thoughts drifted through her mind. *I can't have you, I'm sorry. Your daddy's a monster… he can never know about you. It's not your fault… here I am, protecting you, and yet I'm not sure I can have you… I don't have to have you. If I have you, I'll love you, no matter what. But I can't bring you into all this… I might wake up one day and blame you and it's not your fault.*

She knew what she had to do. It was the sensible decision – in the circumstances. She made the call.

Chapter 10

The Dark Web

Chloe was at her desk when Amelia arrived at work. She was smiling and could barely contain her excitement. 'I've found some more references to a guy called Davo.'

'Where?' Amelia asked. 'And why didn't ECRIS find them?'

'You do know I was employed by CEOP because of my IT skills, right? There's plenty of places to look if you go beyond the disinfected Google search. You've heard of the Dark Web?'

Great. Something else to shield my kids from. 'I've heard of it.'

'But never dabbled, eh? I'm glad to say most people haven't,' Chloe continued. 'It's not that hard to find if you have the right search tools and operating system. Imagine a group of doors. You just need the exact key to unlock them. I guess the bastards need somewhere to share their child pornography. They can't exactly do it on Facebook or Instagram, although some do. You'd be surprised.'

'And The Devil?'

'He owns a nightclub.'

'Sorry?'

'A nightclub in Brum. His name is Robert Davo. It's a sex

club, basically, but you need the right keyword to gain entry. They change it every night.'

'You're sure it's him?'

'It could be a coincidence but you've got to admit it, Amelia – it's likely.'

Amelia didn't say anything. She was wondering how they could do this without involving Jake.

'Shall I tell Will?' Chloe asked.

'No. Don't tell him yet.'

'There was a menu, too. It described in detail what was on offer. It was quite funny – there were some things on there that I had to explain to Dion and he's been working at CEOP for six months.'

'We need a man.'

'Sorry?'

'We need a man to check the place out.'

'I thought the team would be going in…' Chloe screwed up her eyebrows, confused.

'I'd rather we cased the place first.'

'I don't think they do ladies' nights.'

'That's why we need a man.'

Then it dawned on Chloe. 'You want me to ask Dion. You haven't met him. I'm not sure it's his cup of tea.'

'He won't have to do anything. Just go. Take a look around. Pay some money for drinks, and then chicken out and leave.'

'You've not actually met him, Amelia –'

Amelia smiled. 'You could introduce us.'

'Okay… I'll introduce you,' Chloe got out her mobile. 'You'll understand what I mean when you meet him.'

Amelia enjoyed working with Chloe. It was so easy. She'd been thinking a lot lately about when she worked with Jake on the Sex Crimes Unit. He had informants, then. Yesterday, she realised what that actually meant. She had basically been his facilitator, supplying the women he could abuse. She couldn't ever forgive herself for that.

Chloe put down her phone and said, 'He'll meet you tonight. Come over to mine.' She wrote something on a sticky note and handed it to Amelia. 'Here's my address.'

Chloe lived in a terraced house in Hillfields. Amelia liked this area of the city. She'd spent a lot of time here. She liked the community and its richness and diversity. You could walk down a street and hear many different languages spoken from all areas of the globe. She knew a couple of women who lived on Chloe's street. They'd be getting ready to go out to work at this time of night.

Chloe had seen her coming. She opened the front door as she approached. 'I've told Dion. He's... well, nervous,' she whispered.

Dion sat on the sofa and looked up as Amelia entered. He wasn't your usual police officer. He didn't have that arrogant, authoritative stance. He was slight, wore small round glasses and his hair was tied back in tight, braided cornrows. 'Hi,' he said. 'Chloe's told me what you want. I don't think I'm your man.'

Amelia was thinking, if he just changed his glasses, he'd actually look like a player. 'Do you have any other specs?'

Chloe laughed. 'Yeah. I thought that, too.'

'If you ditched the Harry Potter look...' Amelia was serious.

Dion glanced at both of the women, looking terrified.

'I can take you to Specsavers tomorrow, get it sorted.' Chloe got up and passed around glasses of wine. It was done.

Chapter 11

The Appointment

Amelia had an appointment. She drove up to the building in the middle of an industrial estate. It seemed out of place for an office block. Amelia entered the building and scanned the list of building tenants for the right floor, then took the elevator. A smartly-dressed woman with brown, braided hair sat at the reception desk. Amelia gave her details and sat down to wait, relieved that she was the only person there. She didn't want to be seen.

Five minutes later, the receptionist said, 'Amelia. They're ready for you now in Room 3.'

Amelia stood up, took a deep breath and walked along the corridor. All the doors looked the same, but eventually she found Room 3 and knocked. It wasn't every day that you made such difficult decisions. But she had no choice.

'Amelia, this is Chief Inspector Cotteridge and I'm Inspector Stevenson. What have you got to tell us?'

Amelia had decided to report a fellow officer – the one thing that you never do. She told them everything she could. She told them about Elena, the relationship with Jake and then she stopped.

They were both making notes. Inspector Stevenson looked up. 'Go on.'

This woman has kind eyes behind that tough edge, Amelia thought. *Maybe I can trust her.*

'DS Faris raped me. I went to his home, I undressed. I… I wanted to have sex with him… but what he did…'

Neither of the detectives from the Police Complaints Department spoke.

Why don't you stop me? Why aren't you asking me questions?

'He held me down. He knew the effect it would have. He wanted to control me. He's sexually assaulted me, too, a couple of times.'

'And when did the relationship between you and DS Faris end, Amelia?' Superintendent Cotteridge asked, his pen poised.

'That night. I wasn't going to stay with him after that.'

'Are you sure it wasn't more recent than that?' He was staring at her, waiting for a response.

'I couldn't see him – not after that. He raped me.'

Why are they asking me this? Don't they believe me?

He continued. 'Amelia, think carefully before you answer. What happened in the women's toilets at WMROCU on July 8th?'

They wanted her to describe it. 'I was splashing water on my face. It was a warm day. I heard something metal scraping. I didn't know what it was. It turned out to be a metal bin. Jake had moved it in front of the door so no one could come in.' Amelia paused. She didn't want to cry. 'Can I show you what he did?'

Inspector Stevenson looked up. 'Yes,' she said. 'Tell me where you want me to stand.'

Amelia demonstrated the assault. It was easier than saying it out loud. She didn't touch the Inspector's breasts, but it was clear what had happened, and so was Amelia's response.

'I know I assaulted him. I needed him to let me go. I was terrified he was going to rape me again. I know I should have reported the rape to you immediately. I did all the things that I've told women not to do. But I only wanted sex with him. I didn't want to be raped.'

Superintendent Cotteridge put his pen down. 'Amelia, we have a problem. DS Faris has made a complaint against you. He said that you're stalking him. He admits he had a relationship with you. He regrets it, says he hadn't realised that you were so vulnerable after your husband's death. He said you physically assaulted him at work after he told you the relationship couldn't continue. He has a photograph that clearly shows his injuries.'

And what do I have? Even the bruises on her wrists had gone.

The room spun and spun. She tried to sit down, grabbing at the top of the chair but failing to get a firm hold of it. Amelia fainted.

She came to and found Inspector Stevenson standing over her. 'Are you okay? Superintendent Cotteridge has gone to get you some water.'

Amelia sat up. 'I'm fine. Just a bit under the weather.'

'I'm not supposed to stay in contact with you after an allegation has been made against you, but I will personally make sure this is properly investigated. We won't take his word over yours. We'll look for proof. My name's Debs, by the way. Here's my card.' Inspector Deborah Stevenson gave Amelia her contact details.

Amelia sat back at the desk. A few minutes later, Superintendent Cotteridge returned with her water. She sipped the water and the interview continued.

The Superintendent doesn't believe me.

Chapter 12

Counselling

Amelia had asked for her next counselling appointment to be early in the morning. She had plenty to talk about. Her counsellor began, 'I've scheduled in this and one more session, Amelia. I've had the fee agreed with your HR provider –'

'Thanks,' Amelia interrupted, 'but I'm not sure I can get everything I need to say into two hours.' She stopped talking, expecting her counsellor to say that she'd had six hours and hadn't said anything, and maybe she shouldn't have wasted them. Her counsellor just waited for her to continue.

When Amelia didn't speak, her counsellor said, 'Everything you say remains confidential.'

Hesitantly, Amelia began. 'He was my DS, my partner at work. Had been since before Joe died. A year ago, things changed between us. He started coming round to my house. He fixed the washing machine and put up some shelves. We went round to his – me, my two kids, my mum – but the atmosphere was strained between him and his wife, so we stopped going.' Amelia looked up and paused. 'The first night we had sex, he'd driven me home after an op at a brothel. We stayed in the car. We just both knew it was going to happen. The tension – sexual tension – between us had been building for weeks. It should've been awful – all scrunched up in the car, uncomfortable, but it wasn't. It was… it just wasn't.' Amelia didn't want to talk about the sex, but she couldn't stop imagining it. It was the type of sex you always remember. Not the loving kind – the kind you should remember. This was the passionate, crazy kind when your senses are on fire and you can't breathe with the intensity of it, when your lover seems to know instinctively where to caress you and at what moment. It's not a shared experience. It's all for you.

Amelia blushed. 'We kept it quiet. I didn't want my kids to know. He didn't want his wife to know. I thought it was good. I thought it was what I wanted… what I needed. He told me that we were just having sex but, in any other circumstances, it'd be far more than that. He told me I was the best lover he'd ever had.'

Amelia bit her lip. 'Then everything changed. Out of the blue, he raped me. He held me down and I couldn't move or say anything.' The tears were streaming down Amelia's face and she hadn't even noticed. She didn't brush them away as they slid down her face and dripped from her chin. 'I don't know what I did wrong. He didn't tell me. He didn't speak… I just knew – "Here's your punishment – you deserve it."'

Her counsellor spoke softly. 'Amelia, this wasn't your fault. A rape is not your fault. You didn't do anything to deserve it.'

'I subjugated him, belittled him – get me a coffee, go and do this and that.' Amelia sought agreement, some explanation, a reason. 'It's the only way I can describe the suddenness of it. I thought we were happy. He was getting a divorce, I thought he wanted to be with me. I must have done something wrong.'

'Amelia, listen to me. This is not your fault. You are *not* responsible for his actions.' The counsellor moved forward slightly in her chair. 'Rape is not sex. He didn't do this with you – he did it *to* you. It's a violent act against you. Just like a physical assault – like a beating would be. Some relationships are toxic.' She paused. 'You were the child. He was the parent in this relationship. You're looked after, he's in control. As soon as that's threatened, he punishes you. It's an unbalanced, unhealthy relationship. Whatever he perceived that you did or didn't do, you had no responsibility for.'

'The stupid thing is – I know. I know all the red flags. I've seen them all in my line of work. He was bombarding me with affection to fulfil his own selfish needs and I didn't see it. I couldn't go anywhere without him knowing where I'd be. He'd text me constantly – *I CAN'T STOP THINKING ABOUT YOU. I WISH I WAS WITH YOU.* Then he started controlling me – "Amelia, you look good in green and grey. Those colours go with your auburn hair." Everything in my wardrobe – everything – is green or grey, apart from a couple of pairs of jeans.' Amelia shook her head slowly from side to side. 'I didn't see it coming. I didn't see it coming. I was trained to notice… and I didn't see it coming.'

She couldn't breathe. She stopped speaking, hearing the tick, tick of the wall clock. She knew she'd run out of time and they hadn't talked about the baby. *What was she going to do about the baby?*

Chloe let Amelia into her house at nine that night. They waited for Dion to arrive. They waited and waited.

Amelia broke the tension, 'Did you get the keyword for tonight?'

Chloe chewed her bottom lip. 'It's Virgil.'

'Odd choice,' Amelia said.

'Not really. He was Dante's companion as he traversed the circles of hell.'

'Let's hope it's not too apt, then.' Still no sign of Dion.

'Where is he?' Chloe walked over to the window, shifted the curtain and peered down the street.

'I wouldn't worry, I bet things don't kick off until late.' Amelia thought she would drag her feet, too, if she was having to enter that vile place.

'I do worry. We spent a fortune on those new glasses,' Chloe smiled, determined not to let on how anxious she was. 'He looks rather hot in them, though.'

Amelia wondered if they should just call it all off when Chloe stood up. 'It's okay, he's here.'

Dion did look good, Amelia had to admit. He'd got the upper-class john look just right.

Before, when he was getting ready to leave, Dion had said,

'I'm worried I won't be able to do this. I can't sit by and watch these women be abused.'

'I understand. If you want to call it off...' Amelia didn't want to pressurise him into doing it.

'Dion, in CEOP you do this every day. You watch children and adults being abused. You do it because you want to stop it – for the right reasons,' Chloe had sat down next to him.

Taking her hand, he had admitted, 'I'm going to be honest. I'm scared. I'm usually distanced from the nasty stuff going on by a screen. Yeah, occasionally I get included in raids, but I'm really just a tech guy. That's what I am.'

Amelia tried again. 'We can –'

'You don't have to do anything. There'll be lots of men there just... well... looking, won't there, Amelia?' Chloe looked to Amelia for confirmation.

'I guess. Voyeurism is likely.'

'Go in. Find a good viewing spot and find out as much as you can about the place. If you feel uncomfortable – leave.' Chloe didn't give up.

'And make sure you buy lots of drinks. Make them happy to have you there. We can get some cash on the way. That's if you're sure, Dion,' Amelia stood to leave.

Dion and Chloe followed her. Dion said, 'Okay, I can give it a go.'

The club was in an old Georgian Town House in one of the wealthier parts of the city, the front of which was masked by tall trees. From the road, you could see that there was a driveway, but you wouldn't be able to see who was arriving and exiting . It reminded Amelia of the brothels that were frequented by politicians and celebrities in the seventies. She had raided a number of those type in her time.

Amelia got the taxi driver to drop her and Chloe at a pub half a mile up the road. The taxi would then return to the brothel with Dion. 'If the pub's shut when you've finished, get a taxi back to mine,' Chloe said, kissing him on the cheek.

Amelia and Chloe entered the pub and waited. They didn't talk much, just nursed their drinks. Two hours later, Dion entered the pub, looking pale. He saw them and sat down.

'How did it go?' Chloe asked. 'Are you okay?'

'Not really. I need another drink,' he answered.

Amelia went to fetch him a neat Jack Daniels. He downed it in one and winced. 'Just imagine the most grotesque tableau of evil. That's what I've seen tonight.'

No one said anything. They just waited until he was ready to continue. 'They gave me a questionnaire when I entered the club. It was like the menu, only it included more things on it… more things, involving kids, mostly. You're supposed to tick what you're into. I just ticked the voyeuristic options with women – not kids.'

Amelia got her phone out of her bag.

'What are you doing?' Chloe asked.

Amelia stopped. 'Actually, I'd better ask to use the pub phone or they'll know it's me. I'm reporting the club. Hopefully, the local force will raid it.'

'Don't you want me to tell you who I saw there?' Dion asked. 'I saw Jola. The woman whose photograph you showed me. She was there.'

Amelia let that news sink in and then went to the bar.

'I need to use your phone,' she said to the barman.

'We don't have one for customers, sorry.'

'It's an emergency.'

'I don't care what it is. We don't have one for customers.'

Amelia didn't want to use her warrant card in case the police tried to trace the caller, but she had no choice. She held it briefly in the barman's face. 'Does this help?'

The barman picked up the phone from its cradle and handed it to Amelia. She dialled 999 and reported that there was a massive brawl going on at the address of the sex club and that men with knives and possibly guns had been spotted.

She then went back and sat down with Chloe and Dion. 'I should have done that sooner.'

Dion stared into his glass. 'Jola may need a hospital.'

By 2 am, the club had been raided and the rescued women had been taken to A and E or Poppy's Place. The children had been scooped up, seen by doctors and placed into emergency foster care, while the johns had been rounded up and charged. Very few staff members were caught. There was no sign of Robert Davo, Elena or Christina.

Amelia and Chloe decided to go straight to the hospital. Dion went home, knowing that there was nothing more he could do. Jola had been admitted. Amelia found her doctor, looking exhausted, leaning against the drinks machine in the corridor outside of the ward. The doctor wouldn't tell Amelia anything despite her waving her warrant card under her nose, so Amelia and Chloe just sat next to Jola's bed waiting for her to wake up. The look on Amelia's face scared off any of the nurses who approached in an attempt to move them on. Jola was hooked up to a heart monitor and Amelia watched its steady beat for the next five minutes. Eventually, the doctor returned. 'We're going to have to operate. You really do need to leave.'

'Why do you need to operate?' Amelia asked. She turned to Jola. 'What have those bastards done to you?'

The doctor didn't answer. She just adjusted some of the buttons on the various machines surrounding Jola. 'I'm going to have to insist, I'm afraid. If you call later, I'll make sure that the nursing staff at least tell you whether Jola's stable or not. That's the best I can do.'

'We need to know the extent of her injuries. Crimes have been committed,' Amelia insisted.

'Are there other women at risk of harm?' the doctor asked.

Amelia knew where she was going with this. As a doctor, she could only divulge information about a patient if there were others at risk.

'We need to find the bastards who enslaved this woman and, yes, we know they're holding others captive,' Amelia said.

'Okay... Jola has internal bleeding. This was probably caused by a tubular serrated object being forced into her vagina. Now, we really need to operate.'

Amelia squeezed Jola's hand. 'Keep fighting,' she whispered.

She stood up and left the room with Chloe. At the end of the corridor, Amelia stopped and leaned against the wall. 'We've got to get them, Chloe. Someone warned the traffickers that we were going to raid tonight. They must have done that as soon as I called it in. There must be a number of officers involved. I can't see how else they'd have known.'

Amelia glanced at her phone. She had a number of missed calls from Jake. She ignored them.

'There's a briefing at nine at WMROCU. We've got just enough time to grab a coffee. We can discuss how to do this on the way,' Chloe suggested.

Chapter 13

Suspension

Chloe and Amelia sat in one corner of the open plan office while Will and Jake sat in the other, like boxers waiting for the bell to announce, 'Seconds out'. At least, that was how it felt to Amelia. This wasn't sparring. It was bare-knuckle fighting.

Superintendent Rodgers entered the room and, instead of standing at the front to start the briefing, he strode over to Amelia. 'I need to see you in my office,' he said, frowning.

Amelia stood and followed him. She was relieved to see Chief Inspector Cotteridge and Inspector Stevenson in the office as she entered. There was another officer already seated in a chair, whom Amelia didn't recognise. When she smiled at him, he didn't return the smile.

Inspector Stevenson spoke. 'Amelia, this is Sergeant Davis from the Police Federation. He's here to support you.' Inspector Stevenson paused and then, in a calm, monotone said, 'Detective Inspector Amelia Barton, I have to inform you of your immediate suspension from duty from the National Crime Agency and West Midlands Police on the grounds of alleged gross misconduct and bringing the force into disrepute. I am formally serving you with a Regulation 15 notice. This is not in any way a statement of guilt but we will need to carry out a thorough investigation and it is in your best interests not to be at work whilst we do this. You will need to hand in your warrant card and collect any personal belongings. You will then be escorted from the building.'

Amelia had only heard the word suspension. *How can they have got it so wrong?*

'I was sexually assaulted. You're suspending *me* and not the bastard who did it? Why isn't he sitting here?' Amelia raged at Inspector Stevenson.

'It's been decided that DS Faris can continue to work at this time. I need to take your warrant card from you now.'

'So, he can rape me and carry on as though nothing has happened. How did you come to that decision? Oh, he's a man and I'm just some neurotic woman, is that it? Just look at him! Why would he need to rape anyone who was already willing to have sex with him? Am I on the right track?'

Amelia took her warrant card from her jacket pocket and skimmed it across the table. Then she tore her ID from her neck and threw that down too.

'You must now leave the building. Please take your personal belongings with you as you may not be able to return to the office for some time. You will not be able to continue to work on cases. If you have any paperwork relating to cases you're working on at a location outside of this office, they must be returned immediately.' Inspector Stevenson paused. 'Amelia, do you have any questions related to your suspension?'

Amelia glanced at her Federation rep, knowing she was on the ropes. He looked worried that she might continue jibing Inspector Stevenson. Instead, she answered, 'Not at this time.'

Amelia was led to her desk. Someone had provided a box for her to pack away her stuff. She grabbed a few framed photographs of her girls and Joe and placed them carefully in the box, then added a box of tissues, a spare pair of black court shoes and the cardigan she kept on the back of her chair. When she looked up, Jake was smiling at her from across the office. In fact, he wasn't smiling; he was grinning from ear to ear. Amelia picked up one of the shoes from the box. She considered throwing it at him but decided that she would rather not use it as a weapon. She knew the injuries that could be inflicted through blunt force trauma. In reality, she dropped the shoe back into the box and calmly left the office with her rep, not looking back, not giving him the satisfaction.

At home, Amelia slammed the front door and took her belongings to her home office. An ornament that she'd always disliked went first, smashing into tiny pieces on the floor, then each shelf was emptied of books as she sent them flying. Within seconds, Amelia's mother rushed into the room. She grabbed the silver photograph frame Amelia was holding in her hands ready to smash.

'Not this one,' she said softly.

Amelia looked down at the photograph. It had been taken during an off-road motorcycling adventure weekend before the girls were born. Joe was an engineer for Triumph. He loved all types of motorsport. While many couples had favourite photographs of them brushed up and well dressed, this photograph showed the pair of them splashed with mud, wearing garishly-coloured padded clothes and motocross boots. They were both smiling broadly at the camera, Joe standing behind Amelia, his chin on her shoulder and his arms wrapped around her waist.

Amelia stared at the photograph, tears falling and bouncing off the glass. Amelia stared until she could no longer see the photograph through the blurring caused by her tears. Her mother led her to the kitchen and sat her at the table.

'I'll make us some tea,' she said.

'I've been suspended,' Amelia said, not noticing her daughter, Becky, entering the room.

'Suspended! Wow, Mum, that's so cool,' her daughter grinned. 'Who gets suspended from the police?!'

'Becky…' her grandmother warned.

'Well, Mum went mad when I was excluded from school for two days for thumping Charlotte Murphy. You agreed that I'd done the right thing in the end, though, didn't you, Mum?' Becky looked to her mum for clarification.

Amelia thought that her daughter may be right. Thumping Charlotte Murphy was perhaps not the right thing to do, but it stopped the bullying. She got up quickly, planning to go straight to her car and round to Jake's. Perhaps thumping him good and proper would have the same effect. Her blood pressure dropped and, instead, she clattered back into her chair.

'You okay, Mum?' Becky asked.

'I think you should go and do your homework, Becky.' Jane looked concerned. As soon as Becky left the room, she turned to her daughter. 'Amelia, how many weeks are you gone?'

She'd been just the same when pregnant with her other two – all-day sickness, dizziness and actual fainting. It was obvious to her mother. She hoped it wasn't obvious to everyone else. Amelia couldn't lie to her mother. She'd told her plenty of truths that hurt her, but she could never lie. 'About ten or eleven weeks.'

'It's Jake's, I guess.' *Did everybody know?*

Amelia looked at the floor. 'We were having an affair.' She paused, not sure how to tell her mum what had happened. In the end, she decided to be blunt. 'Jake raped me, Mum. I reported him, but he'd already reported me for stalking. I wasn't. They believe him, not me, which is why I've been suspended.'

'We'll deal with that in time. Have you been to the doctor? We'll deal with the pregnancy first. Do you want this baby, Amelia?'

It was the first time Amelia had been asked what she planned to do. She'd pushed this problem to the back of her mind as though she had all the time in the world and, as the days ticked by, she had let time make that decision for her.

'I'm going to keep the baby, Mum. I can't face getting rid of it. Deep down, I know I want to have it.'

Amelia waited for the response. She'd had an abortion in the past. She was fifteen and had tried to self-abort by drinking a whole bottle of vodka and taking pills. When her mother found her unconscious in the bath, she decided to support her daughter to get proper counselling and medical help. It was the turning point for Amelia and her mother. From that moment on, Amelia knuckled down at school and, by the time she was at Hendon Police College, her past was pretty much forgotten. Her mother had, at the same time, sought help for alcoholism and had been dry ever since.

'I suppose that means I'll be looking after another of your children.' Her mother didn't look pleased or displeased. She was just stating a fact.

Amelia said, 'I guess.'

Now she had made this decision, she decided to fight, not only for this baby, but for herself. There was no way she was going to let

Jake win. She couldn't wallow in her shame any longer.

Amelia's phone buzzed. It was a text from Chloe. *MEET ME AT MINE TONIGHT AFTER SIX.* Amelia knew this would break the rules of her suspension, but that wouldn't stop her going. She needed to plan her next moves carefully.

Chapter 14

Next Steps

Before going to Chloe's, Amelia visited Jola in hospital. Jola lay sleeping, shrunken and pale against the crisp, white, bedsheets. Amelia took her hand in hers.

'I will get them, Jola. You have my word. Whoever did this to you, I will find them and prosecute them.'

Jola stirred, opened her eyes and blinked in the harsh light. Amelia smiled.

'Where am I?' Jola asked.

'It's okay, you're safe now. You're in hospital.' Amelia squeezed Jola's hand. Jola tried to sit up and winced in pain.

Her doctor entered the room. 'Jola, stay lying down for now. It'll be less painful.' She adjusted Jola's drip, not looking at Amelia or Jola.

'What happened to me?' Jola asked looking from Amelia to the doctor.

The doctor stopped what she was doing and turned to face Jola. *How on earth do you explain this to anyone?*

'You've had an operation to stem some internal bleeding. We had to perform a full hysterectomy. I'm sorry, Jola.' The doctor paused, waiting for Jola to respond.

Jola looked confused. 'I don't understand that word – what is it? Hyst –?'

Amelia spoke. 'Can I suggest that I call our translator? She can explain what's happened to Jola in Polish.'

'We have translators here. I'll sort it.' The doctor was brusque, batting away Amelia's suggestion.

Amelia wouldn't be brushed off. 'But Jola knows Kesia, our interpreter. She may feel more comfortable hearing what's happened from her.'

'Do what you want. I can try to be free in an hour or so if you can get her here by then.' The doctor walked out of the room.

Amelia took her phone out of her bag and called Kesia. Fortunately, she was free and promised to be there in the next forty-five minutes. Eventually, Jola fell asleep so Amelia felt she could leave her for a while.

Amelia met Kesia outside the main entrance of the hospital. Amelia had just lit a cigarette and Kesia waited with her while she finished it.

'I know what happened at WMROCU,' Kesia paused. 'My husband told me that you've been suspended. I can't believe it! What on earth for?'

If Kesia's husband knew and he worked at Steelhouse Lane Police Station, not WMROCU, then presumably everyone in the Midland's force knew.

Amelia sighed. 'It's just a misunderstanding. I'm sure I'll be back within a few days or weeks at worse.'

She couldn't tell this young woman, her colleague, how stupid she had been having a relationship with a subordinate who turned out to be an abuser. She doubted that anyone would believe her if she told them the full story.

'I hope so. I'm always telling Simon what a brilliant officer you are, and how the women trust you and open up to you. There's five new trafficked women at Poppy's Place after that raid yesterday. I don't know how we'll cope without you. Siobhan won't let Jake back in. She can't stand him.' Kesia screwed her face up at Jake's name, which seemed odd to Amelia. She always thought Kesia got on well with him.

She took a shot. 'Siobhan's right to dislike Jake.'

Kesia didn't look shocked. 'He said things about you behind your back. Nasty, vicious things. He expected me to agree with him.

He scared me. I'm so sorry, Amelia, sometimes I didn't tell him he was wrong, I just nodded.'

'What did he say?'

'Just that you're too soft, that you're crap at leading the team. Sometimes he said things about your kids. He said you're basically a bad mum and avoided seeing them as much as possible – that you're more than happy for your mum to bring them up.'

Furious, Amelia berated herself for once again not noticing the methods Jake had used to abuse and belittle her. He never baulked at hitting her below the belt. In fact, he revelled in it.

'Whatever you need, Amelia, I'll help you. Just ask.' Kesia clearly meant it.

'Just take care of Jola. I've got to go to Chloe's now, but Jola's going to need all the support she can get.'

'Yes, of course. Poor Jola. I'll go to her now.' Kesia still looked concerned for Amelia as she turned towards the hospital entrance.

Chloe opened her front door as soon as Amelia's car pulled up in her street. 'Dion's here. I hope you don't mind.'

'No, that's fine. Let's go in, though. I don't want the whole of Coventry to know my problems.' Amelia spotted Jayda walking down the street as she said it. She'd helped Jayda when she was raped by a john two years ago. She tried to avoid having to speak to her, but it was too late. She'd been spotted.

'DI Barton – it is you, isn't it?' Jayda toddled up to Amelia in strappy high heels and grabbed her in a hug. 'I hear you left Sex Crimes to work with those poor trafficked girls. At least I chose this crap, eh?'

'You can always stop. I'm sure they'd have you at Poppy's Place if you wanted a break from your pimp.' Amelia encouraged her.

'Steve's not that bad. He's bought me an engagement ring – look.' Jayda waved her hand around for both Amelia and Chloe to see. It looked like a badly pasted piece of costume jewellery.

Amelia said, 'Very nice.'

Jayda stared at Chloe, sizing her up. 'Are you a working girl, too?'

'It's okay, Jayda, she's a friend. There's no need to get your g-string in a twist.' Amelia didn't want Jayda calling on Chloe in her police capacity every evening, either.

'Any friend of DI Barton's is a friend of mine. Pleased to meet you. Now, I really must start work or Steve'll kill me. See ya!' Jayda hobbled off, leaving Chloe and Amelia still on the doorstep.

'See what I mean. Coventry – small town. Everyone knows your business,' Amelia said.

'Yeah. You'd better come in.' Chloe held the door open for Amelia.

Dion was sitting on the sofa. He stood up when Amelia entered the room.

'Are you okay?' he asked. 'I heard.'

Another affirmation that everyone in the police knew. Every department in every police station. So much for keeping this quiet and confidential. So much for her being considered innocent.

Amelia bit her lip. 'So, what's everyone saying I did?'

Dion blushed. 'I don't really know.'

Chloe urged. 'You might as well tell her. It's only right she knows.'

Dion sat down. 'People are saying that you were having a relationship with DS Faris and he ended it – and you hit him.' Dion paused. 'I've told them that's bollocks. You wouldn't have sex with a co-worker. You're far too professional.'

Even Chloe raised her eyebrow at this.

'Dion…' Amelia struggled to find the right words, 'I did have a relationship with DS Faris. It ended because he raped me. Yeah, I head-butted him but, God, the bastard deserved it.'

'Oh. Is that what you want me to tell people?' Dion asked.

'No, tell them to mind their own fucking business.' Dion looked shocked. Amelia continued. 'Now we're here for more important things. How are we going to carry on investigating if I'm out of action?'

'We could carry on meeting here. I don't mind.' Chloe had made an effort to make her home look more like the office. She'd clearly brought home some of the work files, which were strewn across her dining table.

Amelia was concerned that she was putting Chloe's career at

risk. She gestured at the files. 'I'm not sure that's a good idea. I don't want you both to get suspended, too. Why don't we think of other, safer, places to meet for next time?'

'I don't care if we get susp –' Chloe started to say.

Amelia stopped her. 'But I do, and we need you to carry on supporting the women. Have you got anyone to work with yet?'

'They've given me a Police Constable from Steelhouse — Neesa Begum. It's sorted.'

Amelia thought a PC was better than nothing. The team needed a DI though. She wondered who'd they bring in. It would probably be a hard-nosed brawler who would fit right in with Jake and Will, rather than an officer who would put the trafficked women first and foremost.

'You're probably going to feel even more marginalised.'

Amelia opened the contacts section on her phone. 'Here's the number of DI Carol Jamieson. She works at the Public Protection Unit. If you need any advice or support, she can help you.' Amelia gave Chloe her number. She'd already spoken to Carol, who had readily agreed to mentor Chloe.

'Thanks… yes, I'll call her if I need to,' Chloe said. 'But can't I call you?'

Dion looked worried. 'Chloe… they might be monitoring Amelia's calls. It's best you don't call or text her anymore. I'll set up some secure way of messaging. Yes, I know you have the skills to do that, but I have the time. In fact, why don't I do that now and you two can discuss the case.'

'Great idea.' Chloe said. 'Shall I pour us some wine?'

'Do you have any juice? If not, then water.' Amelia had decided to cut her caffeine and alcohol intake. Better late than never, she thought.

'Sure. I'll get you an orange juice. Dion – Corona okay for you?' Chloe asked.

He was busy on his laptop. 'Great.'

When Chloe returned from the kitchen, Amelia said, 'What I'm most concerned about is how deep this goes. Who tipped off the club? I called 999. I didn't go through to any departments or say that it was a sex club.'

'I've thought about that. Do you think Jake tagged the address if Elena was working there? Then they would've rung him about any reports relating to that address. He may have rung Elena to warn her.'

'And she warned Davo?'

'Possibly. He ran the place. It doesn't mean he ever worked there.'

Amelia was impressed by Chloe's logic. Her thoughts were similar to hers and it felt good to get some agreement.

Amelia continued. 'Of course, Davo might not even exist. The name's used as a cover for so many operations. The child grooming, the sex club, the trafficking... even Elena hinted that she could be The Devil.'

'It seems more likely that Elena's the most abused here. Yes, she gets more freedom, but they repeatedly beat her in front of the other girls as a warning.'

'There must be some reason she stays with them. They've got something over her. It's the only explanation I can think of.' Amelia sighed. 'We need to get to Elena. Maybe Jola knows something. They seem to be close. I'll go to the hospital tomorrow to talk to her.'

Chloe pondered this. 'I'd better do that with Kesia and Neesa, then it'll be official.'

'But then you'll have to write a report on it and Jake'll know we're looking for Elena, too. I've got a bad feeling it'd put you at risk, Chloe.' Amelia frowned. 'I'll talk to Jola first. Then you can do your official interview without directly mentioning Elena. Do you think we can trust Kesia? It would be good to have her interpret.'

'Yes. I'd trust her. She adores you, Amelia.'

'That's our next step, then.'

Dion interjected. 'Sorted. You can chat through this website.' He gave both Chloe and Amelia the address. It's encrypted and I've set up a variety of reroutes, so it won't be obvious you're using it. Oh, and Amelia, I've hacked your home laptop, I hope you don't mind. You might want to speak to your eldest daughter about some of the sites she's using. I've set something up for you so you can monitor them.'

'You've hacked my daughter's laptop, too?' Amelia was surprised.

'Part of my job, protecting kids. Don't worry, there's nothing immediate to be concerned about. Most of her settings are secure.

She's only doing what every teenager does. I know it's a dilemma for parents – how much you monitor your kids without giving them responsibility. How much do you spy on them? If it was up to me, I'd follow them round and spy on them at every opportunity, but, then, I don't have kids.'

'Thanks.' Amelia didn't know what else to say. It was a real dilemma for her. Where do you draw the line between trust and control, authoritarianism and freedom? But she was pleased that Dion had given her more choice on that. If she wanted to monitor everything, she now could.

'I'd better go. When I get home, I'll try this messenger site.' Amelia stood to leave.

'I hate Jake.' Chloe had been clearly waiting to say it. 'I'm not sure I can stay in the office with him. Amelia, I understand why you had a relationship with him. He's very attractive – boyish looks and charm and all that. Please don't feel bad. We've all fallen for bastards in our time. Most people, when they find out the truth, will support you.'

Most people will side with Jake because he's pre-empted and blocked every strike. From what Kesia had said, he'd been talking to her colleagues about her for weeks, rubbishing her, even prior to the rape. Of course, she felt bad, she felt ashamed and wasn't sure she could ever forgive herself for being so stupid.

Chapter 15

Antenatal Clinic

Turning the pages of a magazine, Amelia realised that the wait in the antenatal department was driving her crazy. The fact that she'd even picked up a gossipy, women's magazine was bad enough, but she'd even bothered to read her horoscope. Apparently, as a Scorpio, she should be careful not to be taken in by the lies of a friend or colleague. Amelia had read enough rubbish. She tossed the magazine back on the pile and glanced around the room at the other expectant mothers.

There was one couple that stood out. Something was odd about the way they sat together. The woman recoiled every time the guy moved near. She had her back half turned away from him, nervously biting her nails, eyes darting around the waiting room, not looking at her partner. The woman stood and the guy stood, too. His hand locked around her wrist and he whispered something into her ear. Then the woman walked towards the toilets. The man followed close behind her. This was the confirmation Amelia needed. She stood up and followed them.

The woman entered the toilets. The guy stood guard on the door, his legs slightly apart, arms by his side, like a sentry. Amelia was unperturbed. 'Excuse me,' she said attempting to enter the ladies' toilets.

The guy blocked her way by placing his arm across the doorway. He stared at Amelia and faced her down, obviously considering her to be a weak target. Amelia snapped, 'Get out of the way of the fucking door, unless you want me to pee on your shoes.'

He stood his ground. Amelia knew she had to get the woman to safety. She didn't wait. There was no point wasting time brawling with the guy on her own. She walked away and headed straight to the reception desk, ignoring the queue. 'There's a possible trafficked or abused woman just about to come out of the toilets with her minder. You need to dial 999 and report it. Then let the midwife and doctor who are treating her know. Get them to keep her here as long as possible.'

'How on earth do you know this?' The receptionist asked.

Amelia thought quickly, having no warrant card. 'I work at Poppy's Place. All the signs are there. Please make the call for the woman's sake.'

The receptionist said in a loud, strident voice, 'Please go and sit down, it'll be your turn shortly.' She winked at Amelia and picked up the phone receiver.

Amelia sat back down, now dreading that her name would be called for her appointment before the police arrived. Minutes passed and it was the young woman's name that was called first: Maria Brankova. The appointments lasted anything between ten and twenty minutes. Amelia fidgeted in her seat, hoping she wouldn't now be called to see the midwife. The police still hadn't arrived ten minutes later. Amelia went back to the receptionist, 'You did call the police, I take it? And warned the doctor and midwife?'

The receptionist looked concerned, 'Of course I did, but it often takes up to half an hour for the police to arrive. I've contacted hospital security, too. I'm surprised they're not here yet, but they're based in A and E on the other side of the hospital.'

Amelia went back to the plastic seats and sat down. A few minutes later, Maria and her minder came through the doors to exit the consultation area. He was practically dragging the young woman, his hand tightly grasping her wrist as he led her towards the main department exit. If Amelia followed them, she would have to confront him. She had no authority and would again break the terms of her suspension if she physically prevented him from taking her. She had no time to ponder such things. She stood up and followed.

The couple were now in the corridor between the department and main exit. Amelia didn't care there were others around. She charged at the man, caught him by surprise and forced him, with her arm across his throat, against the wall. With her other hand, she grabbed his flaccid cock and balls. She started to squeeze. This wasn't an agreed Hendon trained procedure, but she needed something effective and immediate.

She hissed into his ear, 'You're going to leave here and not look back. Maria or whatever her name is, will stay here. Do you understand?'

'Yes,' he spluttered.

Amelia squeezed a little tighter. Tears started to appear at the edges of the guy's eyes. Amelia said to Maria, 'Go back to the receptionist. Tell her to keep you safe.'

The woman did not need telling twice. Amelia led the guy by the balls to the exit and threw him out. She wished she could have kept him prisoner and handed him over, but she had no legal protection and could just as easily be arrested for assault. It would only take the woman saying that she didn't need saving, then Amelia would have to explain why she had practically removed the guy's wedding tackle. But she hated the fact that he could get away. The police still hadn't arrived by the time Amelia's name was called.

The midwife apologised for the wait as Amelia entered the consultation room. Amelia didn't attempt to explain that she was, in the end, grateful for it.

The midwife had a set of questions. Was the father of this child the same as her other children? No, but it would be hard, since their father was dead. Did Amelia smoke? Occasionally. Then she should consider stopping. Did Amelia drink? Sometimes. That was not wise either. Was it possible that she had a Sexually Transmitted Disease? That stopped Amelia in her tracks. She hadn't considered it. Jake had pursued many women. This had become obvious over the last few weeks. When he assaulted her, he wasn't wearing a condom. In fact, there had been occasions when, in the heat of the moment, she hadn't insisted on it, which could well explain her current condition. Did she have an STD? Possibly. Probably.

The midwife wrote everything down and said, 'Don't worry,

we do various tests anyway.' She got out the blood test forms and a vaginal swab kit.

Amelia felt disgusted with herself. The last eighteen months, she had been playing with fire. She'd set aside her own health and wellbeing for stolen moments of pleasure and she'd also neglected her children. In fact, the only ball she'd kept in the air was her job and now she'd lost that, too. In those eighteen months, no one could have accused Amelia of being a poor worker. She didn't even want to hold on to that. Her priorities were so skewed, there was so much she now needed to put right and here she was, bringing a baby into the mess. What the hell was she doing?

'I have to ask you this.' The midwife interrupted Amelia's thoughts. 'Are you happy to proceed with this pregnancy?'

'Yes. Definitely.' Amelia wasn't sure where that had come from. She'd made the decision without thought or contemplation. A couple of days ago, she woke up and just knew that was what she wanted to do. There was no wavering, no concern, except for the fact that Jake was the biological father. If necessary, she'd fight him to the death to ensure that he wouldn't get the chance to take on that role. She'd deny him any access. Whatever it took, he was not going to be this child's father.

Chapter 16

Visiting Jola

When Amelia entered the main part of the hospital, she spotted Jola's doctor by the reception desk. She waved Amelia over. 'I'm glad I've seen you, I wanted to apologise. I'll be honest – I thought you were just trying to get information from Jola, but she clearly wants to have you around. If I was a little brusque, it was only because I wanted to protect Jola.'

Amelia smiled. 'I understand. You've got nothing to apologise for.'

'There's something you need to know. Jola's injuries,' the young doctor looked down and sighed, 'I've seen them before a number of times. Too many times recently. I can't give you any details. I probably shouldn't even tell you this, but there's something evil going on.'

'Were they trafficked women?' Amelia asked. So many people didn't even consider this. 'Why didn't you report them?'

'No, they were regular sex workers. Their injuries weren't so severe as Jola's. They weren't very forthcoming and didn't stay long after being stitched up.' The doctor paused. 'We obviously encouraged them to give us permission to contact the police. If I thought for a moment that they were trafficked, I'd have informed you. I've attended training on trafficking, I do know the signs.'

'If you have any more women with similar injuries, at least report it, even if it's after the event. Here's –' Amelia was about to recite her own mobile number and then remembered that she could do little about it. Instead, she gave her Chloe's. 'Sorry, here's my colleague's number.'

If the doctor thought this was odd, she didn't show it. 'Thanks. Let's hope I don't need to use it.'

Amelia took the lift to the fifth floor where Jola's ward was located. Jola was sitting up, looking less pale than she had previously. 'DI Barton. I thought you be too busy to come see me.' Jola smiled. Her English was coming along.

'You can call me Amelia, Jola. It's fine. I wanted to see how you were.'

And quiz you about Elena, Amelia thought. She couldn't feel guilty, though. This was important for all of the trafficked women.

Kesia arrived. She hugged Jola gently before pulling up a plastic chair on the opposite side of the bed.

Jola spoke animatedly in Polish to Kesia. When she stopped, Kesia said that Jola was just thanking her for helping her yesterday.

'How did she take it?' Amelia asked.

Kesia grimaced. How do you take the news at the age of twenty that you can no longer have children and that any sex you have in the future, even if consensual, will be a painful experience?

Amelia couldn't wait for the right moment. She waded in. 'Jola, I'm sorry, I need some information from you. We need to do as much as we can to find the other trafficked women, including Elena and Christina. Can you give me any details about how we could find them?'

Jola answered whilst looking at Amelia. She waited for Kesia to translate. 'I don't know exactly where we were kept. They dragged us into windowless vans when they moved us.'

'Can you tell me anything about the location?' Amelia asked. 'What did you see when moving from the house to the van?'

'The houses were all in a line. There were no gaps between them. We were on a hill. The road went down the hill.'

Amelia asked Kesia to explain gradient to Jola, and Jola showed the angle with her arm. The hill was reasonably steep.

'Jola, we've learned that Elena could come and go from the house. How often did this happen?'

Jola squirmed. 'Yes, she was allowed to get the shopping and go on other errands, but she was the one that was beaten. They slapped her and punched her. She wasn't free. She just wasn't.' Her voice grew louder as she spoke.

Amelia wondered why Jola was so protective of Elena. She still couldn't understand why the traffickers allowed Elena to leave, only to beat her on her return? Why didn't she just go and not come back? 'Elena was a good friend to you, I can see that. Why did she keep returning to the traffickers, Jola? It doesn't make sense.'

'I don't know.' Jola turned away from Amelia. She may well have known and chosen not to say, but Amelia didn't press her. Maybe Jola would tell her in good time. Amelia had other questions to ask.

'Jola, when Elena came back with the shopping, did she ever say where she'd been?'

'No, she wasn't allowed to tell us anything about being outside. Although, she did tell me once that there was a Polish Centre nearby, which she seemed to find funny.'

'Was this a house that you were in recently?'

'No, this was months ago.'

Amelia thought it may still be worth trying to trace the house. She would add a similar question to Chloe's list for her formal interview later, then Chloe could investigate it.

Amelia wanted to know more about where Elena shopped. It could provide vital clues. 'Did Elena bring the shopping home in bags?'

Jola thought about this for a moment. 'Yes, always blue ones.' Corner shop bags, not a supermarket chain, then.

They needed to get this right. 'So the last place you were staying was a terraced house on a steep hill and Elena shopped at the local corner shop?'

'I guess so, yes.' Jola pulled the white sheet on her bed up to her chin and then rubbed her eyes. She looked exhausted.

'One last question, Jola. How long did it take you to get to the club the other night?' Amelia knew this would tell her whether they were kept in Birmingham or a nearby town.

'Not long. Maybe ten minutes.' Birmingham then; a suburb near the club.

'Thank you, Jola. That was really helpful. Now, is there anything you need?'

'Can you get me something to read in Polish? My English reading is poor and I would love to read a book. I loved reading at home. It's been so long.' Jola smiled for the first time.

Kesia said, 'I can get you some books. What sort of books do you like to read?'

'I love women writers, both classic and modern day.' Jola mentioned some names. 'Eliza Orzeszkowa, Olga Tokarczuk, Katarzyna Grochola.'

'I've some at home. I'll bring you them later. I love reading, too. My husband despairs. We have books everywhere – on the stairs, on the dining room table, in so many different languages.'

'Maybe that's why you're so talented as a translator, Kesia,' Amelia said.

Translators in the force were paid a pittance and Kesia's skills were invaluable. She could earn thousands more undertaking other translation work. Amelia often wondered why she chose to work with the police force.

It was time to leave. Amelia was eager to get home and look at a map of Birmingham. If she could find some possible shops that Elena used, then she might be able to find her.

Kesia rose as Amelia did. She kissed Jola on the cheek and promised to visit her that evening with a pile of books.

In the corridor, she turned to Amelia. 'I know I'm not being paid for these sessions. That's fine, but I just want you to know that my whole family's behind you. Whatever you need, we can help. We'll do it for nothing.'

'I can't thank you enough, Kesia, but I can't involve your family –'

'I mean it. My whole family. My husband, uncle, cousins, grandfather. All of them.' Kesia stood her ground. She wanted Amelia to know how serious she was. The men in her Roma family were all boxers. They ran a boxing club in Coventry – a very successful club. Her cousins were both regional champions.

Amelia hoped that she wouldn't need their support, but she was grateful that Kesia had offered. 'Thanks. I can't tell you how much I appreciate your help.'

Kesia nodded and walked away.

An hour later, Amelia was sitting in her office at home. She'd moved her laptop and various files off her desk, which was now covered by a map of Birmingham. She'd marked the location of the sex club with a huge cross and had drawn a circle to mark a fifteen-minute journey border. She would increase this if necessary. She just hoped that they hadn't moved the women again or all of this would be a waste of time.

Amelia rubbed her eyes. She'd highlighted a few possibilities including Small Heath, Camp Hill and Balsall Heath. Then she made a separate list of corner shops. There were hundreds. She needed to narrow things down. She threw her pen down.

There was a faint knock on the door. Amelia opened it. Becky was standing there, chewing her bottom lip.

'What do you want?' Amelia asked, still feeling frustrated.

Becky looked to the floor and shuffled. 'Can I go out tonight? It's my mate's birthday party.'

'Which mate?'

'Sara. You know her. She lives up the street,' Becky raised her eyebrows, pleading.

Amelia did know Sara. That was true. 'Give me her mum's number so I can check.'

'Her mum'll be really busy getting the party together. And –'

'Becky, if you want to go, I'm going to have to speak to her mum. Sort it.' Amelia shut the office door on her daughter and went back to work. She heard her daughter walk away and slam the living room door.

No longer thinking of her daughter, Amelia highlighted the roads she knew were on a gradient. Then she found the nearest corner shops. This cut the list dramatically, but she'd probably missed many key roads. It was a start though.

Fortunately, Amelia had kept the original photographs of the women. She found the one of Elena and copied it on her printer a few dozen times. She grabbed the map, the list of shops and her car keys. As she attempted to leave, Becky stopped her. She passed Amelia her mobile. 'It's Sara's mum.'

Amelia didn't need this distraction. Without any pleasantries, she said, 'Is there a party tonight?'

A quiet, female voice answered, 'Oh yes. It's my daughter's birthday. Don't worry, it'll all be over by midnight.'

'Thanks,' Amelia said and cut the call.

Becky smiled. 'Can I go then?'

Amelia passed the phone to her daughter, 'Be back by twelve or you'll be grounded again.'

'Thanks, Mum.' Becky rushed off upstairs.

As she walked to the car, Amelia wondered if she'd made the right decision, letting her daughter go to the party.

Ten corner shops later, hunting down Elena seemed a waste of time. Not one of the shop workers she spoke to had seen her. She'd left them a photograph and her number. She'd introduced herself as DS Chloe Smith and – fortunately – so far, no one had asked for ID.

She had two more shops in Small Heath before she moved on to Balsall Heath. The next shop was little more than a newsagent, but it did have some rotten-looking fruit and veg on a stand at the front of the shop and a couple of loaves of white bread on a shelf. The shop keeper was a young, slight, Bangladeshi man who was reading a chemistry textbook.

'How can I help?' he asked, barely looking up from his book.

'I'm DS Smith. I'm looking for a Czech woman who was the victim of a crime but appears to have moved without giving her us her address.' Amelia showed him the photograph of Elena. 'Have you seen her by any chance?'

He looked up then and glanced at the photo. Amelia expected him to say no and return to his studies. He didn't. He took a long look at the photo. 'She comes in most days to buy bread and milk.'

'Has she been in today?' Amelia tried to hide her excitement.

'Not yet.'

Amelia said, 'Thanks. That's really helpful.' She could have hugged him.

She went back to her car, which was parked on the opposite side of the street to the shop and settled down to wait.

Amelia was used to waiting around during stakeouts. It was always the same: the desperate need for a toilet, intense boredom and concern that you might have already missed the subject. She didn't know which direction Elena might come from, so Amelia positioned her mirror to cover any angle she might miss. If she could enter the shop quickly, either before or just behind her, then she wouldn't need to risk talking to her in the street. If her minders saw them talking, she would place Elena in severe jeopardy.

It didn't seem to matter how Amelia sat; as the minutes passed, she grew more uncomfortable. It was possible that she had been spotted, sitting in the car, hopefully only by a nosy neighbour, not one of the traffickers. If they reported her to the police, she wondered how she would explain her presence. The shadows lengthened outside, the fading light only adding to her gloom. Her thoughts drifted back to her predicament. Her biggest fear was losing her job. Nothing else mattered. All of the posts she had held over the last eight years involved supporting women. She wouldn't have it any other way. No one had supported her until it was almost too late. Almost. It plagued her. That recurring sensation of being engulfed by water, suffocating and then being hauled out, coughing, spluttering, ejecting water from your mouth and nose, intense darkness turning to painful light. Her dreams were always drowning in water – rainwater… bathwater… consumed, choking, never escaping.

Amelia shook away her nightmares. She needed to clear her head. As she did so, she spotted Elena walking down the hill. There was just enough time for Amelia to enter the shop ahead of her. She stood waiting, perusing the magazines as Elena entered. She put down the copy of Boxing News and approached her calmly.

'Elena, we need to talk.'

Elena didn't blink. 'I've got nothing to say to you, Amelia.' If she was surprised to see her, then she didn't show it.

'Just fifteen minutes. I know you're not a trafficker, and you're not The Devil. Whatever keeps you with them, I can help.'

Elena laughed. 'I hear you've lost your job… how do you plan to do that?'

'I don't know what Jake's told you, Elena. He abused me, raped me. He's as dangerous, if not more dangerous than your captors. You can't trust him.'

'Oh, Amelia, you think I'd ever trust a man?' She laughed again.

One last stab: 'Jola's safe. She was seriously hurt. I can tell you where she is. I know you care for her.'

Amelia noticed Elena soften. 'She's safe. That's all that matters. I don't need to see her.' Elena paused. 'I'll meet you tomorrow at the café on Wright Street at eleven. I can't give you long.'

'Thanks.' Amelia left the shop, surprised and relieved.

Chapter 17

The Devil

It was after nine when Amelia arrived home. Her mother was tidying away the Lego that was strewn over the living room carpet. Caitlyn had got her treat for staying in her own bed for a week.

Amelia smiled. 'Is Caitlyn already asleep?'

'It's late. Of course she is.' Her mother carried on tidying.

Amelia didn't want to wake her but had an overwhelming urge to cuddle up to her youngest daughter. She'd missed that all week. The softness of her pyjamas, the baby smell that still lingered that only a parent would recognise. Amelia hadn't had the same closeness with Becky. She was her daddy's girl, going to Joe for everything when he was alive. Even when Becky was clearly grieving, she didn't turn to her mother. Instead, she spoke to her nan or her school counsellor.

Amelia's mother broke through her thoughts. 'What time did you tell Becky she could stay out 'til?'

The disapproving look said it all. She shouldn't have caved in, in her mother's view. 'Midnight.'

'Well, you'll have to stay up. I'm exhausted. I'm going to watch Casualty then turn in.'

Amelia never watched television. She used to watch

motorsports with Joe, and the occasional film, but she hadn't even done that in years. She decided to leave her mother to it and contact Chloe.

Entering the kitchen, she made herself a coffee and put the meal her mother had left out for her in the microwave. When it was ready, she took the food with her to the office. Dion's instructions for logging on to the message site were on a scrap of paper. It took her five minutes to find it, between forking in the odd mouthful of hot food.

Eventually, she got online.

Amelia: *Hi Chloe. I've found Elena. She's willing to talk to me tomorrow. It would be helpful if you could interview Jola. Take a map of Birmingham with you and see if she can narrow down the places that she and the other women were kept. Start at Blackwood Road, Small Heath. That's where the shop that Elena uses is located . We'll need some formal identification from Jola, though.*

There was no immediate response. Amelia didn't expect there to be. She reached into her desk drawer, hoping that she still had a pack of index cards. When she was younger and in the depths of a case, she'd often spend a few hours creating her own case log. She'd use it to map out links between facts but would also add her own thoughts on investigations that she wasn't yet ready to share with colleagues. She hadn't needed to do this in her current job. Her main role was to interview and support the trafficked women. Will's role was intelligence gathering. Between them, they set up a thorough case evidence board that was stored online rather than pinned up on a wall. It worked well because both of them trusted each other to add relevant details. Of course, Jake had access to the board, but Amelia had never allowed him editing access. There was no need since he worked with Amelia and had already heard the same information. He'd also pass his notes onto her, which she would add herself. Maybe this was another sore point for Jake that made him so angry with her. She started writing out key pieces of information on each index card. Attaching Blu-tack to the back of each card, she stuck them to her office wall.

She'd just finished the cards and was looking for a ball of string when she noticed the reply from Chloe.

Chloe: *Thanks. I'll interview Jola in the morning with Kesia. I think you should know that the Super's been looking for Jake all day and no-one's been able to contact him.*

Amelia: *It's only been a day. Why the concern?*

Chloe: *Not sure. But something's happened, as Will looks clearly worried. He's been checking his phone every two minutes.*

Amelia: *Let's hope nothing dreadful has happened to him.*

There was a pause. Chloe was clearly trying to work out how serious Amelia was being.

Chloe: *I'll let you know if he turns up.*

Amelia nearly added "in a body bag" but just about stopped herself.

Amelia: *Let me know how the interview goes. Shall we catch up tomorrow at a similar time?*

Chloe: *Good idea. Speak then.*

Amelia glanced at the clock. It was 12:01. She went in search of her elder daughter. A few minutes later, the front door slammed and Becky walked in. Just as Amelia was deciding whether or not to berate her for being a few minutes late, she noticed her daughter was crying. Without saying a word, Amelia wrapped her arms around Becky and held her, waiting for her sobs to subside. 'What's wrong?' she eventually whispered in her daughter's ear.

'He doesn't… want me.' Becky got out between sniffs. She rubbed the tears from her eyes. 'He said he did… he kissed me… a few times but when I… I told him… I didn't want to do it, he went off with Leah.'

Good riddance, Amelia thought. She wanted to say that, technically, if he'd done anything, he would be breaking the law and she'd arrest the little twerp. Instead, she said, 'This boy, whoever he is, doesn't care about you. He's really not worth crying over. You've done the right thing tonight. I made huge mistakes when I was your age. I thought that sex and love were the same thing. They often aren't. I know it hurts and you feel rejected, but actually, you rejected him because, quite frankly, he's a little bastard.'

'Mum! You can't say that!' Becky laughed through her tears.

'Your dad would have gone after him with a shotgun.'

Becky smiled, 'No, he'd have run him down with the car.'

'True.' Amelia paused, realising what they'd both said about Joe. Neither needed that reminder right now. 'Becky, love, you're just about to turn fourteen. The age of consent is sixteen for a reason. It's so you're old enough and mature enough to make considered decisions. Sex is great… with the right person. You've done the right thing tonight. You should never be pressured into it. I'm proud of you.'

'Thanks.' Becky snuffled.

'But I'm not making good decisions on your behalf – so no more parties or late nights out for a while. Just concentrate on being you… and your homework. Okay?'

'Okay.' Becky looked down at her feet then hugged her mum again.

Amelia didn't want to let her go. She needed the hug as much as her daughter did. 'Off to bed then. I won't tell your nan… this time.'

'Okay.'

Amelia kissed the top of her daughter's head, catching the subtle aroma of her lemon shampoo as she pulled away to go to bed.

When Amelia awoke the next day, she found Caitlyn asleep next to her. She gently carried her back to her own bed. It would be their little secret. It was the first night that Caitlyn hadn't managed to stay in her own room since starting the sticker chart. She'd done so well up until now.

After eating breakfast with her daughters, Amelia returned to the evidence wall she had created in her office. As she made the links between the main players and events with string, she realised that Elena's role was key. Every time, she came back to the same concern. Why stay?

At 10:30, Amelia left to meet Elena, armed with questions that she knew Elena wouldn't answer. The cafe was relatively busy with people eating a full English. Amelia usually loved the smell of sizzling bacon and eggs, but it was overpowering today. She ordered a tea and a plate of toast, which she nibbled at. Elena strode in and went straight to the counter to order a coffee and a sausage sandwich. Then she plonked herself down opposite Amelia. The bruise on her cheek had faded significantly since their meeting in the church. As she took off her jacket, Amelia noticed the rose tattoo above her chest and shuddered.

'What do you want? I can't stay long,' Elena leaned back against the red leather booth.

'Elena, I know you've said you don't need my help and you're right. I'm not in any position to help you at the moment, anyway, thanks to Jake,' Amelia thought being honest was the only way forward. 'But he's putting you and the other women at incredible risk. What happened to Jola nearly killed her. Whatever information you can give me, I can pass on to the right people –'

'I'm already an informant. Whatever I know is being passed on. Jake's got a handle on it. The only reason I can see for you to be here is to tell me to stop fucking him so you can win him back.' Elena sneered. 'You're basically just a jealous bitch. Why don't you just admit it? What is it you really want to know? What positions we've done so you can fantasise about it?' Elena laughed.

Amelia ignored her sparring. 'Why, Elena? Why do you stay with them? You could walk down the street and never go back. What the hell have they got over you?'

'Nothing. They have nothing. Maybe I just like sweaty men wanking over me.'

'Have you ever thought that maybe they lied to you? Maybe your mother didn't give you up. Maybe they stole you from her. Maybe she's sitting back in the Czech Republic crying over you every night.'

Elena's mask fell. It was for the shortest moment, but Amelia saw the anguish briefly caught in its net. 'A child. They have your child, don't they?' It was a punt and Amelia had no idea where it came from, but it made so much sense.

Elena didn't say anything, she looked past Amelia at the counter. Then she jumped up, searching around for an escape point.

'Shit!'

Amelia realised, too late, that someone had entered the café from the back of the shop. She turned to see two men with their faces covered by hoods and scarves. The tallest was waving a knife. The other grabbed Elena round the neck and started dragging her out of the café. As Amelia attempted to run, the man with the knife grabbed her hair and pulled her back towards him. As her arms flailed, trying to grab or punch any part of him, he turned the knife in his hand and held it near to her neck. She sensed the cold steel and stopped struggling. The café fell silent. Then Amelia heard Elena: 'Let go of me, you fucking bastard! I'm coming with you. Look, I delivered her…'

No one in the café moved. They crouched in the corners of

their booths, staring at the developing scene. Not one reached for his mobile. It was just Amelia and the man with the knife. He made no attempt to move her. He whispered in her ear, 'I hear I'll be killing two today. You and your baby. That's what you expect, isn't it? That I'll slit your throat.'

So this was it. There were no bright moments of clarity. No vital grains of truth. No angels or trumpets. No movie playing her life's best bits. He continued whispering in the softest of voices. 'I'm a roaring lion, Amelia. I'm here on this earth to devour women. You're far too pathetic to stop me.'

Amelia waited, her eyes tightly shut, knowing this man was The Devil and not wanting to see the horror on the faces of those watching. She waited and realised she could no longer feel the iciness of the knife on her skin. Then he hit her. He punched her hard on the side of the head. She dropped to the floor, out cold.

When Amelia came to, there were a couple of men in green kneeling over her. 'I'm okay,' she said putting her hand to her head. Squinting, she tried to sit up. The pain hit her like an express train and she sank back down.

One of the men in green said, 'Good to see you awake. You're not going anywhere just yet. My name's Charlie. What's yours?'

'Amelia.'

'It's DI Amelia Barton, isn't it?' A voice boomed from behind her. She'd recognise it anywhere: DS Clive Sutton. He used to work in the Sex Crimes Unit. 'What sort of mess have you got yourself into now?'

DS Sutton was not known for his tact or diplomacy. It was a good job that she hadn't just blurted out to the kneeling paramedics that she was pregnant.

'I'm okay. Someone tried to mug me, that's all. I'm sure these kind gentlemen will just take me for a nice ride to the hospital to check me over before I go home to my girls. I can pop down to the station later to give a statement, if you like.'

'Ummm.' He didn't look convinced. 'What about the other woman? The witnesses said one of the men dragged her away.'

'I've no idea. Look my head's killing me. Can we talk later?' To prove her point, she turned her head to one side and started vomiting, just missing one of the DS's shiny, black brogues.

'We'd better take her in now. It could be a concussion,' Charlie said. 'Can you walk, or shall we get the stretcher?'

'I think I can walk,' Amelia said and leaned on the paramedic as he helped her up, avoiding eye contact with DS Sutton.

'I'll see you at the hospital then,' DS Sutton boomed, looking down at his shoes as she left.

Later, in the hospital, Amelia sat in bed surrounded by her mother, her daughters and Chloe. The doctors had decided to keep her in overnight for observation. She'd had a brain scan that showed no abnormalities, but they were still concerned that she might be concussed. Then, of course, there was the baby.

'Amelia, you shouldn't even be investigating. What on earth were you doing at that café?' Her mother fussed around her. She'd straightened her sheets five times and poured her countless cups of water.

'I've told you, I only went in for a cup of tea. I was mugged.' What Amelia really wanted was for her mum and the girls to leave her be so she could talk to Chloe, but she didn't have the heart to tell them to go.

'Should you be here, Chloe, if Amelia's been suspended?' Her mum just couldn't leave it.

'It's okay. Who's going to dob me in? You, Mrs …?' Chloe looked slightly concerned as though she wasn't sure if she'd do it.

'Just call me Jane. I'm Mrs. Henson. But any colleague of my daughter's…' She was clearly thinking of Jake. *Go on, Mum, say it,* Amelia thought, *any colleague of my daughter's except that fucking bastard.*

'Don't worry, Chloe, my mum won't dob you in. Will you?'

'No, of course not. It's nice that you're here.' She was still fussing. Now she was attempting to fluff up Amelia's pillows. The movement was making Amelia feel nauseous again.

Caitlyn looked like she was about to cry. She scrambled up the side of the bed and lay down next to Amelia, who hugged her close.

'I know this may seem an odd request, but can someone get me a Bible?' Amelia's thoughts returned to the café. There was something she had to look up. It was itching away at the back of her skull.

Everyone looked at her as if she'd gone mad. Her eldest daughter piped up, 'Has the blow to the head made you go all religious? Please don't say we're going to have to go to church each week. I'd rather vomit.'

'God forbid…. No, it's not that. I just need to look something up.' Amelia didn't add that it was for a case, but looked at Chloe, who seemed to get her drift.

'Why don't I take a look in the hospital chapel? I'm sure they'll have one there.' Chloe left in search of a bible. Amelia hoped that her mother and daughters would take it upon themselves to leave, too, so she could talk to Chloe in private as soon as she returned.

Minutes later, when she'd all but given up hope of that happening, her nurse walked past her bay. 'You know we can't have visitors on the bed, can we?' the nurse said, looking mildly annoyed.

Caitlyn didn't stir. Eventually, Amelia's mother said, 'Let's leave your mum in peace. They'll release her by the morning when they find that there's nothing wrong with her brain. She's always been this mad.'

Her attempt at humour didn't work. No one laughed, but Amelia was glad that she'd finally decided to take her girls home. The hospital was no place for them.

'You can go home and play with your new Lego, Caitlyn. I'll see you in the morning.'

They all said their goodbyes, and the girls and her mother left. Chloe came back from the chapel a few moments later. She passed the bible to Amelia. 'What exactly are you looking for?' Chloe asked.

'References to the devil. I think it was him who attacked me at the café. He said something – well, rather odd.' Amelia answered, thumbing through the Bible. 'Do these things have an index?'

'If you're looking for something specific, you might be better doing an Internet search.'

'I guess you're right. This is like looking for a needle in a haystack.'

Chloe took her mobile out of her pocket and opened up Safari. 'What am I looking for?'

'He said something about being a lion and devouring women. It was really odd.'

Chloe typed 'devil'+'lion'+'devouring women' into the search bar. It didn't take long to find the right verse. 'It's obviously a popular quote. There are even memes for it. Here it is – Peter 5:8 "Be sober-minded; be watchful. Your adversary the devil prowls around like a roaring lion, seeking someone to devour." No mention of women, but he'd obviously added that for effect.'

'What an odd thing for him to do – quote Bible verses.' Amelia touched the side of her head, still shocked by the size of the lump generated by his fist.

'I think maybe this whole devil thing has gone to his head. But you're right, it is odd.'

Thinking of devils, Amelia conjured up another. 'Has Jake turned up yet?'

'No, there's no sign of him. The Super's got everyone out searching for him. I'm supposed to be checking in with the hospitals.' Chloe winked.

'Let me know if he turns up. Elena didn't say anything or appear worried. I'm really not sure if she set me up or was just covering for herself when we were attacked in the café. She said, "I delivered her," as though the traffickers had ordered her to give me up.'

Amelia and Chloe didn't have time to discuss this as Amelia spotted DS Sutton entering the ward. She whispered to Chloe, 'We'll have to speak later. I'd better give him a statement.'

She then made a show of saying goodbye to Chloe. 'I'll see you tomorrow. We'll have lunch at mine.' She hoped that DS Sutton would see Chloe as a friend, not a fellow officer, as she didn't know if he was aware of her suspension.

Thankfully, the statement did not take long. DS Sutton making it very clear that he was no fan of hospitals. This left Amelia free for the rest of the evening. She was lost in her own thoughts, not sure if she cared if Jake was in danger or not, wondering if she was right and The Devil really did have Elena's child.

Chapter 18

Missing

Amelia woke early the next morning. She heard the nurses shuffling around getting the drugs trolley ready and writing up notes in preparation for the ward round later. Her phone beeped next to her. It was a reminder that she was supposed to have a counselling session that afternoon. Before she could decide whether to cancel it, one of the nurses came over.

'You had a message late last night.' She passed Amelia a piece of paper. It simply stated: *Elena told me she met you. Glad you're both still alive to tell the tale. Jake X*

Not dead, then. Amelia wasn't sure what upset her most about the message: the fact that he'd put Elena and her together in that way, or the kiss at the bottom. She imagined him dictating it to the nurse, probably flirting with her in the process.

The nurse, still standing next to the bed, watched Amelia read the message then confirmed her suspicions. 'He seemed nice. So, is he your bloke?'

'No, he's not nice at all. He's a bastard.' Amelia ripped up the note. 'Here, you can put this in the bin for me.'

The nurse took the paper without comment and walked away.

Amelia couldn't contact Chloe to let her know that Jake was

alive and well. She didn't have her laptop and she didn't trust her phone. God knows why Jake hadn't checked in with the office. Presumably, he knew what he was doing. What did she care if he was in trouble, anyway? What she needed to do was get out of the hospital. She called the nurse back over. 'What time can I leave?'

Whether it was the way she'd spoken to her earlier, or for some bureaucratic reason, the nurse was far from helpful. 'It's not up to me. You'll have to wait until you've seen the doctor.'

'I've got a counselling appointment at one o'clock at the Martens Clinic. I can't miss it.' Amelia hoped the mention of a medical appointment might help.

'Ward round's in two hours. You'll have to see what the doctor says. Sorry.' The nurse didn't look sorry, just fed up and worn out.

Amelia realised that she must have been on shift all night and changed her tone. 'I'm sorry. I just want to go home. Can I sign myself out?'

'You'll have to wait until the next shift starts in an hour. There's so much paperwork involved and I've got other patients to deal with before then.'

Amelia knew she wasn't getting anywhere. She got up, took her clothes from her locker and went to the nearest bathroom. Once she was dressed, she left the bathroom and, instead of going back to bed, walked out of the hospital. She hoped she wouldn't get the nurse into trouble, but that was the least of her problems.

When she arrived home, she entered by the back door and went straight to her office. Five minutes later, her mother knocked on the door and said, 'There's no use pretending you've been discharged. The hospital rang to see if you were here. I told them you were pig-headed and they'd have to chain you to the bed to keep you in it once you'd decided to leave. They're going to send you some forms through the post to cover themselves in case you drop down dead in the next couple of weeks. I told them we wouldn't sue them if you did – it'd be your own fault.'

'Fine. Thanks.' Amelia didn't want to spend more precious time discussing it, but her mother wouldn't stop.

'It's not about you now – it's about your baby. You can't carry on like this. Someone else is going to have to save those women.'

Amelia knew that, apart from Chloe, there was no one… no

one saving those women. The other officers at the NCA were more driven by beating the traffickers than saving the women, and it wasn't the same thing. Jake, in particular, didn't care who he destroyed along the way. Elena and the others were still at risk. Amelia had to speak to Chloe. 'Mum, I've got stuff to do, so…'

'Amelia, you can't save them all. Sometimes you've got to save yourself. These kids have only got you left. You can't put yourself in danger anymore. Promise me you won't.'

'I promise.' *With my fingers crossed behind my back*, Amelia thought, feeling ten again.

Finally, her mother left her in peace. Amelia shut the door and fired up her laptop. A few clicks later and she was in the message site Dion had set up:

Amelia: *Chloe, I've had a message from Jake. He's fine. You can call off the cavalry.*

Amelia waited. There was no response.

Amelia: *How did you get on talking to Jola?*

After getting no response, Amelia left the message hanging in the air and relaxed, exhausted by the fight.

When she hadn't heard anything by 12.30, she shut down her laptop and got ready to go out for her counselling session.

Her counsellor looked more concerned than usual when she arrived. She kept taking off her glasses and pinching her nose as Amelia told her that she was fine.

Finally, her counsellor said, 'I've been told by your employer that you've been suspended.'

So much for confidentiality. 'Are they allowed to do that? Tell you, I mean.'

'Yes, when there's a concern for your welfare. It means you can have as many sessions as you need and,' she paused and took a deep breath, 'even if the force lifts the suspension, they'll come to me to decide if you're fit to return to work.'

'Did they tell you why I was suspended?'

'No, they… they didn't. Perhaps you should tell me.'

'Apparently, I assaulted a fellow officer. I bet you can't work out who.' Amelia was getting angry and wasn't hiding it in her voice, which rose sharply.

The counsellor didn't answer for a few moments and then said, 'I've been thinking about what you told me in our last session. I'm concerned for your safety.'

'You're concerned for my safety? Didn't you hear what I said? Apparently, I go around thumping people, and you're concerned for my safety?' Amelia's voice became louder and harsher.

'What caused you to hit him?'

'He locked me in the ladies' toilets and groped my breasts. Then he had the cheek to go to internal affairs to say that I'd assaulted him.'

'Then you have every right to be angry.'

'Too right, I do!'

'Listen, Amelia. I said I'd thought about what you told me about your DS. He could be very dangerous. Obviously, I can't diagnose him without assessing him personally, but his behaviour – I've seen it before. I've written papers on it, in fact. He clearly has issues with forming healthy relationships. It sounds like a typical cycle to me of someone with a personality disorder. Narcissism springs to mind. The way he treated you was an extreme form of a phase often referred to as the discard phase. He'd completed the cycle of abuse with you and moved on to someone else. He'll no doubt do the same with her.'

Amelia listened, knowing that whatever Jake had done to her, she had survived – just. But, Elena…

'He'll start the new relationship with love bombing, as you previously described. Then, once he knows she's captivated by him, he'll start devaluing her emotionally.'

'She's already damaged.' Amelia knew her survival had depended on her strength. She'd been able to break away, but only when she'd reached rock bottom. Elena was far more damaged to start with.

'I'm not sure what I can do. I'm happy, with your permission, to report back to your employers and say that I believe you're telling the truth and that you were defending yourself.'

'Thanks. I appreciate that.'

'Amelia, you must be careful. He'll keep trying to get back at you. He may even try to get you back onside. He could use triangulation – try and play you off against the other woman if he hasn't done so already.'

Amelia thought about it. Jake had certainly talked about her to Elena. He'd even suggested that he'd happily see them both at the same time. The mere thought repulsed her.

The counsellor looked up at the clock. Time had run out again.

Amelia rushed back home. She wanted to see if Chloe had replied. The answer she finally got from Chloe wasn't what she expected.

Chloe: *Jake's still not reported in. I can't stop and chat. They've found another body: another woman with a rose tattoo.*

Amelia's heart sank. She slowly closed the lid of her laptop. It could be anyone but, if she had a rose tattoo, it was likely to be one of the trafficked women. It could be Lucia's sister, Nikola, or maybe it was Elena. If it was Elena, then Amelia would blame herself for arranging the meeting at the café. She'd basically lured Elena to her death, if that was the case. She couldn't live with that.

There was nothing she could do to find out what was happening. She had to wait for Chloe to get back in touch. For an hour, she paced the room, getting more and more angry that she was so powerless. Then she grabbed her jacket, bag and car keys. There was nothing she could do here, but there was one place where she might be useful.

When Amelia arrived at Poppy's Place, she pressed the intercom and waited for Ellie to answer. It took her a few moments. 'Can you say your name and reason for visiting?'

'It's Amelia.' Not DI Barton. Just Amelia.

'I'm just opening the gate,' came the reply.

The iron gate swung open and Amelia got back into her car. She drove along the winding drive slowly, wondering what she was doing here.

Siobhan greeted her at the door. 'You've heard the news, then?'

'Yes. Another body. I wanted to be here for Lucia.' Amelia walked into the hostel and sat down at the kitchen table.

'Kesia's here, too. She's upstairs with Lucia. How are you? I wanted to come to see you, but it's been mad here.'

'Chloe's kept me in the loop. She shouldn't have, but she insisted,' Amelia said.

'I've spoken to your idiot of a superintendent. Told him he's a fool for believing Jake over you. I may have used other choice words. Sorry.'

Amelia smiled. She could well imagine that conversation. 'I suppose we'll all have to wait for information.'

A police car arrived a couple of minutes later. Amelia waited in the living room until they'd left for the morgue with Lucia and Kesia.

Siobhan was sitting in the kitchen. When Amelia entered, she stood up, clearly not sure what to do with herself. 'Shall I make some tea?' she asked.

'Yes, thanks.' Amelia sat back at the kitchen table. 'They think it might be Nikola, then?'

'Possibly. The body was found on waste ground, near to where the other body was found. She was branded, though, like our women.'

'Did they say how long they thought she'd been there?'

'No. They just asked if Lucia would go with them. I know this sounds horrible but I'm hoping it is Nikola. Lucia has been distraught. She's barely eaten. She sleeps all the time. We've suggested she go to Peterborough to live with her family, but she refuses to leave without her sister. It's a bloody tragedy. Now I feel horrible for saying it.' Siobhan sat down and poured the tea. She looked exhausted.

'Don't, it's only what we've all been thinking. If someone's dead, you need closure. If she's alive, you want her found and brought to safety as soon as possible. I can understand that.'

Siobhan sipped her tea. Her phone started to buzz on the table next to her. Chloe's name glowed from the display. Siobhan answered. 'Hi, Chloe. You okay?' She offered the phone to Amelia. 'Chloe knew you were here. Kesia told her. She wants to speak to you.'

Amelia took the phone. 'Hi, Chloe.'

Chloe spoke quickly. 'It's not Nikola. This girl's far too young. We're just following procedure. I wanted to pre-warn you. I'd say she can't be more than fifteen, if that. Her throat was slit,

Amelia. I… I thought you should know.'

Amelia didn't answer, the shock struck her dumb. Her legs were shaking and she felt icy cold. Siobhan must have noticed. She took her phone from Amelia's hand and spoke softly and quietly to Chloe. Amelia wasn't listening. This child had died because of her. Her throat was cut. The Devil didn't kill Amelia. He killed a girl in her place.

Chapter 19

Siobhan's Support

'It's my fault,' Amelia said.

Siobhan put down her phone. 'Of course it's not.'

'He killed the girl because of me. He threatened to slit my throat. It was easier to kill one of the people he'd enslaved and then dump her.' Amelia visibly shook. 'She was a child... Chloe said she was just a child.'

'Why don't we go to my office? Lucia can't see you like this.' Siobhan took Amelia's arm and led her up to the top floor of the hostel.

On entering the office, Siobhan said, 'There's a bottle of whisky in the top drawer over there and a couple of glasses. Help yourself if you need to.'

Amelia's legs were still shaking as she took the bottle from the filing cabinet. She poured herself a large whisky and offered one to Siobhan, who took it. Amelia normally drank it straight, welcoming its burning passage. The shaking stopped after she drank the second glass. Neither woman spoke.

Siobhan's office was her sanctuary. The place, of the whole building, was hers alone. She shared private space: a bedroom and lounge with Ellie, but this was clearly Siobhan's personal haven. On the desk was a photograph of Poppy, taken before she was ravaged by drugs and the mental anguish of being a sex worker. Her long, brown, wavy hair and relaxed smile belied her future fate.

'She was beautiful,' Amelia said.

Siobhan took a large gulp of her drink before answering. 'Yes, she was. Beautiful up until the day that bastard got his claws into her.'

'Her pimp?'

'Yeah. He started out as her boyfriend. They met at a nightclub. I knew she was doing coke and probably other stuff, but what eighteen-year-old isn't?' Siobhan paused, twirling the whisky glass in her hands. 'She moved in with him a few weeks later. I told her it was too soon. I told her that she should stick with her A levels, go to uni, have a life… but, of course, she didn't listen.'

Amelia listened as intently as she could. There were voices screaming in her head. Women's voices. She tried to block them out, concentrating on Siobhan's every word.

'Within a matter of weeks, they'd run out of money and he forced her to perform favours, at first just for the landlord to pay the rent and some of his friends for cash. Soon after, she was walking the streets turning tricks down the Barras. I did everything I could to stop her. Everything. Nothing I said… nothing mattered. She loved him. That's what she said, "But I love him, Mum," as though this was an excuse or a valid reason.'

Amelia knew the rest of the story. Her boyfriend – her pimp, the man she loved – strangled her in a fit of rage in a side street one Saturday night. Amelia was a detective constable in the sex crimes unit at the time. Some of her colleagues had worked the case.

If she'd been on duty that night, she might well have been the one to break the news to Siobhan.

As Siobhan stopped speaking, the voices in Amelia's head grew louder. She couldn't stop them. She started hitting her forehead with the flat of her hand. Blow after blow until Siobhan grabbed her wrists.

'It's… all gone wrong.'

'I know.' Siobhan waited for Amelia to continue.

Eventually, Amelia forced the voices to the back of her mind and said, 'I'm pregnant. I shouldn't be drinking.' She pushed the glass away from her. 'It's Jake's. I couldn't get rid of it. I thought about it, I really did. It was such a difficult decision. Have you ever had an abortion?'

'No, I lost a couple of babies though. Miscarriages. All with Poppy's dad. I wouldn't admit I was more attracted to women in those days. He wasn't a bad man and we had some good times for the first few years, but to be honest, I could take or leave the sex.'

Siobhan smiled at this as though a happier memory flitted through her mind.

'Joe was worth a million Jakes. Oh God, Shiv. Why didn't I spot that he was abusing me? Jake, I mean, not Joe. Joe was the strongest, most secure person I've ever met. He wanted everyone around him to be happy and strong. Oh, he wasn't perfect. He could be a moody sod when he wanted. He'd rather fix his car than go on a date. But, compared to Jake –'

'You won't be the first or the last not to notice a man's abusive behaviour, Amelia. I just wished I'd warned you sooner.'

'He's abusing Elena. I can't do anything to stop him. I've tried, but he's always one step ahead and now my actions have led to this. A girl, Shiv. A girl… she's been murdered because of me.' The tears came then.

There was a knock at the door. Siobhan got up to open it. It was Ellie.

'Lucia's back. It wasn't her sister. I thought you'd want to know. Chloe brought her back. She's downstairs.'

'Thanks. Can you ask Chloe to come up?' Siobhan turned to Amelia. 'That's okay, isn't it.'

Amelia wiped the tears away with her sleeve. 'Yes, yes, of course.'

A few minutes later, Chloe sat down next to Amelia. She looked pale and exhausted. She took Amelia's glass, unconcerned that it had been pre-used, and poured herself some whisky without waiting to be asked.

'That was horrific,' she said eventually.

'You said it was a child.' Amelia hoped this wasn't true, that she'd misheard or Chloe had been mistaken.

'Yes, a child, or young woman… but a child would be a better description. A child lying in a pool of blood. The way he'd cut her! It looked like an open mouth with lipstick badly applied around its edges… like a toddler would draw. Horrific.' Chloe drank some more whisky. 'She was branded with the same rose. It must have been Davo or whatever he's called, or one of his traffickers.'

Amelia took a deep breath, trying to retrieve her professional composure, 'Are they linking her death with the woman who was found in a similar area of town?

'I believe so. There's been no firm decision made yet, as far as I know. The same DCI and DI are involved in both cases. The DI – Branfield – he's a bit shit, though. He kept referring to her as a prostitute and never once looked on her as a child. It was bloody obvious. There's no way she was older than fifteen! She could've been much younger!' Chloe thumped the whisky glass on the table, creating waves of amber liquid that threatened to slop over the top.

Siobhan said, 'We've met loads of bastards like that in our time. You should've –'

Amelia knew what was coming: a long diatribe of what Siobhan would have done to him. It would have been entertaining to listen to, but not constructive.

'Chloe, can you get me the files? For both girls. I want to help.'

Chloe seemed to ponder this. Amelia thought that was good, at least she was considering the ramifications of sharing the file with a suspended officer. She'd have been more concerned if she'd immediately said yes.

'I'll get Dion to copy them and send them to you. He's much more savvy about that kind of thing. I'm better at finding things on the net, shall we say. He's better at hiding them.'

'Thanks.' Amelia knew she had to ask the next question but wasn't sure if she cared about the answer. 'Any sign of Jake?'

'No, he's still not called in. The super doesn't seem that bothered, though. Will flapped a bit but he's gone quiet about it. I reckon he's gone undercover.'

Amelia let that sink in… Jake working undercover with the trafficking ring and screwing Elena. Amelia couldn't work out how he'd managed that. Either he was incredibly devious or incredibly stupid. If he got caught –

Siobhan interrupted her thoughts, 'I'm guessing you'll both either want me to call a taxi or stay the night. Which is it? You've worn this old woman out.'

Amelia guessed that all this talk about the murdered young woman had unsettled her. She was right, though. It was time to call it a night. Chloe decided to get a taxi to Dion's. She'd pick up her car in the morning. Amelia decided to stay at Poppy's Place. The settee in the office was already furnished with a duvet and pillows. Siobhan left her to rest there.

After texting her mother to let her know she'd be back in the morning, Amelia lay down, knowing she was likely to have a restless night.

Chapter 20

The Boxing Club

When Amelia woke the next day, the rest of the women seemed to be already awake. She could hear them chatting on the main staircase, along with the constant stream of the shower in the bathroom below her. There'd been no nightmares. Maybe since she now seemed to have them during the day, they'd departed from her at night.

There was a soft knock on the door. Amelia rose to answer it. Aware that she only wore her blouse and knickers, she pulled the bottom of the shirt down as far as it would go.

It was Siobhan carrying a tray of breakfast. 'I wasn't sure what you wanted so I brought you a bit of everything. Natalia dressed the tray. She wanted it to be special.'

Amelia felt a lump form in her throat. It reminded her of all those occasions when her daughters had made her "a mummy breakfast". This one looked far more edible, if not quite as heart-warming. Natalia had made a special effort at presenting each dish. There was even a small vase containing a single red rose sitting next to the boiled egg in its own china egg cup. Siobhan set the tray on the opposite side of the desk and sat down in her office chair.

'Aren't you having any?' Amelia asked.

'I've already eaten.' Siobhan looked out of the window at the pink, morning sky.

It felt odd, eating in front of Siobhan, but Amelia was ravenous. She hadn't eaten the previous evening. In fact, she couldn't remember when she'd last had a proper meal. *This can't be good for the baby,* she thought, mentally scolding herself.

As Amelia finished the last of the toast, Siobhan said, 'I've been talking to Kesia. We're worried about you. We both think you need some protection. I'd give you Ellie, but we need her here. I've been getting emails again.'

Siobhan had often had periods when some troll decided she was an easy target for abuse. She had a public profile that was essential for her charity work. The house needed constant maintenance and the food bills were astronomical. They didn't get any financial aid from the government as they didn't hold the housing contract for trafficking victims – that honour went to the Salvation Army – nor were they given money to support women leaving the sex trade. Instead, part of Siobhan's life involved organising high profile events to raise money. It was a never-ending process.

Siobhan continued. 'Kesia wants you to go and speak to her uncle at the Blue Corner. She's arranged it for this afternoon. He's expecting you, Amelia. You wouldn't want to let him down.'

'What would I need at a boxing gym? Is he offering lessons? I've got my own technique for dealing with lowlifes.' Amelia wasn't sure how she felt about the offer. She knew Kesia's family were well known in the city. No one would dare cross them, but the thought of having someone following her around and looking after her just didn't appeal.

Siobhan sighed. 'We can't force you to accept the offer. Just meet with Michal and see what you think. Promise me that at least you'll do that.'

'Okay, I'll meet him. Maybe he'll teach me how to knock someone out with one punch or at least how to skip. I've always wanted to be able to do that,' Amelia laughed.

Siobhan smiled. 'Can't you skip?'

'Not very well. Two left feet. My dancing's not up to much, either.'

'I've heard he's a great dancer, too.' Siobhan raised an eyebrow.

'I feel like I'm being set up on a date now.'

'Did I say that he's rather handsome?'

'Believe me Shiv, the last thing I need is a man.'

Just after midday, Amelia drove into the car park of the Blue Corner Boxing Club. It sat at the end of a row of shops. It had a side door with a simple sign showing a blue square with a pair of black boxing gloves in the centre of it. Around the edge of the square, the words Blue Corner were repeated. Amelia had been to many boxing matches. She hated the sport, but it was some kind of initiation for West Midlands Police. *You've got to go to the charity boxing matches or you're not one of the lads.* Amelia never wanted to be 'one of the lads' but it wasn't like they gave her a choice.

The gym was on the second floor. Walking up the stairs, she could already hear the *thud.d.d.d, thud.d.d,d, thud.d.d.d, thud,d,d,d...* of the repetitive punching of a leather speed bag. Amelia expected to open the door to a room full of sweaty, sparring men. She was surprised to see a young woman alone in the gym in training gloves. The woman didn't falter or break into a sweat. She continued her routine without pause. This left Amelia feeling awkward and unsure of where to go. Then an office door to the right of the boxer opened. It seemed strange to see a man in a suit in a boxing gym, but this had to be Kesia's uncle. He beckoned Amelia over to the office.

As she reached the office door, he pulled her into a hug. She caught the citrus tang of his aftershave. It was the same as the one Joe had always worn. Normally, she hated being hugged by strangers, but she didn't want to let this man go. He pulled away too soon and smiled.

'Come in, come in.' He gestured her into the office. The *thud.d.d.d, thud.d.d.d, thud.d.d.d...* continued. 'Kesia's told me so much about you. She says that you're not a bad person for a *gadji*.' He laughed and Amelia found herself blushing.

'I'm not sure how you can help. I don't really need minding.' Amelia glanced at the photos around the room. They were of a younger Michal. This man had been described as handsome, even by a lesbian. Amelia could see why, but she'd been fooled by that before.

Michal interrupted her thoughts. 'Did Kesia ever speak to you about her father?'

'No, she doesn't speak much about her family. There's rarely time to be sociable.'

'He was a police officer in the Czech Republic.'

'Was?' Amelia was surprised that he was a policeman but was more interested in why he'd stopped.

'He was murdered. Stabbed once in the chest by a Neo-Nazi. A gang recognised that he was Rom and chased his car for a mile before forcing him off the road and killing him. No one was ever charged.'

'Kesia never said anything.'

'So many Roma have been killed over the years. You can slag off gipsies, call us dirty scroungers, even kill us. No one cares. We left the Czech Republic soon after, bringing Kesia with us. Her mother went back to Poland.' Michal grimaced. 'My wife died of cancer five years ago. I've got five boys. Kesia means everything to me. One thing they never tell you about the Roma – family is everything.'

'I'm sorry. I wish I'd known all this. Kesia always seems so composed. I had no idea of her history.'

'She was very young when it happened. Only four years old. She's had a happy life here. We all have. There's not many Roma that own a boxing club.' Michal smiled that broad smile of his.

'As I said, I don't really know why I'm here.'

'Kesia told us that you needed some support. My door's open. Whatever you need.' He opened his arms as if encompassing the whole gym.

'I can fight my own battles.'

Michal laughed. 'I don't doubt that. Look, Amelia, I don't want to bully you. Take a look round the gym. Meet my boys. See what takes your fancy.'

Amelia blushed again. 'I'd like to see the gym.' She didn't want to seem ungrateful. 'One thing… I've always wanted to do that skipping thing'

'Really? Oh, there's no trick to that.' He got up from his chair. He didn't even look surprised. 'Wait here.'

Michal left the room. Amelia stood and took a closer look at the photos. In each stood a lean, dark-skinned boxer with wavy black hair and that broad, friendly smile that could only belong to Michal. This may have been his younger days, his belt-winning days, but he'd barely aged.

The door clattered against the wall as Michal returned to the office. Amelia jumped and turned to face him. He'd changed into long black, boxing shorts and a vest top. In his hands were similar women's clothes. 'Alicia said you can borrow these. What size shoes?'

'I'm a seven.' Amelia, not for the first time, felt self-conscious about the size of her feet.

'That's great. I'll just get you some boots. The women's changing room is next door.' He ushered Amelia out of the office and into the changing room. She noticed that the gym was now full of young men warming down. As if reading her mind, Michal said, 'Oh don't worry about them, they've just returned from a training run.'

The shorts would have been super long on Alicia. There were tight on Amelia, but just about comfortable. The vest top rose up and showed her stomach as she moved. In the mirror in the changing room, Amelia noticed the rounding of her abdomen. If you didn't know she was expecting, then you'd have thought nothing of it. Amelia placed her hands on the gentle bulge, standing still for a few moments. Then she reached into her bag and hunted around for a scrunchy to tie her auburn hair back. The boots Michal had found for her were flat and springy. She pulled the laces tight and tied them in a double knot. Amelia the boxer; the reflected image looked tough and athletic in equal measure. For the first time in weeks, Amelia felt content.

Michal was waiting for her in the gym, holding a boxer's weighted skipping rope. When he handed it to her, it seemed very different from the skipping ropes she'd held as a child. The handles were a deep mahogany leather, creased with age. When she gripped them, she sensed their history.

'This was my father's rope. It's the only one I'll use. It's heavier than some modern ropes,' Michal said softly. 'Hold it loosely, not too tight and with your arms out to the side. Your elbows need to be slightly bent.'

Amelia did as she was told. Michal gently took her wrists and moved her hands further away from her side by just a touch. 'Perfect,' he said. 'Just a flick of the wrist should get the rope turning.'

The rope turned fine, but for the first couple of revolutions her feet let her down. They tangled in the rope, as she failed to raise them in time. Then the rhythm took hold and Amelia skipped. Slowly at first, but then she became braver and skipped faster and faster. The click of the rope on the gym floor drummed like a dripping tap. Michal smiled, crunching up the skin at the corner of his eyes. 'A natural,' he beamed.

That tore it. Amelia lost the rhythm and nearly tied her feet in knots. Luckily, she stayed standing – just. She burst out laughing, causing many of the male boxers to turn in her direction.

Michal had taken her arm to steady her. 'Maybe you need a little more practice.'

He took the rope from her and proceeded to demonstrate how it should be done. Amelia was transfixed. He changed rhythm without faltering, barely raised his feet and then added a number of tricks explaining as he did them: crossovers, side swings, double-unders, until finishing with a number of skips at an unbelievable speed. He wasn't even out of breath. Amelia laughed and clapped. The others in the gym paid little attention.

'Here.' Michal handed the rope back to Amelia. 'Have another go.'

Amelia took the rope. 'You want me to follow that!'

'You can do it. Take it slowly.'

Amelia started to skip, noticing that Alicia had finished her routine and was sitting on a bench, warily watching her. Michal didn't seem to notice. He offered occasional words of encouragement, his smile growing each time Amelia put a set of more than ten skips together. She didn't want to admit that she was both enjoying the gym and being in Michal's company but she was soon too exhausted to continue.

Michal put the rope back on the shelf above a set of black and white photographs.

'Is that your father?' Amelia asked.

Michal nodded. 'Yes. His ambition was to get to the Olympics.' He then walked behind Alicia, who was still sitting on the bench, and put his hands on her shoulders. 'Just like this one.

The Blue Corner's Nicola Adams. The only thing holding her back is having to cut her hair.'

Alicia blushed but said nothing. Amelia had noticed the young woman's long, black plait. You couldn't not notice it. It swayed with every punch.

'I think it's time I got out of both your hair.' Amelia turned to Alicia. 'Thank you for the loan of the clothes. I'll wash them and return them to you.'

Amelia didn't expect her to be so softly spoken. 'Please, I'll wash them.'

Michal explained. 'Alicia likes to do things the Romani way. She'll be happy to wash them. Don't worry yourself.'

After changing, Amelia put her hand out to Michal. He didn't shake it. Instead, he hugged her tight. 'Don't be a stranger. Come, eat with us soon. Kesia can arrange it.'

For the second time, Amelia willed him to continue holding her but he let her go and she knew it was time to leave.

'Thank you. That would be wonderful. I'll speak to Kesia.'

Chapter 21

Evidence

Dion had sent through both files for the recently murdered women. Amelia arrived home to find them already uploaded to her computer. The file was labelled: *Davo the murderer?* It was saved to her desktop and it even winked at her when she fired up Windows. She didn't know how Dion had managed it, but it made her laugh. As soon as she clicked on it, clear instructions for how to delete the file and its contents were given. Amelia made sure she printed the files then deleted them in exactly the way Dion described. She wrote one word on the messenger site for Chloe. *Done.*

After making a pot of tea and grabbing some custard creams, Amelia sat on the sofa in the office with her laptop on her knees. She opened the first file. A woman's digitally modified photograph appeared first. It looked nothing like the woman that she had seen. She appeared young and attractive, with long, dark hair and flawless, olive-brown skin. The woman they had discovered was barely recognisable as a person. A beating like that results in the face blowing up, becoming disfigured and distorted. It's horrific. They couldn't use that photograph as a means of identification, hence the digital reconstruction.

Amelia wondered why this woman hadn't been branded with a rose tattoo. She opened the autopsy report and five lines in got her answer. She had been branded, but not on the shoulder. There was a small rose, which had clearly become infected at some point, on her inner thigh. Perhaps the traffickers had realised that it was, in some way, better to tattoo the shoulder? The Murder Investigation Team had not managed to identify the woman. They'd contacted Europol but had no joy. Amelia sighed. There were so many dead, nameless women across Europe and the rest of the world.

Putting down the laptop, Amelia stood up and went to the window. She opened the blinds and glanced down the street. Who knew what went on in people's homes? She hoped if anyone heard these women's screams that they'd reported them, rather than putting it down to a domestic or a television left on loud. These two women weren't killed where they were found. The post-mortems and scene of crime evidence made that transparently clear. Amelia's gut told her they were killed in houses, maybe like these in her street, maybe at a sex party or maybe in the dirty, seedier brothels where anything goes for a price and no one cares if the sheets are clean. She'd seen both and many in between. Very few were reported, but the neighbours must surely know, or if they didn't, they must have heard the women's screams and wondered about the goings-on. Those women's screams seemed to now be punctuating her waking moments.

Two women now, three if you included Nikola Markova – three women murdered by this group of bastards. Amelia had never felt so angry and frustrated. What Jake had done had rendered her powerless unless she took it as an opportunity to work outside the law. It wasn't worth thinking about. She could search the whole of Birmingham and not find either Davo or Elena. It was pointless.

Amelia heard the ping of a message reaching her inbox. Knowing that this was a message from Chloe by the tone, she sat back down on the sofa and picked up her laptop.

Chloe: *So you got the files?*

Amelia: *Yes, thank Dion for me.*

Chloe: *We're not getting much input into the case. I'm surprised they even shared the files with us.*

Amelia: *I'm thinking of visiting the two dumping grounds. Are they still cordoned off?*

Chloe: *Not that I'm aware of.*

Amelia: *I'll take a look tomorrow.* After my scan. Another

visit to the hospital. Hopefully, this one will be less eventful, Amelia thought.

Chloe: *Let me know if you find anything.*

Amelia signed off moments later and returned to the files. The two dumping grounds were less than a mile from each other. Both were waste grounds next to semi-derelict industrial estates. The more Amelia knew, the more she wondered if Robert Davo was actually local. The way he spoke to her, the menace, hissing tone, hadn't given too much away about his accent. He could have come from Bourneville or Kyiv for all she could tell.

There had to be something about him that she could remember. His height, the way he walked, his smell. Amelia let herself sink back into the sofa. She relaxed and closed her eyes, shivering as she pushed her mind back to the café. Her heart began to beat faster as she recalled the pressure of the blade on her neck. She heard the man's voice as he threatened to kill her and her unborn child. What else could she remember? Her heartbeat slowed back to normal. Concentrating on his hand twisted through her hair, she guessed that he was as tall as her, maybe even taller. He'd pulled her head back so he could keep the blade at her throat. Blocking all other senses out, she tried to recall what she could smell on his hands or body. There was something. It took her back to when she had first met Joe as a nineteen-year-old, obsessed with fast bikes and cars. *Two-stroke engine oil.*

Amelia hadn't spoken to Joe's dad in six months, not since Caitlyn's last birthday. She hoped he was fine. He had lived alone since Joe's mother had died of cancer, in a rambling, four-bedroomed house in Sutton Coldfield. He would know what engines used two-stroke oil. It couldn't be many these days. She found his contact details in her phone and pressed call. He answered on the third ring.

'Hi, Frank. It's Amelia. I'm sorry to disturb you –'

'Disturb me? Don't be daft, love. You could never disturb me. How are you and the girls?'

'We're all fine, Frank. We'll come over soon. It's your birthday next month, isn't it?' Amelia hoped she hadn't got this wrong. She was rubbish with dates.

'Yes, the 20th. Come over and we'll go out for a meal. There's a Jamie Oliver place opened in town. The kids'll enjoy that.'

'Yes, it's a date.' Amelia wondered if this was sufficient small talk. 'Frank. I need to know what uses two-stroke oil. Is it just bikes?'

'Not just bikes. Old lawnmowers, leaf blowers, chainsaws, other garden equipment. Why do you ask?' he sounded curious.

'It's just for a case, nothing to worry about. Thanks, Frank. I'm just putting the 20th in my diary. We'll see you then.'

'Bye, love. Look after yourself. It was so good to hear from you.'

Amelia ended the call.

A chainsaw. She hoped it wasn't that. Perhaps he enjoyed gardening, but she couldn't see it. If it was motorcycle oil, then it was probably for a motocross bike, go-kart or a vintage bike. She could try the motocross clubs and go kart centres, but she didn't know what Davo looked like, so she wasn't sure how that would help. She wrote, 'Two-stroke oil' on a record card and attached it to the wall, linking it by string to Robert Davo. It was just another small piece of the puzzle.

Chapter 22

Dumping Ground

As Amelia parked her car at the hospital, she hoped that she wouldn't be in for another long wait. She was even tempted to go to the hospital shop and buy herself a magazine or a book, but it had taken so long to find a parking space that she didn't really have time.

Luck must have been on her side because, almost as soon as she'd arrived, she was called in to see the sonographer. She lay down and braced herself for the cold gel, followed by the pressure. Her head turned straight to the screen. Excitement wasn't an emotion that Amelia commonly felt, but she had to bite her lip to stop herself from grinning like a mad woman. The sonographer finished taking measurements, then turned the screen towards Amelia. It didn't take long for a picture to form. She made out a little body, legs, head, then arms. The baby was real. A boy or a girl. A wriggler, by all accounts.

'Let's see if we can hear the heartbeat.' The sonographer placed what looked like a microphone on the gel and moved it around. There it was, the unmistakable fast heartbeat of her child.

A few minutes later, after leaving the scanning room, Amelia felt almost bereft. She placed the two photographs taken during the ultrasound between the pages of her notebook, then decided she would tell the girls tonight.

The contrast couldn't be greater: new life and death in one day. Amelia had seen the first dumping ground before. The white tent had been removed. If you didn't know that a woman's body had lain here, you wouldn't know it because there were no visual clues. Maybe the ground was flatter, but it had rained a number of times since that day. Amelia was more interested in the local area. Why had they chosen this place?

Last night, she'd marked on her map of Birmingham the location of the houses where they knew the traffickers had imprisoned women. Then she'd added the warehouse where the rescued women had been picked up on their journey to Coventry. Elena and Christina were, to Amelia's knowledge, back in Birmingham, so it looked like the traffickers had scrapped that plan. Maybe other women were moved there. This wasn't a small operation.

The area where the first woman was dumped was, despite being on the edge of a housing estate, mostly commercial and pretty run down. In recent years, there had been little car production in the Midlands. This area was a relic of that. Most of the buildings, including the pub on the dumping site, were boarded up or in the process of demolition.

Amelia walked across the road away from the waste ground. Any van or car that had been used to dump the body would need to come this way. As she walked by the perimeter fence of a small bearings factory across the road, she was greeted by the wild barking of a huge Alsatian, its jaws snapping at the metal fence. Amelia stepped back. Someone must be caring for this animal. Then she spotted a partially-hidden white sign near to the gate: 'These premises are protected by Marston Securities.' They may have been around on the night. It was a long shot, but it needed investigating.

There was nothing else of interest at that location, so Amelia drove to the next. It only took her a few minutes. The photographs in the second report had given her a precise location of where the body was discovered. A postal worker had found it as he walked to the sorting office for his shift. The girl had been deliberately displayed so that she would be seen from the path. Amelia knew that the postal worker would see the dead girl whenever he shut his eyes. Chloe had described the girl's injuries, but the photographs were even more disturbing. Seeing it in the flesh would have been horrific. It didn't take long for Amelia to spot the place where the girl had lain. There were still patches of brown-stained grass. You could see where her neck and head had been propped up.

Amelia didn't linger at this spot. Instead, she sought out any possible areas from where the vehicle used to transport the body would be seen. The Murder Investigation Team would have found CCTV from the area, but the chances were that the cameras might not have been working or, if they were, they may not have been directed on this particular spot. Whoever dumped her here knew what they were doing. There were so few businesses still open and operational. She'd struck lucky with the dog, but wasn't likely to again at this spot. At least she had more of a feel for the place. That was important, too.

When Amelia got home, she started searching the drawers of the desk in her office. Somewhere, she had her ID from the time she worked for West Midlands Police. She recalled forgetting to hand it in when she'd moved across to the National Crime Agency. At the time, she thought she might still need to use it as she was officially on secondment but, in the first few months, there had been a flurry of emails from the Communications Officer at her old station asking for it back. Then, when she failed to get round to returning it, he'd given up and stopped asking. As long as the security company didn't ask for her warrant card, she might get away with just this ID. She rang them and made an appointment to visit later that afternoon.

Marston Securities was based in an office above a row of shops in Marston Green. Amelia didn't know the area well. It was on the edge of Birmingham and had its own railway station about 100 metres from the shops. She decided to park her car there, rather than try – and fail – to find a parking spot in front of the block of shops.

By the time she reached the office of Marston Securities, Amelia felt confident that she could blag an interview with her old ID. She knocked and waited. A few moments later, a short, bald man with broad shoulders opened the door and ushered her into the office. If the size of the office was anything to go by, this was not a large business. Amelia wouldn't be surprised if this guy was both the owner and the only person offering a security service to his clients. The room contained a small desk with a laptop and piles of paper on it and one filing cabinet that looked like it had been rescued from a skip.

The man's face reddened as he noticed Amelia scan the room. 'I'm Dave Marriott. Marston Securities is my company.' He cautiously extended his hand.

Amelia shook it. 'DI Amelia Barton, West Midlands Police.' She sat on the only extra chair in the room. It creaked. She didn't wait and dived right into the reason for being in this shabby office. 'I'm sure you know that a woman was murdered and her body dumped on waste ground on Shelton Road. You have a dog-protected factory on that road, I believe.'

'Y… yes, we do. Sheba's there. I feed her once a day.'

Once a day, Amelia thought. *No wonder the poor dog nearly took my arm off.* 'You must remember the day the murdered woman was dumped, then.'

'I saw it on the news. I had to persuade some copper… er… one of your colleagues to let me through the cordon to feed Sheba that evening.'

'What time did you feed her the previous day?'

He paused and looked at the ceiling, as though this was a particularly difficult calculation. 'Well, I have ten dogs at different locations. I feed them in the same order. Sheba's the furthest away from my house, so it would have been after eight that night. It was a Sunday and I had to take my mother home first. She always comes for Sunday lunch. She likes a roast.'

Amelia wriggled in the chair. She really didn't need to hear this guy's life story. 'Did you hear or see anyone near the site at this time?' It was early, but anyone would have seemed out of place there on a Sunday evening.

'There was someone,' he scratched his head. 'I could hear a bike engine touring around. I was trying to work out from the sound what sort of bike it was. I used to have bikes before I married, but the missus hates them. I reckon it was an oldish Aprilia. A two-stroke. Maybe a crosser.'

Surely this guy wasn't mad enough to ride around looking for a dumping site on such an unusual machine?

'A motocross bike? Did you get to see it?'

'No. By the time I'd fed Sheba, it had left. You don't think –'

'Thanks for your time, Mr. …' Amelia looked at her notes.

'Marriot. Dave Marriott.'

'Mr. Marriott.' Amelia stood to leave.

'There was something else… odd.'

She waited. 'What?'

'The pub's been empty since before I took on the security job. I keep expecting them to demolish it or the local lads to burn it down. It looked like someone was using it in the weeks before the murder. When I went to feed Sheba, I'd see a light on in there.'

'You didn't think of telling the police?'

'I just thought it might be some homeless guy. I'm not paid to keep an eye on that place, too.'

'There was a murdered woman found right next to the pub. Didn't you think that it might have been relevant?' Amelia's voice rose in line with her growing anger.

'That lad you left guarding the place wasn't much interested in what I had to say. He nearly didn't let me feed my dog, for Christ's sake! What sort of bloke would let a dog go hungry?'

'Next time you're in a similar situation, you might want to think a bit further than your customers, Mr Marriott. You're very lucky I'm not charging you with withholding information from the police.' Not that she could currently charge him with anything.

Amelia left the office and cast her mind back. She couldn't remember if DI Branfield had ordered a search of the pub. She'd go back there herself now. It was locked up when she went there earlier but there might well be an easy way in and she had a crowbar in the boot of her car.

It was a thirty-minute drive, the last ten minutes through central Birmingham, the usual stop-go nightmare. The light was beginning to fade by the time she reached the pub. She would probably do better to wait until the morning. She could at least find the way in that the intruders had used, then come back tomorrow and search the place properly.

At the front of the pub, cut into the path, were the old metal doors leading to the cellar where the barrels were kept. These were rusted together and didn't look like they'd been moved in years. To the side of them was the main entrance to the pub. This was covered by a metal security gate that covered the space where the doors would have been. It was locked and chained. It was possible someone had removed the old lock and replaced it with this when they'd finished, but behind it were boards that had been bolted in. The bolts didn't look damaged.

The only other entrance was a much smaller door at the back of the pub. This, also, had boards bolted across it. Amelia ran her fingers over the edges of the bolts. She could feel the rough edges of the board. It seemed that these screws had been taken out and re-bored a number of times, unlike the ones in the front. She would need something to remove them if she was going to get in this way tomorrow. Joe's tools were still in the garage. She'd barely looked at them since his death. He'd kept them in pristine condition. She dreaded to think what they looked like now.

Amelia glanced at her watch. It was just after seven. She texted her mum. *I'M JUST ON MY WAY BACK. I SHOULD BE ABOUT HALF AN HOUR. IT'D BE GOOD FOR US ALL TO EAT TOGETHER.*

Within seconds came the reply: *I'LL TURN EVERYTHING DOWN. SEE YOU THEN.*

An hour and a half later, the meal eaten, Amelia smiled at her two daughters who were sprawled on the sofa in the living room. 'I've got some news.'

Caitlyn sat up, rubbed her eyes and stared at her mum. Becky pulled her feet up and hugged her knees, waiting for her mother to speak.

'I'm having a baby. You're going to have a brother or sister,' Amelia bit her lip and waited for the response.

Caitlyn got up off the sofa and squeezed next to her mum on the chair, hugging her. Becky didn't look at her mother. She said, 'How?'

'I don't think we need to go into that now,' Amelia answered softly.

'Okay. Who?' Becky now turned to her mother and waited for an answer.

Amelia stared back at Becky while stroking Caitlyn's hair. 'It doesn't matter.'

'Well, it's not Dad's, is it?!' Becky shouted and stormed out of the room.

Amelia heard her stomp upstairs and slam her bedroom door. She hadn't known what to expect when she told them. Perhaps she should have guessed this would be the response.

Amelia's mother was sitting in the other chair in the room. She picked up her knitting. 'It's time for bed now, Caitlyn.'

Caitlyn reluctantly got up, hugged her nan, then followed her sister upstairs.

'That could have gone better,' Amelia said.

'What did you expect?' Her mother carried on knitting.

There was no point sitting here with her mother, so Amelia went to her office. She'd left her phone on her desk and noticed a missed call from Kesia.

Amelia rang her back.

'Hi, Kesia. You called me.'

'Yes. My uncle asked me to. He wants you to come to Alicia's next match on Saturday.'

'That's lovely of him, but —'

'I'll be there, and my husband. In fact, the whole family.'

Amelia wanted to say that she was not a big boxing fan, but she feared this would be seen as an insult and that was the last thing she wanted to do. 'Okay. I'll come for Alicia's bout, but I can't stay the whole evening. What time is she on?'

'About nine, I think. I'll get my uncle to ring you with the exact time. Can I give him your mobile number?'

Could she give Michal her number? For some reason, Amelia's heartbeat quickened at the thought. 'Yes, of course,' she managed to say.

'Great, I'll see you on Saturday, then. Bye, Amelia.'

'Bye.'

The call ended. Amelia smiled. She hated boxing, but she was glad she had agreed to go. She dismissed the thought that she'd be more than happy to see Michal again. The whole thing was ridiculous... but she couldn't get his beaming smile out of her head.

Chapter 23

The Pub

The garage was a tip. It had been months since Amelia had bothered to even enter it. Someone had dumped the girls' bikes on the floor. Amelia lifted them up and propped them against the wall. There were boxes stacked haphazardly. She had no idea what could be in them and no inclination to look. The metal chest containing Joe's tools stood neglected. The bottom drawer was slightly open, reminding Amelia that Jake had been the last one to use them when he fixed the washing machine. It was easy now to see how he'd made himself appear indispensable and useful. Amelia shuddered. The torque wrench that she sought was in the second drawer of the chest, along with every size bolt and nut imaginable.

Joe had spent a lot of time in the garage fixing various vintage motorcycles and cars. His favourite was an E-Type Jaguar that he'd completely restored. Amelia couldn't remember what happened to it. Maybe it was sold. The first year after his death was a complete fog. She'd gone to work and come home each day, not sensing or feeling anything, all her concentration spent on keeping herself together at work. If her mother hadn't insisted on moving in, then none of the everyday, important events would have occurred. No one would have eaten, the washing would've remained dirty and the house never cleaned. In many ways, they had come a long way. In others, they had barely moved forward. Amelia knew this had to change but had no concept how to achieve this. Perhaps there was an adult version of Supernanny who could swoop in and sort her life out.

She put the wrench in her bag along with some thin rubber gloves, then left for the pub. One thing she could do was find out what had happened to the dead women. She still had a purpose. No one was taking that from her.

It was early morning when Amelia arrived back at the pub. The streets were empty of traffic. It was fairly light, but she'd brought a torch; the inside of the pub would be darker than outside as little natural light would enter.

She put on the tight rubber gloves ready to enter the pub. It didn't take long to remove the bolts using the torque wrench. Amelia had checked the report the previous night and the DI on the case hadn't ordered a search of the premises. This was a ridiculous decision. The only reason for not doing so that she could come up with was that they weren't taking the woman's death seriously. How was this even possible?

On entering the pub lounge, Amelia shone the torch in an arc. There were various stools strewn around like fallen chess pieces. The tables remained next to the wall-mounted benches. It reminded her of the morning after a fight in a saloon in an old western. She scanned the floor of the pub for any signs of recent occupation. In the lounge area, she found an upturned chair with scuff marks and scratches on the sides of its back. She looked closer and discovered various dark spots that could have been blood on the wooden rungs. Amelia imagined the poor woman who might well have been held here, with her arms stretched behind the chair and tied, the blood caused by the constant rubbing of the ropes that bound her as she struggled to free herself, and the absolute fear that she must have felt before her death. Was this woman later found outside, dead? As soon as she left the pub, Amelia knew she would need to contact the Murder Investigation Team.

But there was more.

In the cellar, Amelia found that the traffickers had attached metal leg and arm cuffs to the walls with chains. They'd kept people here. Most likely, they'd kept other women here. The stench was indescribable. There were no toilet facilities and, even though there had been an attempt to clean up, they clearly couldn't get rid of the smell. Amelia covered her mouth and nose with the top of her hoodie, but she couldn't stand being down here for long.

It was likely that, while the women had cried and screamed in fear, the men had stood and drunk in the bar. On her return upstairs, she found glass marks in the dust. The optics looked corroded and the upturned bottles were drained empty. They could have brought their own spirits and cans.

Amelia left the pub. She could bear it no longer. As she drove home, she switched on the radio. She played whatever band was on, as loud as she could, in an attempt to drown out the voices in her head. As soon as she reached home, she contacted Chloe on the message site.

Amelia: *You need to get MIT to search the pub at the first murder site. Say that you remember it being there and were surprised a search report wasn't in the file. If you get no joy from the DI, then go higher. Chloe, they'll find evidence of women being held there. It's horrific. Do it now.*

Then she sat and cried.

A few minutes later, her phone rang. She didn't recognise the mobile number. She answered apprehensively. 'Hello.'

'Amelia. It's Michal,' a hesitant voice said.

Amelia croaked. 'Michal. It's good to hear from you.'

'Are you okay? You sound –' Michal's voice was full of concern.

Amelia wiped away her tears. 'Sorry… I'm fine.'

'Kesia asked me to call you to let you know that Alicia's bout is on at nine. I'll save you a seat next to mine and Kesia's, so you can arrive late.'

She composed herself. 'Thanks, Michal. I'd love to come.' The thought of seeing him warmed her.

'Great. I look forward to it.' Michal paused. 'Are you sure you're okay?'

'Yes. I'm fine.' What she really wanted to say was. *I'm not fine. I'm not fine at all.* But she barely knew this man and, in the state she was in, she didn't trust herself to behave appropriately.

'If you're sure? I could come over. Alicia's training's nearly finished for the day, if you need me.'

Need him? Yes, I need you.

Amelia said, 'I'll see you Saturday at nine.'

'Great ... yes, I'll see you then. Bye, Amelia.'

'Bye.' Amelia cut the call then added Michal's number to her contacts. She hoped he'd call her number again and didn't want to be surprised next time.

Two hours later, Amelia received a response from Chloe.

Chloe: *I've convinced them to search the pub. A team's been selected. What a shock – I'm not on it!*

Amelia wondered if Chloe was getting support from DI Jamieson. She knew how isolating working in a male-dominated environment was. She made a mental note to contact Carol later and get her, if necessary, to make the first move by calling Chloe.

Amelia: *Believe me, in this case, you wouldn't want to be on the team.*

Chloe: *I'll request a report, though, and get Dion to send a scan to you as soon as possible. Do you really think they held women there?*

Amelia: *Unfortunately, yes, I do.*

Chloe: *By the way, Jake's definitely working undercover with the traffickers. Will has pretty much confirmed it. I wonder what he did to get accepted by them?*

Amelia didn't want to consider this. Whatever it was, it would have put Elena at more risk, and her daughter, if she had one.

Chloe: *Gotta go. My phone's ringing. Speak soon.*

As soon as Chloe signed off, Amelia texted Carol on her private mobile. Dion had set up an account from which she could send texts that were unlikely to be picked up. *HI. FANCY A GIRLY NIGHT OUT? MEET YOU AT THE USUAL. 8 PM. A XX.*

Amelia had been friends with Carol since Hendon. They graduated together and became sergeants in the same cohort. Then Amelia lagged behind while she had the girls. Carol became an inspector two years before her, but Amelia didn't mind. Working at the Public Protection Unit was ideal work for Carol. She was multilingual, having studied languages at university and, like Amelia, was able to be supportive and a frank speaker at the same time. Carol knew where the usual was: The Shepherd on Craven Street.

Amelia arrived first and sat on one of the leather bench seats in the back room. The Shepherd was a quiet pub, off the beaten track behind a row of terraced houses. It had its usual bunch of regulars who sat in the front bar. The back room was less busy. It was often empty, which had always suited Carol and Amelia. It meant that they could discuss work and the misogyny in the police force without fear of interruption. It helped that the pub had a fine array of independently produced beers, too. Tonight, though, it made her choice of an orange juice even more unappealing.

Carol walked in a few minutes later. She raised an eyebrow when she noticed what Amelia was drinking. Amelia simply announced, 'I'm pregnant.'

'Ah,' Carol said. 'Just let me get a drink and you can tell Aunty Carol all about it.'

Amelia always loved the way Carol took control of situations. She may only stand just over five-foot-two, but she had an easy confidence and strength about her.

Carol returned from the bar with a pint of real ale. She took a good gulp and wiped the froth from her mouth. 'I've missed this place,' she said. 'Now, then. Pregnant. It's that fucking bastard's, I'm guessing.'

Amelia blushed. 'Yes, he doesn't know, though –'

'Don't worry, I'm more likely to kick him in the bollocks than tell him.'

'I can believe that.'

'Amelia, I've written to Police Complaints. I've told them exactly what I think of their ludicrous decision to suspend you. I'm sure I'm not the only one.'

'You didn't need to do that.'

'Too bloody right, I did. That little prick! I'm sorry, Amelia, but I really don't know what you saw in him. Okay, he's a good-looking bastard, but even so.'

'I actually invited you here to talk about Chloe.'

'Your new DS?'

'Yes, I'm worried she's becoming increasingly isolated. I'm sure she could do with some support. Has she been in touch with you?'

'No. No, she hasn't.' Carol appeared more sombre. 'Do you want me to get in touch with her?'

'Would you? I'm sure she'd really appreciate it.'

'Okay. I'll ring her.' Carol took another gulp of her beer. 'Now, what are we going to do about your situation? You keeping it?'

'Yes, I'm keeping it.'

'Fair enough. What'll you do when it really starts showing? Jake's going to want to know if it's his.' Carol looked genuinely concerned. 'If he wants access or whatever, I can see him turning nasty.'

'I haven't really thought that far, to be honest. At this rate, I'll have had the baby before they let me back into work. I haven't even had an investigation meeting yet. And Jake's working undercover, so I'm not likely to see him.'

'It's the injustice of it that makes me mad. Surely they should have suspended him, too!'

'I'm his superior officer. I knew what I was getting into. I decided to have a relationship with him.'

'I know he raped you, Amelia. Kesia told me.'

Amelia had forgotten that Kesia knew Carol. She did some interpreting for the PPU. There wasn't a response that Amelia could make. She stayed silent until Carol continued talking. 'He can't get away with it. There must be something I can do to help.'

'Look after Chloe. That's help enough.' Amelia looked down at the remnants of her orange juice and wished she had a pint like Carol's.

'Why don't I get you a half? How many weeks are you anyway? I've never really understood the drinks ban. I remember when a Guinness was recommended for pregnant women. It's full of iron, isn't it?'

'Thirteen. And I've no idea about Guinness. Don't tempt me.'

'Well, I'm having another pint.' Carol stood up to go to the bar. 'What can I get you?'

'An orange juice. Thanks.'

While Carol was at the bar, Amelia considered sharing her concerns about the case.

When Carol sat back down, she quickly put these fears to rest. 'Kesia told me about your Devil. I might have some information on him. I've got a file in my car. I've been debating whether to show it to you.'

Amelia stared at Carol. It was rare for her to be unsure of herself and what to do. 'Why didn't you pass the information directly to the Trafficking Unit or contact Chloe?'

'It's sensitive information and I wasn't sure of its relevance. Is Jake working undercover on this case?'

'Yes, as far as I know. He's sleeping with one of the trafficked women, too.'

'He's what?! For fuck's sake! How's he getting away with it?'

Amelia couldn't explain it. 'I guess it's just another example of how the boys' club works.'

Carol stood up. 'I'm going to get you that file. See what you make of it.'

When Carol returned with the thin manila file, Amelia noticed how tired she looked. Carol had always been as hardworking as Amelia. They were both more likely to pull a late shift than their male colleagues. They both spent more time with the victims of crime and then spent unpaid time catching up with paperwork.

Carol, also, drank – a lot. Amelia knew that she would finish her current pint and drive home without incident. Then she'd probably drink some more. Amelia also knew that you can't stop an alcoholic drinking. Only they can stop themselves. When everything fell apart, which it invariably did in an alcoholic's world, Amelia knew she would be there for Carol.

Carol placed the folder on the table in front of Amelia. 'It's a child protection case. It came through the Safeguarding Board. They weren't sure whether to pursue it, so they came to us first.'

Amelia opened the file. The photograph on the first page was of a ten-year-old girl. Her skin was light brown, and hair and eyes were a deeper brown, almost black. She looked a little like Elena, but Amelia wasn't one hundred per cent sure that she wasn't seeing that purely because she wanted to. The girl was standing next to a small pony and was dressed in jodhpurs and a black hoodie. She was holding a riding crop and black helmet.

This wasn't a girl that lived on the estates. Her address was Gibbet Hill, one of the most expensive areas of Coventry. Amelia said, 'I'm surprised by the location.'

'Why? You know as well as I do that abuse can happen in any

household.'

'That wasn't what I meant.'

'I know I'm just teasing you.' Carol pointed to the file. 'If you turn to the next page, you'll see what the girl alleges to have seen and heard.'

A statement had been taken at the child's school, a private prep school in Kenilworth. It had been countersigned by a social worker, so they were concerned enough not to include the parent at this stage. Amelia carefully read the statement, feeling more anxious as she read each paragraph. The girl, Lillian Davies, described how her father had threatened her that she would succumb to the same fate as her mother if she didn't comply with his requests. The fate of her mother, which Lillian went on to describe in detail, was being shackled and kept prisoner. His demands were the usual: do your homework, tidy your bedroom, be polite. She then went on to describe how her stepmother was often bruised and, on occasion, 'couldn't walk'.

Amelia looked up at Carol. 'What's the father's name?'

'Robert Davies.' Carol turned the page. 'This is his statement.'

The child's father had laughed off the whole incident. He talked about his daughter having a highly developed imagination, and how she'd won competitions at school for her 'stories'. He said that the girl didn't get on with her stepmother and that her own mother had returned to Albania many years before. She clearly missed her, that was all.

'What work does he do, the father?' Amelia wondered how he could afford a private school and such a good address. She also noted the similarities in the names Robert Davo and Robert Davies.

'Doesn't it say?' Carol scanned the page. 'I'm not sure. It wasn't my case.'

'So how did you come by it?'

'Kesia asked me to look at it. The stepmother's Polish. Kesia translated her statement.'

The stepmother's statement was on the next page. She described in detail how she'd had a car accident that had caused damage to her face and legs. Apparently, Lillian had been in the car at the time and had been distressed by it. But it was one line that stood out: 'Her father is no devil, he's a kind, caring father.'

It was probably just coincidence, but Kesia had thought it was important enough to contact Carol. Amelia wondered why Kesia hadn't told her or Chloe. She made a mental note to ask her at the boxing match.

Before closing the file, Amelia asked, 'What action's being taken?'

'None, the file was closed. There wasn't any evidence that anything bad had actually happened or that the child was at risk. There were concerns that maybe she'd been watching some inappropriate television. Her description of the way her mother was treated was pretty graphic.'

Amelia took photographs of the statements, the address and the picture of the girl, and gave the file back to Carol. 'It could well be the guy we're looking for.'

'Okay. I'll keep this file safe in case you need it later. I'll also send a copy to Chloe. If it is your guy, then Trafficking might be better looking at it.' Carol stood to leave. 'It was good seeing you, Amelia.'

'Let's stay in touch. And please take care of Chloe for me.' Amelia hugged Carol. She stayed in the pub for a few minutes after Carol left. She wondered if she'd actually found Elena's daughter. If she had, she feared she was at risk, just like her mother.

Chapter 24

The Boxing Match

It took Amelia ages to decide what to wear. In the end, she decided on a pair of jeans and a pale green top that showed off her figure. She almost changed her mind about this, too, but thought she might as well flaunt her assets she had whilst she still had them. It wouldn't be too many weeks before she'd need a whole new wardrobe. She wasn't sure what impression her choice of clothes would give Michal but decided that, either way, it didn't matter.

True to his word, he'd saved Amelia a seat between himself and Kesia on the front row. He smiled as she sat down next to him. The bout was about to start, so his attention quickly switched to his niece in the ring. Amelia studied his profile as he did so. His features were sharp, yet his eyes were kind and even the lines on his face portrayed how often he smiled. She didn't even mind his bumpy boxer's nose. Kesia nudged her. Amelia turned to her. 'You might want to watch the bout. There'll be questions after.' She winked.

Amelia blushed. Was it that obvious?

As soon as the fight began, everyone stood. Amelia watched as Michal soon became animated, following every one of Alicia's punches, shouting at her to keep her guard up. Alicia dodged a blow and danced across the ring. She was clearly the superior boxer, even to Amelia's untrained eye. She dropped her arms, goading her opponent to attack. As her opponent lunged forward, Alicia struck the young woman hard to the side of her head, her long ponytail whipping behind her. The poor opponent couldn't have known what hit her. A few minutes into the fight, she was down and out for the count.

The whole place erupted. Michal jumped up and down and slapped Amelia across the back. She wasn't quite sure how to take that. Then the sports hall fell silent, waiting for the floored girl to get up off the canvas. She did so, slowly. Finally, both girls stood together so the referee could hold up Alicia's arm in triumph. The hall erupted for a second time. Amelia was ready for the back slap this time, but it didn't come. Instead, Michal grabbed her in a hug. He was wearing the same cologne as he had on their first meeting and Amelia held him close. He whispered in her ear, 'Let's get some champagne.'

They broke apart and made their way to the bar together. Michal shook many people's hands along the way. Amelia said, 'I thought you might be in the ring, helping.'

'We've got some great cornermen. I'd rather watch the fight.' He smiled. 'She was magnificent, wasn't she?'

'Yes, not that I can judge, but, yes! She was stunning!'

When they reached the bar, Michal ordered bottles of champagne. Amelia asked for an orange juice. He looked surprised. 'I thought your lot always drank like fish.'

'Not always,' Amelia said, not wishing to divulge the real reason for her abstinence.

As they waited for their drinks at the bar, Michal moved closer to Amelia until their shoulders touched. Neither of them spoke. Amelia felt her pulse begin to race. She wasn't sure if the feeling in her stomach was the first movements of her unborn child or the butterflies of attraction. It made her feel uneasy. She didn't need this. Not now. But she wanted it all the same.

Michal began to speak. 'I'd like to see you again, Amelia. But I can't. Not alone, anyway, which is what I want.'

'I'm sorry... I don't understand.' Amelia stared at him, looking for clues. Did he feel the same?

The barman put the orange juice down on the bar and Michal passed it to Amelia. Their fingers brushed and the quickening started again.

'If I saw you…' Michal looked away and began nervously stepping from foot to foot, '… I mean, if we went out, I'd have to keep it a secret from my family. You deserve so much more than that, Amelia.'

'Oh.' Amelia didn't know what to say. She was attracted to Michal. There was no doubt about that, but he was right; the last thing she wanted or deserved was another clandestine relationship.

'You're probably wondering why. It's because you're not Roma. If you were… well… I'd sweep you off your feet right now and…' he grinned, his eyes scrunching. 'But then I'd have to marry you, so…!'

He laughed then. So did Amelia. She wasn't sure why when she actually felt disappointed. The bottles of champagne were ready in their buckets. Michal paid for them and asked for one of them to be delivered to the changing room.

The next bout was about to start. Amelia said, 'I'd better go. Congratulate Alicia for me.'

Michal raised his eyebrows. 'So soon?'

Amelia wasn't sure what to say. She didn't want to take her leave, but he'd made it clear that they were never going to be more than friends. That was fine but, at some point, she was going to have to tell him that she hated boxing. 'My mother's unwell and she's looking after the girls, so I said I wouldn't be too late back.'

'Okay.' Michal kissed Amelia on the cheek. 'Come to dinner – soon.'

She smiled. 'Bye, Michal.'

As Amelia walked towards the exit, Kesia called out to her. 'Amelia, are you going?'

'Yes, sorry. I saw you were enjoying the moment with your family, so I didn't want to interrupt you.'

'I'll walk you to the car.' Kesia held the door open for her. 'I can see you and my uncle are getting on well.'

Amelia blurted out without thinking, 'But I'm not Roma –'

'Did he say that to you? The idiot!' Kesia looked shocked. 'He's had women lining up outside his home ever since my aunt died. He's taken no notice of them whatsoever. Then, when we can all see that he's finally… well… interested – he says something as ridiculous as that! We're not living in the dark ages. He can go out with who he wants. Honestly!'

'It's okay.' Amelia quickly changed the subject. 'I spoke to Carol Jamieson the other day. She showed me the file you directed her to.'

'Oh, that.' Kesia looked away. 'I'm sorry. I work for different departments. I only get paid when I work. I couldn't give you the file. I hoped Carol would mention it. I'm glad she did.'

That made sense. 'It's fine. I understand. I'll tell Chloe about it. It means we have an address to follow up. Thanks.'

Kesia looked anxious. 'I'd better go back in. I'll see you later, Amelia.'

'Yes, of course.'

Kesia went back into the sports hall. Amelia was tempted to drive to Chloe's. She could do with the company and she really wanted to have a proper discussion about the case, not the stilted one you had on a message service. It wasn't worth the risk. Instead, she looked up an address on her phone and drove to Gibbet Hill

Chapter 25

The Devil's Home

It was dark. Amelia knew she wouldn't be able to see the house from the road, but she knew the area. All the houses on Gibbet Hill were set back and had long, winding drives. They were in a variety of styles from mock Tudor to modern, all individually designed and built, and none of them worth less than a million.

Amelia stopped her car in front of the address she'd photographed from the report. There were lights on in the house and she made out the hazy shapes of windows. She counted six upstairs. They clearly didn't have to worry about their electricity bill.

The women were shackled or guarded in dirty, dingy terraced houses or the cellars of derelict buildings, while their jailer lived like this. It sickened Amelia. She had to stop herself getting out of the car and confronting him, knowing that it wouldn't get her anywhere. But they *would* get him. They had to. It was only a matter of time. He would make a mistake.

There was nothing else she could do here, so she drove home.

On Monday morning, before her family were awake, Amelia drove back to Gibbet Hill Road. She pulled into a side road near the main junction that the family members would have to use to take their daughter to school. She sat and waited, wondering who would be driving. The stepmother? The Devil? A nanny? And would she get to see Lillian? Would she recognise her as Elena's daughter?

She didn't have to wait long. Five minutes later, a new Range Rover drove past with the raven-haired girl sitting in the passenger seat. Amelia had imagined her with blonde hair. She had the same bone structure as Elena: high cheekbones, long thin nose and small pointed chin. It could be her daughter but, equally, it might not be. The driver was a woman with blonde hair tied back in a braid. There had been no photograph of the stepmother on file, so this could be her. A thought flashed through Amelia's brain. She could pull out suddenly and hit the side of the car, then she would get a closer look at the occupants and, maybe, get a chance to talk to them. But then, she would be putting herself and them at risk. She dismissed the thought as ridiculous. Instead, she watched the car cross the junction towards Kenilworth. She followed it. There was no rush. She knew where it was going.

Ten minutes later, Amelia decided to overtake the Range Rover. She wanted to try and get some photographs of the girl without arousing suspicion. It was going to be difficult since she was on her way to school, but there may be somewhere she could view the school from.

On arrival at the school, she immediately spotted a vantage point. It was quite obvious. Across the road was an apartment block. One of the windows faced out from the stairwell onto the street. She would have to be quick, but she might get a good view from there. The apartment block had a key code entry. Amelia pushed buttons at random. Eventually, a male sleepily answered, 'Who is it?'

'Sorry to disturb you, sir. I'm Detective Inspector Amelia Barton and I need access to your stairwell.' She still had her ID card if she needed it.

The man didn't seem to care. The door buzzed and she was in. By the time she reached the window, the Range Rover was pulling up at the school. Using her phone, Amelia was just able to get a quick photo before the girl entered the school building. It wasn't too bad a picture, considering the circumstances. She'd decide what to do with it when she had a chance to speak to Chloe.

When she got back to the car, Amelia's phone buzzed. It was a text from Michal: *SORRY FOR THE WAY I BEHAVED. WHY DON'T YOU COME FOR DINNER ON FRIDAY? BRING YOUR GIRLS IF YOU LIKE. I'D LOVE TO MEET THEM.*

Amelia wondered why he was apologising, as he'd done

nothing wrong. She pondered whether it was a good idea taking her girls to dinner with her. On the one hand, it might be good for them to meet some of her mother's friends. On the other, what would be the point? It wasn't like she was having any kind of relationship with Michal. Besides, Becky would soon get bored and become annoying in her usual teenage manner.

THANKS, MICHAL. I'D LOVE TO COME. MY GIRLS HAVE OTHER PLANS, UNFORTUNATELY.

Maybe she should go shopping while she was in Kenilworth and find herself something new to wear.

An hour later, Amelia was starting to regret her decision to go shopping. She wasn't in the right mood, but then she saw the driver of the Range Rover enter the boutique. She purposely stayed out of sight behind a rail of dresses and watched as the woman perused the designer underwear. The woman finally chose a black lacy bra and matching panties. She paid with a platinum credit card and left the shop. Amelia waited a few moments and followed her. The woman hadn't gone far. She was staring into an estate agent's window. It appeared that she'd spotted a property that she liked because she then entered the shop. As Amelia stared in through the shop window, she saw the woman being given the particulars for a couple of houses. After the woman left the estate agent's, she made her way to the café next door. Amelia waited until the woman was sitting at one of the tables, then she went back to the estate agent's office. She used her ID to attract attention. 'I need information about the properties that blonde-haired woman was interested in, the one who just came in. It's part of an ongoing investigation into property fraud.'

The agent went to a drawer and quickly found the property details. She handed them over. They were both for rambling Victorian properties with cellars similar to the Birmingham sex club that they'd raided. Amelia gave the estate agent her number and asked her to get in touch if the woman returned. Then she went back to the café.

There was a table free next to that of the blonde woman. Amelia quickly bought a coffee and sat down.

The woman was on the phone to someone: 'There are two properties both in Leamington town centre… yes, they're both big enough. Why don't we view them and see… there's room for all of the activities… yes, even that. It's not far to travel from Coventry, either… for what we offer, the men would travel that far, surely…. Okay, I'll show you them later and we can decide.'

The woman ended the call and glanced over at Amelia, who was reading her emails on her phone. A few minutes later, the woman stood to leave. Amelia considered following her but decided that she had enough information. It was obvious that the woman was looking to buy or rent a new property for their sex club. The implication was that they'd moved some of the trafficked women to Coventry. She would pass all of this information on to Chloe when she got home. Amelia sighed and stroked her stomach, then left the café.

When she reached her car, her phone began to ring. She didn't recognise the number, so answered with a degree of hesitation. A strident voice asked, 'Am I speaking to Mrs Barton, the mother of Rebecca Barton?'

Amelia answered, 'Becky's mother, yes.'

'This is Mrs Jessop, headteacher of your daughter's school.'

Amelia's heart sank. If Becky was ill or had hurt herself then it was likely that her form teacher would ring her. For the headteacher to ring, then this had to be serious.

The Head continued. 'I'm afraid we need to speak in person about your daughter's behaviour. Are you able to come to school now?'

'Yes, I can be with you in the next half an hour. I'm currently in Leamington.' Amelia got in and started her car as she spoke.

'Fine, I'll see you then.' The head ended the call, leaving Amelia free to drive back to Coventry. She forced herself to relax so she didn't drive too aggressively.

Twenty minutes later, Amelia arrived at her daughter's school. The receptionist stared at her when Amelia introduced herself as DI Barton. She then had to explain that she wasn't there in an official capacity. She'd never really been 'Mrs. Barton'. The receptionist phoned through and asked Amelia to take a seat. The chairs were much plusher than the ones she remembered from school. Her stomach churned, just as it had on those numerous occasions that she was called to the Head's office as a child, usually after she'd called some teacher a fitting name or refused to follow some ridiculous instruction. Amelia had wanted her children to have a degree of confidence and assertiveness, but not to the point of insolence. It had got her into far more trouble than was necessary.

Eventually, Mrs. Jessop put in an appearance and politely asked Amelia to follow her to her office. It didn't take her long to get to the point. 'I'm afraid we're going to have to suspend Rebecca for two days.'

Amelia shuffled uncomfortably in her chair. The Head had insisted that they sit at the table rather than in the more comfortable chairs around her desk. The only thing she could think of saying was: 'What on earth has she done?'

'She smashed a phone belonging to one of the male students. It's very possible that she may also get a bill for the damage. Becky won't tell us why she did this, but it was clearly no accident.'

'There must be an explanation. Why not let me talk to her before you jump straight into a punishment?' She'd nearly said, 'Let me interrogate her,' but stopped herself just in time.

The Head sighed. 'She's in the Deputy's office. I'll go and fetch her.'

Becky looked angry when she was brought in – defiant, even.

'Why? Why on earth would you do such a thing?' Amelia asked her daughter.

'He deserved it, Mum. He really did. Don't make me say why in front of everyone.' Becky looked at the floor then.

'Will you tell me if we're alone?' Amelia asked. The Head nodded. This must have seemed a reasonable idea. She turned and left the office.

Amelia waited until the door shut, 'Well?'

'He'd taken dodgy pics of my friend Leah and sent them round the whole school.'

Amelia guessed what sort of photos she meant, but she needed confirmation. 'Intimate photos?'

'Yes. From the party the other night, when I left, and he had sex with Leah. He took some photos. I couldn't tell a teacher. Leah would kill me, but I was so mad, I took his phone and smashed it.' Becky started crying. All Amelia could think was how lucky her daughter was that he hadn't done it to her.

'I'm going to have to tell Mrs. Jessop what you've said. They may contact the police or social services, but it's the right thing to do. Your friend needs protecting.'

'She'll be so upset and angry with me for telling –'

'And she'll thank you later because you'll have stopped the abuse. Let me get Chloe or someone from CEOP to come to school. They can help all of your friends to stay safe. Sexting is abuse, Becky.'

'I know. The pictures were vile. Why would he do that?'

'I've no idea.' Amelia hugged her daughter. 'I'm just glad it wasn't you, love.'

Amelia went to find Mrs. Jessop and told her what had actually happened. The suspension was lifted, but Amelia still took Becky home.

Amelia's mother took over looking after Becky when they got home. She made her hot chocolate with whipped cream and marshmallows while Amelia spent some time trying to get hold of Chloe using the messenger service. When that didn't work, she decided to go to Poppy's Place. She knew Siobhan would contact Chloe on her behalf and they could meet there like last time.

Before she left, Amelia decided to do one last thing. She hadn't used the hacking facility that Dion had set up for her up until now. She'd decided that it wasn't necessary. She trusted her daughter to make the right decisions after the conversation they had following the party, but she feared for her safety after today's events.

So many girls were being systematically abused online. A minority of teenage boys seemed to think they could threaten and bully girls into performing sexual acts for them by blackmailing them. They would have persuaded them to send them pictures of their breasts or even vaginas online, or they would have taken photographs, sometimes without the girl's knowledge, while they performed sex acts together. Then they would threaten to publish these on social media if the girls stopped having sex with them or even their group of friends. It was a vile practice that CEOP couldn't keep track of and schools seemed at a loss to prevent.

The hacking tool allowed Amelia to search through her daughter's computer files and internet search history. She started with Facebook. There were already some pretty nasty comments levelled at her daughter by both teenage boys and girls. She was being called various names for speaking out about the abuse. What shocked Amelia the most was that many of them were girls who were clearly defending the lad who had published Leah's photos – 'snaking' as they called it. What drove them to that? When did abuse of this kind become so acceptable? It sickened Amelia. She couldn't even block them on her daughter's behalf as she would know she'd hacked her account. All of her social media accounts were the same. But the abuse that Becky was getting was nothing as to what her friend, Leah had received.

Amelia turned off her computer and went in search of her daughter. She found her in the living room, wrapped in her duvet, eating chocolate biscuits and watching That 70s Show. Amelia turned off the television and sat down next to Becky. 'Have you checked your phone? We might need to block some students. I've seen what happens in cases like this.'

Becky rubbed her eyes. 'It's in my schoolbag. I haven't dared to look.'

Amelia fetched her bag and found her phone in its sparkly pink case. 'Why don't you open your phone for me? I'll do it for you.'

'Will you? I really can't bear to see it.' Becky took the phone and typed in her passcode. She gave the phone back to her mum. 'Here. Just delete and block everyone. I don't care.'

She lay down and pulled the duvet up around her. She looked so young and defenceless. Amelia was tempted to go and seek out the boys involved and arrest the lot of them, but the school would hopefully be sorting that.

'I'm going to visit Chloe. I think we need her help. Don't worry, love, I'll sort your phone out for you.' She kissed her daughter on the cheek and left for Poppy's Place.

Chapter 26

Siobhan's Attacker

Ellie opened the gates as Amelia's car approached them. This was a first. She was usually so fastidious, expecting all visitors to use the intercom and checking IDs. Amelia sensed that something was wrong.

When Amelia entered the house, she found Ellie in the kitchen. She had clearly been pacing the floor. 'I'm so glad you're here. Maybe you can talk some sense into Siobhan.'

Amelia could see the stress lines in Ellie's face. 'Why, what's happened?'

'She's in her office, hiding away from me. She can tell you.'

Had Ellie and Siobhan argued? Was she needed as a mediator? That would be another first, Amelia thought as she climbed the stairs to the top floor.

Amelia felt that she needed to knock on the office door before entering. She heard the faintest, 'Come in.'

She saw Siobhan's curly hair first, as she had her head down on the desk. She sat up slowly as though every part of her ached. Amelia noticed she had been crying. Her face was red and blotchy, but there were bruises too – purple, angry bruises.

'Who did this to you?' Amelia was ashamed that her first

thought was that it might have been Ellie. She dismissed that.

'I've no idea… a stranger.' Siobhan brushed her hand through her hair. 'Shut the door. I don't want Ellie to hear this.'

Amelia shut the door and sat down opposite Siobhan. 'Tell me.'

'I was at the indoor market. We needed some veg and I wasn't going to pay supermarket prices.' Siobhan rubbed her eyes and winced. 'I was just leaving and sensed someone was behind me as I left through the automatic doors. They grabbed my arm and forced me into the alley opposite the market.'

Siobhan paused. Amelia gently touched her arm, urging her to continue.

'He hissed at me. Called me a whore supporting whores. Said I deserved all I got and pushed me into the wall. He grabbed the back of my hair and smacked my face against the bricks.'

'Did you call the police?' Amelia knew what the answer would be.

'And what would they do? Probably say I deserved it.'

Amelia sighed. She was well aware of Siobhan's stubbornness. 'You were attacked in the street by a stranger! Of course they'd investigate!'

'I've not had the best experiences with the police, as you know. I couldn't see the point. I just wanted to come home.' Tears were rolling down Siobhan's cheeks.

Amelia got up and hugged her friend. 'For fuck's sake, Siobhan. Let us get the bastard…'

'If only you weren't suspended. You're the only honest cop I've ever met.' Siobhan sniffed, not looking directly at Amelia.

'Now, can I tell Ellie you're okay? She's worried sick about you.'

Siobhan wiped her tears with the back of her hand. 'Yes, you'd better or she'll start wrapping me in cotton wool. I can't have that.'

'I'll be back in a minute. Oh, and can you text Chloe for me and ask her to come over? There's something I need to talk to her about.'

Siobhan picked up her phone. 'Consider it done.'

Amelia went down to the kitchen, knowing that Ellie would be in her office wringing her hands. She wasn't wrong. Ellie looked up as soon as she entered the office. Her eyes were hooded with fear.

Ellie might have muscle, but Siobhan was the strong one in their relationship.

'Is she okay? She won't even speak to me.'

'She'll survive, stubborn as she is. I was going to make coffee. Do you want one?' Amelia realised how exhausted she was. It would take more than coffee to perk her up. What she really needed was a good night's sleep.

'Thanks. That'd be lovely.' Ellie must have noticed Amelia's tiredness. 'Let me make it. Why don't you sit down?'

Amelia didn't need asking twice. She sat down at the kitchen table. Running her hands through her hair, she started to yawn.

Just as Ellie was about to pour the coffee, the intercom buzzed. Ellie finished pouring, passed Amelia her mug and went to answer it. It was Chloe. Amelia recognised her cheerful voice.

Chloe entered the kitchen moments later. 'I was on my way here when Siobhan texted me. What's up?' she asked, looking straight at Amelia, who filled her in with the events at her daughter's school. Chloe promised that she would contact the school in the morning and offer her professional help. Amelia sighed, relieved that at least that would be sorted. But she was still worried about Siobhan. She didn't want to worry Ellie, but hoped that Chloe would be able to convince Siobhan to go to the police.

'Is there another coffee going?' Chloe asked.

Ellie got up to make her one. Amelia whispered, 'Someone's got to get through to Siobhan. Are you willing to give it a try?'

'Oh absolutely,' Chloe responded. 'Why don't I contact Carol? I can see her being more than a match for Siobhan.'

Amelia considered this. It wasn't a bad idea. Pitting Carol against Siobhan would be a bout people would pay to watch. It also meant that she had a reason to meet up with Carol.

'That's a great plan. Why don't you text her?'

Chloe took out her phone and contacted Carol. Ellie passed her a mug of coffee. 'Let's go and keep Siobhan company. Ellie, do you want to join us?'

'No, it's fine. I'd better carry on doing my job. Keep the women safe.' She stared at the floor as she said this. She looked defeated. Amelia was tempted to hug her but didn't think that would fit with the tough image that she was trying so desperately hard to project.

'DCI Carol Jamieson should be joining us at some point. Can you send her up?'

Ellie smiled. 'Yes, of course. Maybe, between you you'll be able to convince Siobhan to report the attack.'

The two women climbed the stairs to Siobhan's office. She was sitting in the same spot but at least she'd stopped crying. This appeared to make her bruises even more vivid.

Chloe sat down in front of her. 'For fuck's sake, Siobhan! You've got to let me get a uniform down here to take a statement. Have you seen the state of your face?'

Amelia had never seen Chloe so angry. Siobhan just looked back at her without emotion.

Amelia added, 'Chloe's right, love. You've got no choice. You need to let us help you.'

Siobhan folded her arms. 'Maybe he was right. I whore myself every day to get money to finance this place. Suck up to wankers to assuage their guilt. What do you want to bet that half of them only give us money because they use prostitutes to meet their needs? And the women we help? Half of them go back on the streets. The ones you bring us end up being deported or worse. What's the fucking point?'

Chloe sat open-mouthed throughout Siobhan's tirade. Amelia knew there was truth in what she said, but it was so unlike her friend to admit defeat.

Amelia spoke calmly and with clarity: 'The point is you give women a real choice, Shiv. They can stay here and have a break from their pimps. Even if only one or two decide to make a complete break, you've allowed them the space to make that choice. Poppy never had that chance. She was financially and psychologically attached to her abuser. You can't save all the women. None of us can, but even if you save just one –'

'Just one. I only ever wanted to save one.' Siobhan sighed.

'I know… and we can't bring them back, Shiv. None of us can do that.' Amelia knew that turning back the clock was not an option. If it had been, both women would do so in a heartbeat.

'Jeez. Have you two ever thought of being partners? You'd break down anyone.' Siobhan grimaced rather than smiled, but Amelia saw this as a breakthrough.

There was a knock on the office door before Chloe could make the call to the local station to request a uniformed, preferably female, officer. It was Ellie, with Carol.

Carol didn't stand on ceremony. 'Hi, Siobhan. You don't know me but, if you need a ball-breaking cop in your corner, then I'm your woman.'

For the first time that morning, Siobhan smiled. She held out her hand. 'Pleased to meet you. Welcome to the coven.'

Carol shook Siobhan's hand and sat down on the only available chair.

Chloe spoke first. 'It looks like you've had a wasted journey. Siobhan's agreed to give a statement. I was just about to ring a colleague at Little Park Street.'

'Oh, I wouldn't say it was wasted. Let's hold our inaugural Let's Get Amelia Reinstated meeting. It's long overdue.' Carol sat forward in her chair and clasped her hands together. She clearly meant business.

'I think that might actually be harder than it was to persuade Siobhan to report her attack,' Amelia said.

'There's got to be a way we can work together and get that bastard Jake Farris to withdraw his statement against you.' Carol slammed her hand on the table. 'Just give me five minutes with him.'

'And then you'd be suspended, too. I appreciate all your support, but this is a hopeless cause.' Amelia sat back in her chair. She'd accepted that she was likely to stay suspended for the foreseeable future.

'He's still working undercover, is he?' Carol looked to Chloe for confirmation.

'Yes, we get irregular reports from him, but it seems he's posing as a local trafficker while he tries to find evidence against Robert Davo or Davies or whatever he's called.' Chloe raised her eyebrows, implying that it was a lost cause.

This seemed the most opportune moment to fill Chloe in on what Amelia had discovered that morning. Having Carol there meant that she could tell her what she knew about Robert Davies, too. It made it all the more difficult to understand why they were getting so little from Jake. Without evidence, it would be the wrong time to arrest Robert Davies, but they could still lean on Jake.

'Who's he reporting to?' Amelia asked Chloe.

'Will,' Chloe sighed, 'when he can be bothered.'

The room was silent for a moment as the women considered the options.

'What if we tried to get Will on our side? Do you think he'd help us meet with Jake?' Carol wasn't giving up on him yet.

'What if he does? Are you going to take him on?' Amelia asked. 'He's not going to withdraw his accusation against me just because you ask him to.'

Carol smiled. 'I can be very persuasive.'

'I don't doubt that, but he's an evil bastard. It's going to take more than words.' Amelia knew this tack was useless. 'I really appreciate the moral support from you all, but I'm just going to have to try and persuade the powers-that-be when the time comes. What we really should be focusing on is how we can protect the trafficked women from Davies.'

'Despite everything you've told me today, the investigation appears to have stalled. It's not our top priority anymore,' Chloe admitted. 'We've been assigned a new group of women who've been trafficked across the UK. It's a major case as they're all under eighteen and the traffickers are all white English guys. The powers-that-be want to showcase it to take the spotlight off previous cases.'

Amelia knew what she meant. There had been a small number of high-profile cases involving male traffickers of Asian heritage. These were used by far-right organisations to stir up hatred in local communities. The traffickers involved were mainly British citizens, educated in British schools. In Amelia's experience, it mattered not one jot what a trafficker's culture or skin colour was. A trafficker did it purely for the money and cared little about the girls and women, who were just commodities to be bought and sold. There were far too many women being abused in this way. It was no surprise that a new case was being given priority. The fact that there were murders linked to Davo's gang meant that the case would be shifted to the regional murder squad and away from the NCA.

'Are they considering recalling Jake?' Amelia guessed that they probably wouldn't. They'd wait to see how deep he could infiltrate and how useful his intel was.

'I've not heard anything. Will's still keeping contact with him. I'd expect this to switch to someone in the MIT at some point.' Chloe yawned. Amelia noted how tired she looked. She was only a DS and she was basically fulfilling the role of a DI.

'They can't afford to keep him out in the field forever. They'll be pressuring him to come up with a quick result. Knowing Jake, he'll put himself and others at risk in the process.' Amelia grimaced.

Carol understood what Amelia was implying. 'So, if we leave him to his own devices, he'll bring about his own demise…?'

'True, but he'll also put the women at risk. To him, they'll just be collateral damage.' Other women, particularly Elena, would be caught up in his game and he wouldn't be bothered by that at all.

'Chloe, contact Will for me. Tell him you need to meet him about a case.' Carol balled her fists. 'He's the weak link here. We need to exploit it.'

She then raised her hand before Amelia could interject. 'I won't change my mind, but I'll try to be a little more subtle in the way I handle him.'

There was no further argument from any of the women. Chloe called Little Park Street Station and then rang Will to request a meet at a nearby café. She left shortly after with Carol. Amelia stayed with Siobhan until the police constable arrived, leaving through the back door so she wouldn't be noticed. She didn't want to be accused of breaking her suspension.

Chapter 27

The Dinner Party

Friday came and Amelia had heard nothing from either Chloe or Carol about their meeting with Will. She hoped no news was good news. Becky had returned to school that morning. Amelia had heard nothing from her, either. She was tempted to text her but guessed that, if there was a problem, she would be the first point of contact. It left her feeling restless all day.

It wasn't until lunchtime that she remembered she was seeing Michal that evening. She considered cancelling it, concerned that Becky might need her but, later in the afternoon, she got a text from her saying that she was going to stay at a friend's after school and go for pizza.

Now all she needed to do was decide what to wear. Her trousers were getting tighter by the day. Rarely did she wear dresses or skirts, but she did have a loose fitting, blue, lace dress that she'd worn once to a wedding. It seemed to have survived her green and grey period. She tried it on and stared at herself in the mirror. Rushing into the relationship was her mistake with Jake. If she hadn't wanted everything immediately, maybe she'd have paused and realised what he was really like.

What did she know about Michal? He was Roma and didn't want a relationship outside his culture. He was a boxer and owned his own club. She hadn't investigated whether there was any intelligence about him or the club. Boxing was known to attract criminals. Now she was being paranoid. She sighed and shook her head to clear it. She was going to dinner, that was all; she wasn't marrying the man.

When she went downstairs in the blue dress and a pair of heels. Her mum was in the kitchen with Caitlyn.

'You look nice.' Jane smiled.

'Too much, d'you think?' Amelia looked down at the dress, then flicked off some imaginary dirt.

'No, not at all. Perfect.'

Amelia was surprised. She'd expected a hint of disapproval, but not these words of encouragement.

She picked up her bag, kissed Caitlyn on the cheek and said, 'I won't be late.'

Michal's house was on the other side of town. It was larger than Amelia's, detached and with double-fronted bay windows. Clearly, the boxing business was doing well. There were a number of cars parked on the drive. Amelia guessed that she wouldn't be the only guest but didn't expect the whole family to be there.

Michal opened the front door as soon as she got out of the car. He kissed her on the cheek and ushered her in. He whispered, 'Sorry, I didn't invite them all. They just turned up. Fortunately, my daughter-in-law made enough food to feed an army.'

Michal sat at the head of the table. Amelia sat on his right. Kesia sat next to her, almost as a buffer from the rest of the family. Kesia's husband sat opposite. He noticeably blushed when Amelia glanced at him. He was either embarrassed at being at a meal with a superior officer, or with a suspended one. Amelia guessed it was the latter.

There was an upside to having all the family there. They talked to each other, followed their usual patterns of behaviour and laughed at the in-jokes. This left Amelia free to chat to Michal about neutral subjects: what kind of music they liked, countries they'd visited, films they loved. The meal ended far too soon. Amelia was surprised when Michal took her hand and led her from the table. 'Let's leave them to the washing up and go outside.'

The garden was stunning, Mediterranean in style, with a covered seating area. Michal led her there and sat down on one of the cushioned wicker chairs. Amelia took the seat next to him. 'I thought you'd want some peace from the clan,' he said, smiling.

'Is it always this busy at yours?' Amelia leaned in so their shoulders were lightly touching.

Michal laughed, 'Yes, it often is. They've all left the nest but not flown far.'

Amelia smiled. She hadn't felt this relaxed in ages. Part of her hoped that he'd got past the fact that she wasn't Roma. Maybe that was why he asked her here? Perhaps Kesia had spoken to him to persuade him that it didn't matter. Besides, Kesia had married outside her race and Michal didn't seem bothered by it.

While she contemplated this, leaning in closer on his shoulder, he suddenly stood up and held out his hands to her. 'Let's dance,' he said.

'But there's no music – and, besides, I'm a rotten dancer.' Amelia didn't know what to do. Was this some kind of test and if she couldn't dance would that be the end of their budding romance?

'I guessed as much. I've seen you skip remember, although, with my tutelage, you did improve… slightly.' He was still holding his hands out and grinning now.

Amelia sighed and stood up. Michal pulled her towards him, their bodies comfortably close. Both being tall, they naturally moulded together. Amelia smelled a hint of Michal's cologne and instantly relaxed. They moved slowly at first, Michal leading and Amelia following. He had one hand on her hip and the other wrapped around her hand resting on his shoulder. Amelia sensed Michal's breath on her neck and closed her eyes.

'See, I knew you could dance,' he whispered.

Amelia didn't reply.

The peace was soon shattered by the others when they all came pouring into the garden. One of Michal's sons held a violin and another an accordion. It seemed odd that two burly boxers could hold and play instruments with such delicacy but, when they played, the softness and precision of the notes was breath-taking.

The tempo increased tenfold and, even with Michal's

leadership, Amelia couldn't keep up. 'I need to sit down. Sorry,' she whispered in his ear and he led her to a vacant seat.

Amelia watched as the others danced, aware that Michal was staring at her, and she felt herself blush.

She could barely hear him over the noise of the music when he asked her, 'When's the baby due?'

'Sorry?' Amelia leaned closer, hoping she'd misheard.

'You're pregnant, aren't you? I recognise the signs.'

Amelia was unsure what to say. There was no point in lying as it would be obvious to everyone soon enough, but she really didn't want to lose this man when she'd only just found him.

Eventually, she said, 'I'm nearly four months pregnant.'

'And the father?'

'We're not together anymore. He abused me.'

Michal took hold of her hand. 'Amelia, you don't need to tell me anything until you're ready. This doesn't change anything. I'd like to see you again.'

Amelia didn't believe him. Of course, it changed everything.

Michal continued. 'It strikes me that you need someone to take care of you. My whole family have offered to do that, don't forget that. It's hard to accept help when, often, it's exactly what we need.'

The independent woman in Amelia baulked at this. She nearly got up to exclaim, 'I don't need your help!' Instead, she started to cry. She had no clue where the tears came from. They fell hot and urgently. Michal pulled her close and held her until they subsided.

Amelia had never felt more embarrassed. She hoped no one had seen her, particularly Kesia. When she was able to look up, she saw that everyone was dancing, engrossed in the music, which was a relief.

'I've no idea why I did that. I'm sorry.' Amelia pulled away from Michal and wiped her eyes.

'You don't need to apologise.'

'I think it might be best if I go. Thank you, though, for a lovely evening.'

Michal stood up as she did. For the first time since she'd met him, his brow was furrowed and he wasn't smiling. 'Let me show you out.'

When they reached the front door, Michal reached for her and drew her close. He kissed her then, slowly and a little unsure to begin with but, as she responded, the intensity grew. When each of them stepped back, they were breathless.

Michal grinned. 'I've wanted to do that all night.'

Amelia didn't need to admit that she had been thinking the same. They both stood apart staring at each other, neither sure what to do next. Eventually, Amelia broke the silence. 'I'd better go. Until next time.'

Michal kissed her again. This time the kiss was slower, more exploratory. He stroked her face when they'd finished.

'Until next time,' he said, smiling.

As Amelia walked to her car, she bit the tip of her finger to stop herself grinning like a schoolgirl.

Chapter 28

Will Takes a Side

Amelia awoke early the next day. She felt more relaxed than she had for a while. Pulling the duvet closer, she wrapped her legs around it and, for a brief moment, imagined she was sharing the bed with Michal.

The one good thing about being suspended was that she was in no rush to get out of bed. She could lie here dreaming for as long as she wished. She'd always worked harder than anyone on her team; long, luxurious lie-ins were unheard of, and it felt unnatural to stay in bed and dream once the sun was up. Amelia stretched, her hands reaching up to the ceiling, and then pushed herself up and out of bed.

The house continued to slumber. No one else stirred as she went down to the kitchen. Amelia helped herself to cornflakes and waited for the coffee to brew. She decided that, if she didn't hear from Carol or Chloe today, then she would contact one of them, probably Carol as it was unlikely that they were monitoring her calls. She didn't want to risk Chloe not picking up the message using the online service.

Becky entered the kitchen a few moments later, yawning.

Amelia held out her arm and gestured for a hug. It was strange how the dreadfulness of the last few days had brought them closer. As Becky hugged her back, Amelia stroked her hair.

'I thought you were staying over at your mate's?'

'She's got swimming practice this morning, so her dad dropped me off early.' Becky moved away from her mum and helped herself to some cereal.

Amelia held up the cafetière. 'Coffee?'

'Thanks.'

Amelia poured the coffee and they both went to sit at the kitchen table.

'How was school yesterday?' Amelia asked, concerned that the bullying might have continued.

Becky sighed and twirled her mug in her hands. 'At first, no one would look at me. I think… I hope they were embarrassed. By lunchtime, everyone was behaving like they usually do around me, like it had never happened.'

'That's good,' Amelia said and placed her hand on her daughter's arm.

'I s'pose. It's just crap, though. I don't get it. Why would anyone think it was okay to share pictures like that?'

'Neither do I and I prosecute people who do far worse.'

'I've never said, Mum… I know it looks like I've always resented the work you do, but I actually think it's amazing.'

Amelia smiled. Her eldest daughter was usually so confrontational. It was as though she'd grown up in the past couple of weeks.

Becky continued. 'But don't think I'm not going back to hating you from now on though.'

They both started to giggle just as Caitlyn came rushing into the room. Amelia got up and fetched a bowl. 'What do you want for breakfast?'

As she poured her daughter some Coco Pops, she thought about whether now was a good time to mention Michal. As she took the milk out of the fridge, she decided that it wasn't. She wasn't sure yet where the relationship, if that's what it was, would end up. At the moment, she was at that giggly schoolgirl stage where she wanted to share how she felt with everyone, but there was so much holding her back, not least the child that she was carrying.

After breakfast, Becky and Caitlyn both went to their rooms,

Becky to listen to music and Caitlyn to play. Jane still wasn't up, so Amelia went to her room and knocked softly on the door. Her mother opened the door a few moments later. She looked tired and her eyes were red, as though she'd been crying.

'You okay?' Amelia asked handing her mother a cup of tea.

'Sorry. Are the girls sorted?' Her mother held the door open and Amelia entered her room.

'It's not like you to have a lie-in.' Amelia searched her mother's face for clues to her obvious distress.

Her mother closed the door and sat on the bed, patting the space next to her.

Amelia sat down. Neither spoke; their thoughts were gathered in like the drawing-in of the laces on a boxing glove.

Her mother spoke first. 'We really need to start planning for this one's arrival.' She placed her hand on Amelia's stomach. 'I'm not getting any younger and I'm not sure I want to look after another baby while you're at work.'

Perhaps she should have expected this, Amelia thought. Why would her mum want to put her own life on hold any longer? Caitlyn and Becky needed her less and less. She was able to pursue her hobbies, meet friends and do chores while they were both at school. A baby to care for would change all of that.

Police officers of Amelia's rank didn't take extended maternity leave. Amelia had returned to work when Becky was two months old and Caitlyn was three months old, the extension only because she had difficulty finding a childminder. That was when Joe was alive and her irregular hours were complemented by his regular nine-to-five. He was able to drop the children off to childminders, leaving Amelia free to work whatever hours she chose. After his death, there was no way she could cover her hours with a childminder, which was when her mum had stepped in. Now she wanted to step back. Who could blame her?

'I guess we could look for a live-in nanny.' Amelia stared at the floor.

Her mother stood and smoothed her skirt. 'Yes, I think that would be the best option.'

It was time to start considering the baby. They'd need two bedrooms, one for the nanny and one for the baby. Years of junk would need clearing out of the box room. The spare bedroom would need painting to make it attractive for someone. Mind you, the thought of having a stranger living with them didn't really appeal.

A germ of an idea began to grow. Jola would be out of hospital soon. You couldn't wish for a kinder person to care for your children, but would a woman who's just been told that she can never have children want to help bring up someone else's? She couldn't ask her straight away because that would mean telling Kesia about the pregnancy... but maybe Michal had already done that? Then there were Becky and Caitlyn. They would be sharing their home, too. She'd discuss it with the whole family this evening. They could have a takeaway and sit around the table like a proper family and make some plans.

Just as Amelia reached this decision, her phone vibrated in her trouser pocket. She took it out to find a text from Carol: *MEET ME IN THE PUB IN AN HOUR.* Carol didn't need to say what pub.

Amelia arrived at The Shepherd a few minutes late. Carol's car was already parked by the entrance to the back bar. Just as she was getting out of the car, she received a text from Michal: *I'D LOVE TO SEE YOU AGAIN. A MEAL? OR WOULD YOU LIKE ME TO TEACH YOU DOUBLE CROSSOVERS AT THE CLUB?*

Amelia smiled. If he wasn't put off by the fact that she was carrying another man's child, then perhaps she should meet him again. She might give the skipping a miss though; a meal sounded much more inviting.

Carol was sitting at their usual table, drinking a pint of a dark ale despite the fact that it was only eleven o'clock in the morning. Amelia ordered a lime and soda and went to join her.

'Still on the pop, I see. Good girl,' Carol said with just a hint of sarcasm.

Amelia decided to skip any small talk. 'How did it go with Will? Did you manage to turn him?'

'Well...' Carol put her pint down and leaned forward, '... it was two against one. That DS of yours is pretty savvy, too. She's a credit to you.'

'Tell me more.' For the first time in ages, Amelia felt that things might be turning in her favour.

'Chloe duped Will by feigning some deeply held lust for him and inviting him for a drink. Here, as it happens,' Carol grinned. 'Of course, he didn't expect to see me. I thought he was going to bolt at first, but actually there were a number of things he wanted to get off his chest.'

'So, he's not best pals with Jake, then?' It was likely that Jake had taken his manipulation too far and Will was feeling uneasy.

'Far from it. He thinks he's dangerous – to himself and everyone else he comes in contact with. They've been told to move on to other cases, yet he's still working undercover. It doesn't seem to matter how many times Will's told him he needs to come back in. It's always "We're so close. I can't. This is going to be massive," or words to that effect.'

'Surely Rodgers has ordered him directly by now? Will can't cover for Jake forever.'

'Rodgers is weak. You know that. He's one of those over-promoted idiots who's never particularly brilliant at any of his roles but knows who to brown-nose.'

Amelia stopped to think for a minute. Maybe if she spoke to Police Complaints about this then they would see what Jake was like and investigate him more closely.

Carol interrupted her thoughts. 'Will won't say anything openly. That's the problem. We told him to go to Police Complaints. Begged him, even, but he thinks that'll put Jake in even more danger. He may well be right.'

'So, what does he suggest? That we sit around waiting for Jake to mess up? Get someone, even himself, killed? And all this time he gets away with raping me!'

'I don't think Will believes that, unfortunately. He knew about your relationship. I think he still believes the woman-scorned line. We did try and convince him otherwise. Bloody men!'

'So, Will knows that Jake's fucking Elena, who's probably one of the most vulnerable women you could ever meet, and he's doing that to get information, but he doesn't believe he's capable of rape?'

'He has agreed to keep us in the loop about what's going on with Jake. It's a start.'

'I suppose so.' Amelia sighed. She needed to get back to work. This was ridiculous. How could anyone think that she was so desperate for a bloke that she'd beat up a guy after he dumped her?

Carol put her hand on Amelia's arm. 'Listen, I'm going to speak to Police Complaints on your behalf. I'll tell them exactly what I think of this investigation. They need to know what Jake gets up to. It'd be better if Will did it as he's directly involved, but they know my reputation. Hopefully, they'll take me seriously.'

'They also know you're a good mate of mine, Carol. Don't put your job at risk for me. You know what they're like. If they think you're lying, they'll make your life hell.'

Carol took a long slug of beer. 'But I'm not lying, am I.'

Amelia knew that if anyone wanted rid of Carol from the force, it would be simple. They'd only need to breathalyse her after midday when she was driving her car. No one would touch her at the minute because she was such an effective officer but, if they wanted to, they could bring her down in seconds. This was Amelia's biggest concern. She'd rather stay suspended than put her friend at risk.

'Carol, thanks for offering to go to Complaints. Let's leave it for now. I'm sure we'll find more evidence against Jake, and Will might change his mind when he's thought about it.'

Carol finished her pint. 'If you're sure?'

'I'm sure.'

'Okay, I won't do anything yet.' Carol grinned. 'On a lighter note, Kesia tells me you have a new man in your life.'

Amelia felt herself blush and took a sip of her drink in an attempt to hide it. 'I wouldn't go that far. I barely know him.'

'A Roma boxer. How romantic!' Carol laughed.

She couldn't hide her blush this time. 'He *is* rather handsome but nothing's happened… yet.'

'But you clearly want it to. Good on you. I scare blokes off. It's a shame. I wouldn't mind a shag.'

'I thought you normally went for very young, handsome PCs who were a little wet behind the ears?'

'Yeah, I like to grab them before they find out about my reputation.' Carol snorted at this.

'Well, good luck with that. I'd better go. We'll keep in touch.'

After a brief hug, Amelia returned to her car. She sat in the driver's seat and texted Michal back. *A MEAL SOUNDS PERFECT. WHEN?*

Chapter 29

Elena's Cry for Help

The last person Amelia expected to hear from was Elena. She still wasn't sure if Elena had given her up to the traffickers when they last met, so she was more than surprised when she got a call from her that evening. The call came through as an unknown number and Amelia nearly didn't answer it. Her usual practice was to let these go to voicemail unless they came through to her police-issue mobile.

With some hesitation, Amelia answered, 'Hello?'

A quiet, almost timid, voice responded. 'It's Elena. I'm on an errand. This'll have to be quick.'

'What do you want?' Amelia rubbed her eyes.

'I'm scared something's going to happen to either me or Jake. I want to get out. There's stuff you need to know. Can you help?'

'Of course. Where are you? I can pick you up now.'

'No, that won't work. They'll come looking for me if I don't return in five minutes.'

'I could meet you somewhere. Just give me a time and date.' Amelia was concerned that this was another trap, but she'd consider that later.

'Tomorrow. Hillfields Square in Coventry. I should be there around lunchtime. They'll probably send me out to get their lunch.'

So, the women had already been moved to Coventry. It made sense, Amelia thought, if they were looking to set up a new sex club there.

Amelia was about to agree when Elena cut the call.

Jane announced that tea was ready at that point so Amelia decided to message Chloe later to tell her where the women were now being kept.

It was only when she sat down at the dinner table that she realised how hungry she was. Her mum had made a shepherd's pie with a good range of fresh vegetables laid out in separate dishes. Feeling better, she'd insisted that home cooked food was better than any takeaway. Everyone politely took their share and began to eat.

Amelia had half finished her plate before she spoke. 'I've been talking with your grandma and we've decided it'd be a good idea to get a live-in nanny when the baby's born and I go back to work.'

With her fork halfway to her mouth, Becky asked, 'Do you think they'll let you go back to work?'

Amelia hadn't even considered that. In fact, the thought nearly put her off eating the rest of her meal.

Jane helped herself to more broccoli and said, 'Of course they will. Don't be silly.'

'But they haven't let you yet, have they? What if they don't? What'll happen to us then?' Becky was clearly worried about this. Amelia's salary and widow's pension had kept them afloat financially. In fact, they still had a fair amount of savings, but how long would that last if she was out of work?

'We'll manage. I've got every faith that they'll see sense and let me go back to work soon. Don't worry, Becky.' Amelia smiled to shroud her concerns.

'So, getting a nanny – does anyone mind about that?' Her mum steered the conversation back.

'Will she read me stories?' Caitlyn asked.

She hadn't asked for stories to be read to her for a while, so this came as a surprise to Amelia. 'I can read your stories, if you like.'

'You're no good at doing the different characters, not like my teacher. He's really funny.' Caitlyn finished her food and pushed her plate to one side. 'Is there pudding?'

While her mum went to fetch the apple pie and ice cream, Amelia asked the girls again if they'd mind having a nanny staying with them. The consensus seemed to be that they didn't, but they'd want to meet any potential applicants first to see if they liked them, which seemed to Amelia to be a sensible idea.

It wasn't long before the dessert had been finished and everyone was itching to leave the table. Becky offered to put the dishes in the dishwasher and Caitlyn was sent to tidy away the toys she'd left strewn on the living room floor.

'I think I'll go and watch TV. What are your plans this evening?' Her mother wasn't accusing her of anything, but her tone did give Amelia pause. What she was really saying was – stop investigating, you're suspended. Amelia was well aware of how much trouble she would get in if she was caught.

'I've got things to catch up on in my office. Stop worrying. I know what I'm doing.'

But did she? Really? Meeting Elena again was a massive risk. She didn't want to do it alone. She fired up her computer and found the messaging app.

Amelia: *Hi Chloe. Elena's contacted me. She wants me to meet her at Hillfields Square tomorrow lunchtime. Could you be there, too? She also said that the women are in Coventry. I thought you'd want to know.*

There was nothing more she could do but wait for a reply. In the meantime, she considered ringing Michal. He hadn't got back to her yet about going for a meal. There was no reason why she shouldn't call him first.

She was just about to do so when she received a reply to her message.

Chloe: *I'll meet you there at 11. Why Hillfields Square?*

Amelia: *It's where Elena gets the lunch for the traffickers. It's possible the girls are being kept local to there.*

Chloe: *If I was keeping them anywhere in Cov, that's where it'd be. To think – there could be trafficked women living next door to me!*

Amelia: *Yes, but you'd know what signs to look for. Most people don't look further than their front door.*

Chloe: *True. Listen I'm going out now with Dion. I'll see you tomorrow.*

Amelia: *Yes, see you tomorrow.*

Now that was settled, Amelia couldn't help but feel an impending sense of doom. She switched off the computer and glanced at the clock. It was gone nine. She could phone Michal, but she wasn't sure she had the energy. Yawning, she went to make herself a coffee. Her phone rang as soon as she got up.

It was Michal.

'Hi, I was just thinking about you.' Amelia found herself yawning again.

'And it put you to sleep?' Michal laughed.

'Sorry, don't know what's up. I'm really shattered today.'

'I can let you go and have an early night.'

'No, please, it's fine. It's good to hear your voice.' Amelia settled on to the sofa and put her feet up.

'I'm glad you think so. A meal then. Any preference? Italian, French, Czech home cooking?'

'With the whole family again?'

'I was thinking, just me. But if you like, I could invite –'

'No. I prefer the just you option.' Amelia smiled, crossed and uncrossed her legs.

'Good, tomorrow evening too soon?'

'No, I'd love that.'

'Great. It's a date. 7:30 okay? I'll let you get to bed now. Sweet dreams.'

'7:30's fine. Goodnight, Michal.'

Amelia wasn't sure she'd sleep if she went to bed, so instead she took another look at her case board. What would drive Elena to want to escape? And why wasn't she getting Jake to help her? That would have made more sense, unless she'd realised how dangerous he was. What exactly was Jake doing? How had he ingratiated himself into the gang? Perhaps she should get Chloe to ask Will for more details now that he was being more cooperative.

The next day started badly. Caitlyn was running a temperature and Becky had received a text from the lad whose phone she'd smashed, threatening to kill her for reporting him. Amelia knew that she should contact the police but then she'd be stuck at the house waiting for them to arrive and that would leave Elena at risk. So, instead, she rang around some of Becky's friends' parents until she finally got the boy's mother's phone number. Amelia rang her and made it absolutely clear that a threat to kill would be taken very seriously by the police and if it happened again then she'd have no choice but to report him. Then she dosed Caitlyn up with Calpol and found her favourite DVD to watch.

By that point, it was time to leave to get to Hillfields by 11 am.

Chloe was sitting on a bench next to the community centre, reading a newspaper. She smiled when Amelia sat down next to her.

'Any sign?'

Chloe put down the paper. 'Not yet. We could be here a while. Shall we do the crossword?'

'Go on then.'

They were stuck on 12 down when Amelia spotted Elena walking towards them. Chloe stood up, folded her newspaper and walked off. As soon as Elena got close, she bent her head towards Amelia. 'We need to get out of here quick. Where's your car?'

Both Chloe and Amelia had parked in the car park of a nearby block of flats. Amelia stood and half jogged towards it. Elena had no problems keeping up with her. Chloe was already in her car and ready to follow. Amelia left the car park at speed with Elena in the passenger seat.

'Shall I take you to Poppy's Place?' Amelia asked.

Elena was frantically staring out of each of the car windows in turn, clearly worried that they were being followed. They were, of course, being followed by Chloe, but Elena didn't seem bothered by that. A woman in a car was not a threat. It was men that she feared.

'They'll know I'm there. Is there anywhere else?'

Amelia kept driving, trying to decide where else they could go. Eventually, she made a decision and drove to the Blue Corner. It wasn't that far from Hillfields Square and, as a gym, it would be open on a Sunday. Michal might be there but, if not, one of his sons would be and you wouldn't wish to cross any of them.

Elena looked confused. Her brow furrowed. 'Why are we stopping here?'

'You'll be safe here and it'll give me time to think where you could stay, if not at Poppy's.' Amelia got out of the car and went into the boxing club. Elena followed.

There weren't many in the club. Two young men were lifting weights in the corner. One of Michal's sons was punching a floor-to-ceiling ball. He stopped when he spotted Amelia and ambled over to her.

'Hi. My dad's not here. I think he's gone food shopping for tonight.'

'Right. I need somewhere safe for a while. Can I borrow your dad's office?'

He didn't question why she needed it, he just gestured towards it. 'Sure, if there's anything you need, give me a shout.'

At that point, Chloe joined them. Amelia introduced her to Elena. 'This is DS Chloe Smith. She's going to help you.'

Elena switched from being tame to feral. Her whole face shape converted in an instant. All the smooth edges became hard. Her cheeks puffed out and her eyes bulged. A vein in her neck started to pulse. This was the Elena that Amelia knew best.

'Why the hell have you involved her? You've put us all at risk.'

'Chloe's one of the most honest and straightforward officers you're ever likely to meet. To be frank, Elena, you're lucky to have her in your corner.' Amelia didn't hide her anger either. The number of times that she'd tried to help this woman only to have it thrown straight back in her face...

She strode off into Michal's office, expecting the other two women to follow her. Sitting down in Michal's chair and facing his wall of photographs seemed oddly comforting and Amelia relaxed. Chloe and Elena took the other two chairs, eyeing each other warily.

Amelia started, 'Well, what's going on Elena. And where's Jake?'

'Jake,' Elena spat on the ground. 'He's so involved it would be difficult to distinguish him from the traffickers. They treat him like a long-lost brother. Do you know, he even beats me as hard as they do!'

As if to highlight this fact, Elena lifted her shirt sleeve. Her arm was covered in purple and yellow bruising. 'The other girls are frightened of him, more than some of the others. He's a monster. He loves beating us.'

Amelia bit her lip so she wouldn't blurt out that she'd tried to warn her. 'I'm sure he does. We need to know where the girls are being kept. We need to know that now so we can raid the place.'

Elena sat back heavily in the chair. 'I can't tell you that.'

Chloe leant forward. 'We can give you protection. I can organise that, but we need to get in there quick before they realise you've gone and they move them.'

'You don't understand. If I do that, then my daughter will be at risk. If it's just me, then maybe she'll be okay.'

'Your daughter lives with Robert Davies, doesn't she? The Devil.' Amelia needed Elena to know that she knew some of the details and that, with Elena's help, they might be able to rescue her daughter.

'Yes. If you know this, why haven't you arrested him?' Elena hissed.

'We need evidence, and you can help us with that.' Amelia knew she couldn't make any promises.

'It's too risky. Take me to Poppy's Place. I'll take my chances.'

Amelia stood up. 'If you can't help us, then you're free to leave. I'm not taking you anywhere.'

Chloe raised her eyebrows. She stared at Amelia, seeking some reassurance that she knew where she was going with this.

Elena stayed in her seat, 'I'll tell you the address. That's it.'

Chloe took her phone out of her pocket ready to make the call.

'They are at 276, Thackhall Street.'

Chloe contacted both the trafficking division and sex crimes unit. They'd need as many officers as they could get. Then she left to meet them.

Elena lit a cigarette. Amelia wondered what Michal would make of that. She scoured the room, looking for something to use as an ashtray, in the end settling on a mug and handing it to Elena. Then she called Michal.

'It's me. I'm at your club. I've got someone here who needs a safe place to stay. Can I bring her to yours?'

It had taken Amelia all afternoon to agonise over that. It made the most sense. No one would cross Michal and, by tomorrow, Chloe would have found her a safe house.

Michal answered almost immediately. 'Yes, of course. I'm there now.'

The dinner that evening was not what Michal or Amelia had in mind, although Elena seemed to enjoy the food and spoke animatedly with Michal in Czech. Michal seemed quite disinterested in her, particularly her attempts at flirting, which were beginning to annoy Amelia. When Elena put her hand on Michal's knee, Amelia rose and said, 'Let me show you where the garden is so you can have a smoke.'

She took Elena outside to the covered patio. Elena laughed mockingly. 'You want to shag him, don't you? Go ahead, don't mind me.'

Amelia didn't answer her. Instead, she walked back into the house. She found Michal in the kitchen loading the dishwasher.

'Nice company you keep,' he said with a smile.

'Well, you know my line of work.' She wanted to kiss him then and there against the cabinets.

He seemed to sense this. He moved closer to her, taking hold of her waist with both his hands. 'I was hoping we'd be alone tonight.' Then he kissed her, long and passionately. When he paused, he said, 'In fact, I was hoping you'd stay the night.'

Amelia stroked his arm. 'Maybe I should. It'd keep you out of Elena's clutches.'

Elena walked into the kitchen at that moment. 'I hope I'm not interrupting anything.'

Michal motioned to Elena, 'Come, I'll show you to your room. I've given you a towel in case you'd like to have a bath or a shower.'

Amelia stayed where she was, trying to stop her heart from fluttering. He'd asked her to stay and she knew that she could only say yes. Her phone was in her pocket, so she reeled off a text to her mum to say that she wouldn't be home. Let her think of that what she will.

Michal returned moments later. 'So, would you like to watch a film, dance or –'

'Take me to bed, Michal.' Amelia stroked his cheek and then lifted his jaw and kissed him.

Chapter 30

The Raid

Amelia was woken the next day by a phone call. By the time she found her phone, which was on the dressing table on Michal's side of the bed, the caller had rung off. It was Siobhan. Amelia sat up in bed, glancing down at Michal who was still asleep, lying on his front. She really wanted to trace the line of his back with her fingertips, but it was unlike her friend to call her so early.

As she waited for Siobhan to answer, she twirled a length of her hair with her fingers and reflected on the previous evening. Michal had been a considerate lover, strong and in control, yet surprisingly tender.

Siobhan answered and broke into her thoughts. 'Hi,' Amelia muttered.

'Chloe's here. They managed to raid the house before the women were moved. We've got five new arrivals. We've kept the youngest. The Salvation Army has the rest.' Siobhan sounded exhausted.

'I'll come straight over. Put Chloe on, though. We need to decide what to do with Elena first.'

Chloe came on the line moments later. 'I've arranged a safe house for Elena. Shall I send someone to pick her up?'

That would mean her being alone with Michal. This didn't present itself as a suitable plan to Amelia. It wasn't often that she felt possessive, but he'd aroused that in her now.

'No, it's fine. I'll bring her with me and then we can arrange something from Poppy's.'

Amelia decided to make sure Elena was up and getting ready. She crossed the landing to her room and knocked on the door. No one answered. Entering the bedroom, it was clear that Elena had left. The bed looked like it hadn't even been slept in.

'Shit.' Amelia ran downstairs to check that she wasn't there. Chloe asked, 'What's up?'

There was no sign of her. 'Elena's gone. She may well have left last night. Shit.'

'She's probably gone back to them. They'll have rung and threatened her. You know the score.' Amelia wondered when Chloe had become the calm and mature one.

'I know. I'll just let Michal know I'm going. I'll be with you soon.'

'Great. See you shortly.'

Michal was still asleep when Amelia got back into bed. She lightly caressed his back until he opened his eyes. He pulled her in for a kiss. The last thing Amelia wanted to do was get out of his bed, but she had no choice.

'I'm so sorry, Michal. I've got to meet Chloe at Poppy's. Last night was…'

'Clearly not good enough if you're thinking of leaving me.' He grinned that playful grin of his and kissed her again.

Amelia was glad he drew away after the kiss, or she would have stayed.

'Elena left last night. Not a complete surprise. I'll bring you a coffee and we'll speak later.'

Michal mumbled something, rolled over and hugged his pillow.

Amelia dressed, made coffee, drank hers scalding hot, and left.

The first person Amelia saw when she got to Poppy's was Kesia. She wondered if the blush that she felt building was evident on her face. Kesia smiled at her, giving no hint that she either knew or cared that Amelia had slept with her uncle last night. Fortunately, she didn't ask Amelia if she'd had a good evening. Then she would have blushed like a teenager.

'The new group are all very young. It's heart breaking,' Kesia said.

'But they're safe for now, which is important.' It was surprising that they'd been brought to Poppy's if they were so young. Many of them would automatically say eighteen or above if asked their age. The punters knew they were underage but would swear in court, if it ever came to it, that they'd checked that the girls were not under sixteen. It left the girls vulnerable, even after they were rescued. By the time their applications were referred, Amelia hoped that they'd all be more trusting and would reveal their true age. This was always one of her aims during interview. It felt strange that she wouldn't be doing that in this case. The reality of her suspension continued to gnaw.

Siobhan entered the kitchen at that point. Amelia was right – she looked exhausted. Her eyes were puffy and darkly ringed, her curly hair looked more unruly than usual and her first port of call was the coffee urn. Only when she'd taken a few gulps did she speak.

'It's been a long night settling the new ones in, like being on a youth club outing. I thought they were never going to shut up.'

'I guess they were better off here than at the Sally Army. Do you want me to have a word with Chloe and see if we can find a more suitable alternative?' She wasn't sure there was one. Wherever they went, they'd either be at risk in some way or the accommodation would be unsuitable.

'That's true. Ignore me. I'm horrible if I don't get my six hours.' Siobhan smiled and drank some more coffee.

'Is Chloe interviewing?' Amelia asked and helped herself to a coffee. She was tired for altogether different reasons.

'About to start, I believe.' Siobhan went to pour herself another coffee.

'I'd better go and join them, then.' Kesia left, leaving Amelia feeling at a loose end.

'I don't know why I came. It's not like I can do anything.' Amelia leaned on one of the worktops and folded her arms.

'You can help me collect up the washing and we can chat.'

Amelia almost offered to do it for her so her friend could have a lie-down, but realised that she'd no idea where the washing machine was.

In the first bedroom, Amelia collected the bed linen and Siobhan emptied the washing baskets. Neither spoke. They carried their loads down to the laundry room, which was part of a network of rooms off the kitchen. Amelia had no idea that there were further rooms here, having always assumed that the door simply led to a storeroom of some kind.

'I hate coming in here. It makes me wonder what these rooms were used for previously.' Siobhan led Amelia into the first room, which was kitted out with three launderette-sized washing machines and two large tumble dryers.

Amelia shuddered. The paedophiles that ran the children's home had only recently been convicted. These rooms felt disconnected from the rest of the house. You could almost taste the fear that emanated from them.

One of the other storerooms housed the fresh bedlinen. They picked up enough for the room they'd stripped and carried it upstairs. Siobhan started putting a sheet on one of the beds. 'We've got seven bedrooms. I try and keep a rota for sorting the washing for each once a week. The cleaner does the rest. She won't go into those rooms downstairs. It freaks her out.'

'I can understand why,' Amelia said, starting to make one of the other beds.

'It's getting worse out there. The girls are getting younger and younger. I don't just mean the ones we have here. There are so many girls being groomed on their own doorstep.' Siobhan stuffed a pillow into a pillowcase with more force than was necessary.

'And we have a predator on the loose, someone who clearly enjoys inflicting untold pain on women. He's possibly our murderer, too.' Amelia struggled to get the duvet into its cover.

'A sadist?' Siobhan asked.

'More likely a psychopath. The damage he's done to Jola and some of the other girls was quite extensive.' Amelia wasn't sure how many women were damaged in this way. It wasn't like it was being monitored. Many would have refused to report it to the police. Their relationship with the local force was often a strained one. Amelia would have requested that similar injuries were recorded and reported to the police, even if it was done anonymously.

It was lunchtime when they'd finished and Amelia found a chance to sit with Chloe. The first thing Amelia noted was how exhausted Chloe looked. Her spiky hair was sticking out in random directions; she reached for a chunk and pulled at it as though it would give her some extra energy. Then she forked up some chips and beans and shoved them into her mouth. Amelia looked down at the salad she'd chosen and wished she'd picked the chips.

'What have you learned from the new women?' Amelia asked.

Chloe continued to eat for a while before wiping her mouth on a serviette. 'They're new in the country. Looks like they went looking for new, fresh meat. Young, new, fresh meat.'

Amelia put down her fork, no longer hungry. 'Did they give you any information on their captors?'

'One of them described Jake to a tee.'

'Fuck. What did she have to say about him?'

'That he was a bit of a Jekyll and Hyde character. One minute he'd threaten and beat them, and the next he'd be sneaking them extra food and fags.'

Jekyll and Hyde. Amelia could never remember which was the good and bad side of that character, but she couldn't identify any good in Jake. She doubted he offered the girls treats for any other reason than to assuage his own guilt.

Chloe stood up. It was time to continue the interviews. 'Are you sticking around?' she asked Amelia.

'For a while, then I might go and see Jola.'

She hugged Amelia. 'If I don't see you later, I'll catch up with you soon.' Then she sighed and went back to the living room.

Amelia sat and drank her coffee. Siobhan was talking to the doctor at the other end of the table. She'd arrived a few minutes ago. Amelia left them to it and went outside. She texted Siobhan when she reached her car. *GONE TO THE HOSPITAL TO SEE JOLA. SPEAK TO YOU SOON.*

Jola was awake and sitting up in bed knitting when Amelia arrived at the hospital. She'd just completed a purl row of a short piece of knitting. Without prompting, Jola smiled and said, 'It's for you. I mean, your baby.'

'How did you know?' Amelia found herself blushing. She was

here to ask Jola a favour and before she'd even opened her mouth, Jola had put her mind at rest.

'It's getting pretty clear. Quite a bump!' She patted her own stomach as she nodded at Amelia's burgeoning abdomen. 'So I ask Kesia. She say yes, I'm right,' Jola grinned. 'I'm so happy for you… I love knitting. Kesia got me the wool. It give me something to do in this place.'

'When are they likely to let you out?' Amelia had been surprised that they'd kept her here this long, but she'd had a number of complications and they were unsure where they'd house her once released.

'Soon. Couple of days. They try to find me a place in a hostel with twenty-four-hour support. Poppy's is full, unfortunately.'

Amelia bit her lip. She hadn't thought about how much support Jola might need for her health, but she felt that having Jola at hers was the best solution for everyone. Her mum could keep an eye on her while she was healing. By the time the baby was born, Jola should be back to full health and could become the children's nanny. 'I've got a huge favour to ask you.'

Jola put down her knitting. 'Anything. Just ask.'

'How would you like to come and live with me? I'm not just asking because you need somewhere to stay. I'll need a nanny when this one's born.' Amelia touched her stomach and stared at Jola, trying to judge her reaction.

Jola's eyes lit up and she grinned before saying, 'Really? That would be wonderful. Thank you.'

Amelia reached over and hugged her. 'No, thank *you*. It's a load off my mind too, believe me. If you give me a couple of days to sort out our spare room, then you can move in as soon as they release you.'

'Don't worry about me. I can sleep in a cupboard.'

Amelia left her then and rang her mum. Jane wanted everything to be perfect for Jola and the baby and would contact her friend, an interior designer. Hopefully, they would be able to organise something at short notice.

Chapter 31

Saving Jake

Amelia considered stopping at Michal's on the way home. She'd have loved to spend an hour or so back in his arms but there was a great deal to prepare before Jola could come and stay. The sooner it was done, the sooner Jola could leave hospital.

Arriving home, she was surprised to see that her mum had managed to convince her daughters to help her clear out the spare room. They were traipsing down the stairs with cardboard boxes overflowing with books and games. Amelia smiled.

'Thanks for doing this. I'm surprised you haven't moved all the stuff you've found into your own rooms.'

'We're going to put it all in the garage and sort it properly another day. We thought some of the toys might come in handy for the baby would want to play with when it's older,' Becky grinned back.

It was lovely to see how they seemed to accept the current situation. They even appeared to be looking forward to meeting their new brother or sister. Amelia only wished that she could share their enthusiasm. When she reached the spare bedroom, she found her mother staring at the wall.

'I'm wondering if we can get away with one coat of paint,' she said.

Amelia had no clue. 'Best go with two. I should have asked Jola what colour she'd like.'

'I've got Jackie coming over in the morning, then we're going shopping on your credit card.' Jane squeezed her arm as she left the room. 'Dinner shouldn't be long,' she added.

Amelia wondered how expensive this was going to become. She left this room and, without thinking, went into the box room next door. The girls had cleared this, too. There was nothing in the room except for the odd piece of Lego, which Amelia automatically picked up. The room looked so much bigger than she remembered. It had a built-in cupboard that she knew would soon be filled with nappies, wipes and all the paraphernalia a baby required, plus many other things that weren't strictly necessary but everyone bought anyway. Maybe she could pass the job of choosing and ordering to her daughters. They could sit down after school and batter her credit card even more with some online shopping. The mere thought warmed Amelia, not because she was now looking forward to the new arrival, but more that she'd found a joint activity that her girls would enjoy. At least, she hoped they'd enjoy it – you could never really predict what teenagers would find interesting.

As she left the room, her phone rang. Looking at the screen, she saw it was Jake. Amelia paused, her thumb hovering over her phone, ready to swipe or press the red call ended button.

She chose the former and said tentatively, 'You've got a cheek.'

'Listen. I'm in trouble. Serious trouble. I need your help…'

Amelia held the phone away from her ear, poised to end the call.

'Please don't hang up. I'm at Cannon Hill Park. I just need you to pick me up,'

Amelia answered, 'Why don't you contact Will? He might actually give a damn.'

'Amelia, you're the only one that can help me. The only one that might understand the shit I'm in. Do this for me and I'll make sure you're allowed back to work.'

'You're going to admit you raped me, then?'

'I'm sure we could reach some understanding.'

Amelia cut the call, then spent the next five minutes staring at the phone. She knew she couldn't leave him to it if he really was in trouble. It was in her DNA; officer down meant you dropped everything and helped them. But this was Jake. This was different. She didn't hear her mum come into the room.

'Are you okay? You're awfully pale,' her mother asked, placing her hand on her shoulder.

'I'm fine.' Amelia bit her lip. 'I've just got to go out for a while. I'll have dinner when I get back.'

Leaving the house a few minutes later, Amelia's fight mode kicked in and she was soon flooring her car on the A441 towards Cannon Hill Park. She considered calling Carol for back up but decided it would be a waste of time. Carol would just say that he'd got what he deserved. What could have happened? Clearly, Jake had got in too deep with the traffickers and was now at some kind of risk. Amelia realised as she eased off the accelerator for the final roundabout that she was actually more concerned that Elena was the one at risk. If he'd done anything to harm her, then she might end up killing him herself.

A few moments later, she pulled into the car park and chose a parking bay near the exit without too many obstacles if they needed to leave quickly. Only then did she ring Jake back.

He didn't answer at first. Amelia stood next to her car, hand on hip, her fingers tapping her side, willing him to pick up. It went to voicemail. Rather than hear Jake's whine, she immediately dialled again. After three rings he picked up. 'Amelia, I can't move from the spot I'm in. I can see you though. Thanks –'

'I'm doing this for Elena. Is she with you?' Amelia turned full circle in an attempt to work out where Jake might be hiding.

There was a pause and Amelia heard Jake audibly sigh. 'She's dead.'

Amelia thought she'd misheard, or at least hoped she had. 'What –'

'She was murdered. Her body's in the back of the truck facing you in the car park.'

'No!' Amelia thrust her phone in her pocket and sprinted towards the van. Jake must have seen her as he stepped out in front of her from the side of the van, grabbing her arms and pushing her back.

He whispered close to her ear. 'We've got to get the fuck out of here. I don't know where the killers are. They could be still around. Just get in your car. Now!'

Amelia hadn't realised she was crying. Tears of anger or pain streaked her face. She pushed herself away from Jake's grasp and opened her bag to search for her car keys. As soon as she found them, she pushed Jake towards the passenger door. 'Get the fuck in.'

As soon as they were mobile, she tried to call for back up but before she could voice dial, Jake calmly cut her off. 'Please don't.'

'We can't just leave her in the van. What the fuck's wrong with you?' It was all she could do not let go of the steering wheel and punch his lights out.

'There's no choice. Contact one of your minions back at the station if you must. But consider this. I'm still undercover and you're still suspended. Neither of us can be there.' Jake sighed and turned his head to face her. 'We can't bring Elena back.'

'*You've* fucking killed her, Jake, not me!'

'To be fair, she put herself at risk so many times that this was pretty much inevitable. You, on the other hand, can get back into work if you help me out here.' Jake brushed some imaginary lint from his trousers.

Amelia didn't speak. She shouldn't have come and wasn't sure why she had. Maybe she should just shove Jake out of the car and deal with this whole mess professionally? But what if Jake was still willing to put things right? He wouldn't admit the rape; it would need to be dealt with in another way. If she could just get back to work, then maybe, just maybe, she could implicate him in Elena's murder. It would be some kind of justice at least.

'How will you sort it?' Amelia kept her eyes on the road, not able to look at Jake's sneering face.

'Meet with Will and say that things are getting too hairy. Let the chief know I'm willing to drop the assault charge against you. I can claim it was just a misunderstanding between ex-lovers. Of course, you'd have to withdraw your rape allegation for this to work. I'm sure they'd believe me if I said that you're the best officer in the division and we need you back.'

Amelia bit her lip. 'I'll drop you at the station but I'm going to report the truck. I'll just be an interested member of the public reporting a suspicious smell.'

'If they've got any sense, they'll have moved it by now. But do what you have to. It'll be a joy working with you again.'

Chapter 32

Back at work

Why had she let him convince her? Amelia had only been back in the office for two days and she was already regretting her decision. Everyone else seemed to be looking at her differently, treating her as a pariah – a woman who had given up all her principles. No one said anything directly to her face. They didn't need to.

Chloe was the worst. She kept looking across from her workstation and smiling.

Amelia carried on reading the case notes that she'd missed while away, not noticing that Will was beside her until he started speaking. 'That truck hasn't turned up.'

'What truck?' Of course, she knew full well what truck – she'd been the one to report it.

'The one emitting the odd smell at Cannon Hill Park. It had the same plates as one spotted near the house we raided in Coventry. Raised more than a few alarm bells when we got the report.' Why was Will sharing this with her and not Jake?

Amelia glanced around the office, noting that Jake wasn't at his desk.

'He's not here. Phoned in sick a few days ago, apparently.'
Was Will able to read minds now?

Amelia concentrated on her laptop screen and started typing notes into the shared drive. She said calmly, 'Chances are they've changed the plates or shipped it out of the country by now.' *And got rid of Elena's remains.*

'It was probably being used transport trafficked women. Let's just hope the smell doesn't mean anything nasty.' Will left Amelia to her note-making.

Amelia sniffed and wiped her eyes. She needed to get out of the office but wasn't sure where to go. There was so much that she knew, but none of it would convict Robert Davies. Eventually, she gave up and left her workstation.

'Chloe, you're with me,' she said and headed out of the office.

By the time they both were sat in Amelia's car, Chloe was panting. 'Where are we going?'

'Gibbet Hill, Coventry.' Amelia didn't wait for a response.

They'd been driving for ten minutes before Chloe spoke. 'Do you think this is wise? What are we going to do when we get there?'

Amelia thought about this. What the hell was she going to do when they got there? With Elena dead, she was hoping that The Devil would be too busy covering things up to be at home. Maybe if she spoke to his wife, she could convince her that she was in danger, too. If she could at least get Elena's daughter out of there, it would be something.

She eventually turned to Chloe. 'We need a reason to turn up. Something that won't arouse too much suspicion. But we need to make sure Davies isn't there when we arrive.'

'You'd better let me knock the door, then, since he knows you.'

Chloe had a point. He'd tried to kill her once, and that was once too many.

Chloe scratched her head. 'I could use the old "break-ins in the area" line.'

'That might work and if Davies isn't at home, you could always text me.' But then what would she say to his wife? She'd have to think of something soon as they were just minutes away.

The first thing Amelia noticed as they neared the house was the lack of cars. Hopefully, this meant that there was no one at home and they could have a nose around before leaving. Amelia decided to let Chloe drive up alone to the gates. She expected Davies to have some sort of high-security system. If he wasn't home, then she wasn't that bothered if the cameras picked them up. They weren't intending to stay long.

She received a text from Chloe within minutes of dropping her off. *NO ANSWER. I'LL COME BACK AND PICK U UP. MAYBE WE CAN FIND A WAY IN.*

When Chloe reached Amelia, she'd already made up her mind what the next step would be. There was a way on to the property, but it would involve a long trek and there was no guarantee that the family wouldn't arrive home in the meantime.

Twenty minutes and a hill climb later, Amelia and Chloe had reached the stables at the rear of the property. Davies must have assumed that no one knew about it or wouldn't bother to climb the hill to reach this area. It was still at least a half-hour walk to the house.

The first building they came across was a mock Tudor gabled stable block and paddock. Only one of the stables appeared to be occupied by a large, brown pony with a wide girth, the mount for Elena's daughter perhaps. Amelia half expected the rest of the stable to be used as a jail for kidnapped women. It would explain the girl's story of what had happened to her mother. The other stables were full of equine accessories, including a number of grooming brushes, saddles and children's horsewhips.

The walk up to the house was more exposed. At least the stable had blocked their journey so far. In front of them was a flat, well-manicured lawn that led to a children's play area consisting of a wooden playhouse that Elena's daughter would have grown out of a number of years ago, a climbing frame and swing set. Behind the play area, the patio was laid out more for adult entertainment. There was a covered bar area and a matching range of patio sofas, chairs and tables. Amelia wondered how many trafficked women had found themselves at the centre of parties here… or did Davies keep his private life separate?

What concerned Amelia was the wall of glass at the back of the house. They'd easily be spotted if they moved in that direction.

Chloe appeared to read her mind, 'We'd be better off heading towards the garages to the left. I'd hate to be caught in the middle of the lawn.'

'You're right. If we head there, it's possible we could find a better route to the house.' Her heart quickened. Their best bet was to return the way that they had come, but Chloe had already sprinted off towards the garage.

An explosive crack rang out across the lawn. Amelia watched, stunned, as Chloe fell to the ground, her face shattered by a bullet fired from close range. Streaks of crimson blood marbled the lawn in front of Amelia, who dropped to her knees.

Chapter 33

Imprisoned

It was a box, an airless, windowless box with the faintest glimmer of hope around the edges of a single door. Amelia, kneeling, traced the line of mortar surrounding each brick of her cell. For the first ten minutes, she'd counted them. How many across, how many down... 960 bricks. It stopped her thinking... remembering. She'd completed two walls and all that she'd discovered was a lack of symmetry in bricks.

The final wall faced her. She shivered, knowing this wall would be different. She could sense it – smell it, even. A natural earthiness swelled in the heart of these bricks without a pulse.

Tentatively, Amelia raised her arm knowing that, as soon as her fingers reached the beckoning wall, its past would be revealed. Warm flesh met cold steel. Resisting the desire to pull back, Amelia traced the smooth edges of the metal. Lying open, metal bird claws grasped for prey.

Women had been shackled here.

Then it all came flooding in. Her forcefield ruptured. She couldn't stop the pictures played on an everlasting loop. Chloe's blood splattered across the lawn, Joe's face smashed on the steering wheel and all the screaming women who'd been brought here over time. The women that she hadn't – couldn't – save.

Biting her tongue, Amelia stroked her stomach, trying to calm herself. She needed to get out alive for both their sakes. She was a single mother with two daughters who would be orphaned if she didn't escape. Why did she make such stupid, ridiculous decisions? There was no reason to come here. They should have been looking for evidence in other places, building a case with solid and methodical detective work, not acting on impulse. They hadn't even reported where they were going, so a rescue by the cavalry on regal steeds was out of the question. She was going to die here with her unborn child and it was all her own fault. Curling up into a ball, she lay down on the freezing concrete and forced her eyes shut.

Moments later, the door clattered open. A young girl was forced into the room, her long hair entangled in the closed fist of a tall, stern man who hissed, 'This is what you get if you misbehave, you little bitch!'

The girl squirmed, desperately trying to break away. Amelia recognised her. She was Elena's daughter, Lillian. The hissing voice belonged to The Devil. Amelia would recognise it anywhere. She'd been on the end of that fist with him whispering in her ear.

Davies must have regretted not shackling Amelia, as she now sprang into the air, roaring like a lion. Lillian slipped to the floor as he raised his arms to protect himself from Amelia's flailing hands.

'You fucking bastard, leave her alone!'

Lillian shuffled on her knees towards the door as Amelia kicked Davies in the balls. He yelped and clutched his crotch as she dragged the child by the arm out of the cell.

'Run!' she urged.

They didn't get far. Davies had locked the door between the garage and the main house. The cell had been built into the wall of a small room beside the fleet of luxury cars and motorcycles. Amelia didn't have time to admire them. As soon as she realised there was no exit, she pushed Lillian under the Range Rover closest to them.

'There's no point hiding. I bet you're wondering why I haven't killed you yet. You're such a prize, Amelia. That child you're carrying – I have so many plans for it.' Amelia knew he was close.

She looked down into the girl's pleading eyes and placed her finger on her lips. There was no time to contemplate the horrors that lay in wait for them.

The sensible thing might be to hide for as long as possible, but Amelia was rarely sensible. She lunged from behind the car and threw her body weight in the general direction of Davies. She caught him off guard, sending them both sprawling to the floor. At the same time, she heard the approaching sound of sirens.

Davies pushed Amelia off him. He was clearly winded but didn't pause as he raised his hand. Before it could connect with Amelia's head, the door to the kitchen creaked open.

A voice that Amelia recognised shrieked, 'Come here, baby, he won't hurt you now.'

Amelia thought that she must already be dead, or dreaming. The voice that was so distinctive could only belong to Elena, but Elena had been dead for some weeks now. How could this be?

She had no time to consider this as Davies pulled her to her feet, forced her arm behind her back and shoved her in the direction of the kitchen. 'Let's see what happens now I've got a hostage,' he sneered.

On the kitchen table lay a shotgun. This appeared to be normal practice here. Share your lunch with a deadly table ornament. Davies thrust Amelia towards a chair. Elena picked up the shotgun and aimed it squarely at Amelia's face.

Her daughter, ashen-faced, sat at the table. 'Don't hurt her, please. She helped me.'

'I've no intention of hurting her as long as she keeps her fucking mouth shut.' Elena motioned for Amelia to sit.

The intercom buzzed. Davies picked up the receiver on the kitchen wall. A police car and its occupants waiting at the front gates were clearly visible on the screen next to the phone. Davies, unperturbed, said, 'Hello. How can I be of help?'

The young PC spoke into the intercom. 'There's a car abandoned on the street near your home. We're just canvassing the area to see if anyone has seen the occupants.'

Without hesitation, Davies answered, 'No, we've not seen anyone, but we've been away on business and only got back a few minutes ago,'

'That's fine. Sorry to bother you. If you do see anyone, then please let us know.'

Before the PC could give them any contact details, Davies put down the receiver. The PC shrugged and the car drove away. Amelia stayed silent, barely moving on the chair, hiding the fact that she knew they were her only chance of freedom. They'd probably just canvass a few houses and then send up the helicopter. If she was really lucky, Will or someone else would have the sense to consider that she and Chloe were here. Surely they were clever enough to put two and two together? Her car being abandoned near to the home of a suspect in a trafficking case was a huge clue. But then, what had she added to the file about Davies? Practically nothing. A footnote. She'd barely had time since returning to work to make up ground and she couldn't openly admit that she'd been investigating while suspended.

Davies began laughing. 'Stupid pigs. We might as well stick her back in the cell.'

Elena glanced at him, still aiming the gun at Amelia's head. It wavered slightly. 'She needs to eat or there'll be no baby.'

'I'll take her back and you make her something. Nothing fancy, mind.' Davies grabbed the gun from Elena and motioned for Amelia to stand up. He held the shotgun to her back as he marched her back to the cell in the garage. He still didn't shackle her.

Amelia sat on the floor and stroked her stomach. *We've made it this far.*

The police had canvassed the house for a reason. Either they knew she was here and were looking for easy access, or they had no clue where she and Chloe had gone. Jake wouldn't have stepped up, but surely Will would? Or maybe Carol or Siobhan? Someone must be hunting for them. And what about Michal? Maybe there was an army of Roma boxers searching Gibbet Hill for her. It wasn't a small area and they were close enough to the university to make that an area of interest.

Her thoughts were broken when Elena opened the cell door. She shoved a tray at her. 'There you go, bitch.'

'Why are you still helping him? You could get out of here with your daughter, maybe go back to the Czech Republic. Anything would be better than this, surely?' Amelia appealed to her better nature.

'What business is it of yours? You were stupid enough to come here.' It was hard to see Elena's face in the gloom. Amelia had no idea if she was cracking. If she could just get her onside, then she might have a small chance of surviving.

'Eat.' Elena stood and went to close the door. She paused. 'There's no way out for either of us. It's time you accepted this.'

No way out. She couldn't accept that. Her daughters needed her. Lillian needed to escape this hellhole, too. Amelia bit into her sandwich. Ham salad with mayo and a steaming mug of coffee. She didn't care that, once she'd eaten and drunk, there was nowhere to relieve herself in this tiny room. It was the best sandwich she'd ever tasted.

Elena stood to leave. She turned at the door and smiled – not the kind of smile that fills you with warmth. It made Amelia shiver. She needed to remember that this woman had betrayed her many times. She wasn't her sister. They didn't stand in solidarity. She was a broken woman who held herself together with superglue, giving her a rigidity that could never be judged as kindness. But surely even this could be cracked if Amelia kept pushing. She'd helped her child and carried one of her own. Surely this was enough?

There was little time to contemplate this. No sooner had she finished her sandwich than Elena stood in front of her again, this time carrying the shotgun and not a tray. 'We're getting out of here,' she hissed.

Amelia stood. Elena prodded her with the end of the barrel. They entered the garage and went to the Range Rover. Davies stood by the rear door with a length of rope and a set of handcuffs in his hand. He shackled Amelia's hands together, pushed her onto the backseat and then tied her feet with the rope.

'Where are we going?' asked Amelia, not able to hide the tremor in her voice.

She received a heavy slap across the face in response. Davies forced his face into hers. She could feel his rancid breath on her cheek. 'None of your fucking business.'

Then he threw a heavy blanket over her.

Chapter 34

The Drive

Despite being muffled under the heavy, damp blanket, Amelia heard the garage door open. She tried to roll to knock the blanket from her face but only became further entangled. Taking a long, slow breath, she calmed herself and realised that she would hear changes in her surroundings and the road surface if she concentrated. Not being able to make out any objects through the weave of the blanket indicated that it was probably night time. It made sense to move her now. Perfect sense.

They'd been driving on gravel. It had taken a moment or two for Amelia to realise that, thinking at first that it was raining heavily. As she focussed more on the sounds, it became apparent that the noise was coming from below, not above. It felt strangely comforting, like being snuggled up in bed while a storm raged outside. The front gates whirred and they were on Gibbet Hill Road, turning left.

No one had spoken. Did that mean that Amelia was alone with the driver? She began to wriggle in the hope that, if she moved enough, then the blanket would move with her. Debating whether to speak, she rehearsed what she would say. It depended on who was driving.

Tyres screeched. 'You fucking bastard, get out of the fucking way!' Elena, then.

Amelia hoped that she didn't hear her audible sigh. Shifting on the backseat for the second time, the blanket slipped a little further. Her first sounds came out in a croak. 'Elena, is that you? Are you alone?'

Above the engine, Amelia could hear a sequenced tapping of fingers. 'Yes, bitch. Your worst nightmare.'

Amelia paused. Whatever she said could make the difference between surviving or not. Pictures formed in her head of Caitlyn and Becky. She shook them away. The blanket inched further towards the floor.

'Don't even think about trying to get close. I'm just as much a devil as he is. I know your secrets. As far as I'm concerned, you're already dead, Amelia.'

What could she do? Plead with her? Appeal to her feminine side? The only thing that linked them was that they were both mothers, if you set aside the fact that they'd been used by the same man. Whatever thoughts she had, Amelia knew that they weren't brutal enough. She had to show strength to this woman. Any show of weakness or vulnerability and she would pounce like the lioness she was. It was no good trying to appeal to a soft side that had not been allowed out of its tough skin for many years. A lioness may well be a mother, too, but it didn't stop her fighting to the death when under attack. The same was true here.

'Lost your tongue? I thought you'd be begging me to let you go by now,' Elena cackled.

The car gained speed. They were on a motorway or at least a dual carriageway. Amelia tried to calculate where they were, but it was impossible. They made it look so easy in films. Count how many times the wheels turn, humps in the road and they'd be able to say at any point that there were at a certain location.

The drumming fingers grew louder. 'You're a fool, you know that? It was so easy to trick you into believing I was dead. So easy to get Jake off my tail. He's dead, by the way. I thought you'd be happy to know that.'

Happy? Was she? It made sense then, the fact that he hadn't been at work for a few days. Why hadn't anyone checked on him?

Surely Will would have done? As Jake's minder, he should have, but maybe he was just relieved at not having to face Jake's contempt during his absence. Amelia had wondered if he'd been transferred but hadn't even bothered to ask.

'All I had to do was lie still in the truck with animal blood in my hair. I knew that wanker wouldn't even check if I was alive or dead. He needed to know that his cover was blown. It had been for ages, but it was fun watching you two run rings round each other. With me dead, he turned to you. We didn't need him around anymore. But then you turned up with that dumb sidekick of yours,' Elena laughed.

Tears came, then. She bit her lip in the vain hope that Elena couldn't hear her weeping.

'Have I upset you? I thought you were over that pathetic bastard. But of course, you're carrying his offspring. That devil spawn will never have a child.'

A child. Another child with a dead father. How did she feel about that? Relieved, God help her. There'd be no explaining her bump to him. No court cases. No paternity tests and accusations. Surely this was better. The tears began to form again, betraying her. *You're a police officer. You can't celebrate the murder of a fellow officer. Get a grip!*

Her thoughts drifted back to the child she was carrying. Elena interrupted them. 'If you haven't worked it out yet, that baby you're carrying is the only reason you're still alive.'

What the fuck did she mean? Amelia pulled her feet up towards her chest, womblike.

'There's a market for babies. Some people will pay good money to abuse a child. I should know.'

Amelia shivered and retreated into herself. This couldn't happen. She'd rather they both died.

I should know....

Of course, that made sense. Elena was taken as a small child from her mother's arms.

I should know....

No wonder she had no empathy left. How could you if, your whole life, you'd been used and abused by men. Amelia had to find some chink in her armour and quickly. Or ask for Elena's help. Maybe she still had the shotgun and could shoot her. Rather that.

'Don't even defend your child, then.' Elena couldn't stop goading her. 'You think your silence will save you? Nothing will. They'll take your child and you'll be in a country where you don't speak the language and will be beaten and fucked until you don't give a shit anymore, so ashamed and dead inside that you won't want to return to your family.'

Elena was writing the script of so many women that Amelia knew. No one understood, and many asked, 'Why don't they just leave?' Leave for where? And to what? They'd lost hope; lost any will to live.

'Elena.' It came out in a croaky whisper.

'Finally, you find your tongue. I'm looking forward to your pathetic attempt at pleading for your life.'

It came out in a rush. The bell sounded for the first round.

'Is this what you want? We can get your daughter away. Protect her. Sure, it's too late for you, but let me go and we'll protect Lillian.'

'She's safe. As long as I do as I'm told, her father will keep her safe.'

'And if he's arrested? It's only a matter of time. I can make sure she's looked after. No one else will.'

'You? You'll be far away before then. You won't care for anything, not even your own babies,' Elena sneered.

Amelia heard the sound of the indicator blinking. They were leaving the motorway and slowing.

'I need the toilet. Don't fucking move, bitch.'

The driver's door opened and shut. Amelia tried to sit up. She moved her feet to the edge of the seat. The blanket was caught around them. She tried lifting her feet, but they were locked tightly together. The more she moved, the more tangled she became. Then she tried rolling over but that made things worse.

The passenger door opened. Elena tore off the blanket from her head.

'Here.' She thrust a bottle of water towards her face and dripped a few drops into Amelia's open mouth. 'Can't have that baby dying yet,' she muttered.

This didn't mean she cared, just that she saw the baby as a commodity to be protected. Elena wrapped the blanket tighter around her and covered her face again.

Amelia needed more time to think. Whatever she'd said so far had not broken the surface. She was miles away from freedom. In fact, she was probably making things worse. Silence fell.

Darkness enclosed the space. Shadows formed at the edge of Amelia's vision. The horsemen were leading her to her fate. She needed a miracle.

Darth Vader's theme tune rang out. Amelia physically jumped, unaware that she'd dozed off.

Elena answered the call. 'We're on our way. Stop panicking. We should be there by three. There's barely any traffic.'

Amelia almost smiled. This was the car usually driven by Lillian's stepmother. The ringtone for Davies was obviously chosen by her. She clearly had a sense of humour.

Elena didn't press the speaker button, clearly not wanting Amelia to hear the conversation.

'What do you mean? You said you'd meet me there... I'm not going with her. You can't force me to... Don't threaten me, you bastard! I'm dropping her off, that's it. Then I'm coming back to Coventry.'

There was a long pause. The tension was palpable. 'If you're not there with Lillian then I'll go to the police. We have a deal.'

Elena had just signed her own death warrant. Surely she understood that. This was the miracle that Amelia could only dream about.

The call ended abruptly.

'You know he's never going to give Lillian to you.'

'Shut up, bitch.'

'He's probably taken her halfway across the country by now. You've been travelling in one direction, she'll be heading in another.'

'What do you care? You'll be on a boat soon.'

A boat. So, that was where they were going – to a port and on a boat. Where to? France, then somewhere in Europe? Maybe further afield. She couldn't let that happen.

'I do care, Elena. I've always tried to do my best for you. You've betrayed me at every turn, but the offer still stands.'

'There's nothing you can do. Just accept your fate.'

'If you let me go, there's plenty I can do and you know it. We can get the police to Gibbet Hill before he leaves if we're quick.'

'He's already left. It's too late.'

'Then they'll put out an APB on him. He'll be Britain's Most Wanted. He's abducted one police officer and killed two others.'

There was a short-lived silence. Then Elena spoke steadily and calmly: 'How do you know it wasn't me that killed them?'

Amelia let this sink in. She needed a knock-out blow now more than ever.

'I don't know, but at least in prison you'd still see your daughter. You have my word, Elena.'

It always came back to that.

Amelia waited for a response. The speed of the car increased for the next five minutes and then slowed. She heard the indicator. They left the motorway and, after a few minutes, the car came to a halt. It could be just a coincidence and they'd come to the end of the motorway.

The driver's door opened and then the passenger door. Cold air rushed in, which made the edges of the blanket flutter.

Amelia sensed Elena's warm breath above her. She tore off the blanket. The first thing Amelia noticed was the matted mascara bleeding from Elena's eyes. Had she won?

'I haven't got the key to the handcuffs. Can you get out?'
Freedom.

"I'll try.' Without the heaviness of the blanket, Amelia was able to swing her legs round so she could at least sit up.

'Can you get out of the car?' Elena wiped her nose with the back of her hand.

'Just call the police. You can leave me here and get away.' Amelia couldn't quite believe that she'd suggested that. She bit her tongue.

Elena looked around her. It was pitch dark. There were lights, possibly from a farm, but it could be as far as a few miles away. It must be early in the morning at least. They'd be getting ready to start the day.

Elena got back into the car and said, 'Dial 999'.

Amelia mouthed, 'Thank you.'

Chapter 35

Release

The police took twenty minutes to reach her. Elena had long gone.

The only thing Amelia wanted to do was go home to her family, but that had to wait. They only allowed her to call them. Even then, there was an army of officers in the room and Amelia didn't want to look like a wuss by saying what she really wanted to say. It was clear that she'd been missing for some time. The relief in her mother's voice made that obvious.

Davies had disappeared. The police had gone back to Gibbet Hill that evening to find that the house had been ransacked in the rush to leave. There was no sign of Lillian, either. The stepmother had returned to the house an hour later. She said she'd been working, which Amelia took to mean that Davies was prostituting her, too.

The worst part was explaining that Chloe was dead. Amelia couldn't hold back the tears, then. Whoever had shot her, whether it was Davies or Elena, had killed her instantly, but there was no sign of her body at the property. Surely they wouldn't have taken her with them? Amelia couldn't imagine the pain this would bring – her family not knowing where she was. She wouldn't rest until they'd found the body.

Superintendent Rodgers entered the room after Amelia had finished her statement. He scratched his scalp and ran his hand through his unnaturally brown hair.

'Now Amelia, explain how you got away.'

Amelia stood up, sending the chair she was sitting on flying backwards. 'I'll explain when I've seen my family,' Amelia said through gritted teeth.

'You'll explain now, or I'll have no choice but to arrest you.'

'What the... for what, exactly? For getting abducted and talking my way out of it?'

'That's exactly it, Amelia. Why the hell would they let you go unless you're caught up in it?' His face grew redder and redder. By the time it had reached puce, he blurted out, 'Nothing seems to have stopped you from entangling yourself in this gang. Even when suspended, you were still hanging around them. How do we know if you were investigating or getting more deeply involved?'

Amelia launched herself across the table. She had to be restrained from grabbing Rodgers by the throat. She hadn't noticed that Will had entered the room. He pushed her back into her chair and said, 'I think everyone should calm down. There's no questioning Amelia's motives. Jake's, however...'

Jake. Amelia had forgotten about him. She hadn't even mentioned that he was most likely dead. 'When did you last hear from him, Will?'

Will sat down next to Amelia. 'It's been about ten days. I thought he was on sick leave. That's right isn't it?' Will looked directly at Rodgers, who was doing everything not to look in their direction.

'Well... umm. I haven't heard from him either. I thought he was working undercover. You're his minder.' Rodgers pointed the finger back at Will. He wasn't taking responsibility.

'That operation was over a couple of weeks ago. You knew that. We had information on Davies, but you said that it wasn't enough to implicate him in the trafficking ring and we'd need at least a body or the van that Jake had seen.' Will's retort was sharp.

Amelia stared at Rodgers. 'You knew about the van and *still* you didn't arrest Davies?'

'There wasn't enough evidence, Amelia.'

'We thought there was a dead woman in the back of it and it wasn't enough?'

'Well,' Davies spluttered, sending spit across the table. 'She wasn't dead, though, was she?'

'You didn't know that at the time. Seems to me that none of these women are important to you.' Amelia lay her head on the table. She'd had enough.

'Back to the main question. Why did Elena let you go?'

'Just let me go home. I'll write a statement tomorrow. I need to see my girls.' Amelia stood and headed towards the door. *Arrest me if you must.*

By the time she reached home, Amelia was ready to resign. She'd written the letter in her head and planned on emailing it that night.

As soon as her key turned in the door, her family were hugging her. She couldn't tell where one person started and another ended. When Amelia finally looked up, she noticed Jola sitting on the stairs. Her eyes were hooded, and she kept glancing up towards her bedroom.

'I just need to speak with Jola a minute and see how she's settled in.' Amelia followed Jola upstairs. Caitlyn followed her closely until her grandmother took her to one side and suggested she helped her make everyone a special welcome home lunch.

When Jola closed her bedroom door, she looked directly at Amelia. 'Elena's in your garage. She needs your help. Please, find Lillian. Elena will disappear then, but she'll help you put Davies in prison.'

Amelia mulled this over. Of course, what she should do was to contact Rodgers. She didn't have her mobile. Davies had taken it. 'Jola, can I borrow your phone?'

Jola caught hold of her arm. 'Please… please don't bring the police here.'

'I've got to sort this out, Jola. Don't worry, just give me your phone.'

Jola put her hand in her jeans pocket and pulled out a new iPhone, no doubt a present from Amelia's mother with the justification, 'You'll need to keep in contact with us when you take the girls out.'

Amelia stepped out on to the landing and dialled a number from memory.

Carol answered on the third ring. 'Hi. It's Amelia.'

'My God! You scared the shit out of us all. I thought you were dead!' Carol pulled no punches.

'Good to speak to you, too.'

Amelia explained the problem as best as she could. Who do you call when you want to keep a witness safe? Certainly not an incompetent Super. It was Carol's job at the People's Protection Unit.

Carol was silent for a few minutes. 'I don't know, Amelia. It sounds like she may have committed murder. I can't protect her from that.'

'But we don't know that, and if she can give us a full account of the business, think about what we'd have – the traffickers, the punters –'

'Not my call.'

'We'd be able to free the remaining women, Carol. She's all we've got. We don't even know where they're being kept.'

'I've got to run this past people. I can't just come and get her.'

'I know. I'll keep her here. Please do your best.'

'Always.'

Amelia sighed. The chances that Carol would be able to help were slim. She was probably on the phone to her boss right now and that'd be another stick to beat her with.

Jola was sitting on the edge of her bed, biting her nails. 'Let the girls know that I'll be back shortly.'

'Can't I come with you?'

'Believe me. You don't want to be part of anything I'm involved in.'

Elena was sitting in one of their old camping chairs when Amelia entered her garage. Her legs and arms were crossed as though waiting for a late appointment.

'Well?'

'I've asked a friend to help. Davies is still missing. I think we can assume that Lillian's with him.'

Elena stood. 'A friend?'

Amelia felt herself rise up, displaying her full height like a peacock. 'Carol works for Witness Protection.'

'No –'

'You can't stay here. What the hell did you think would happen?'

'I thought you might know if he's been found. I'll give you anything you need, but I'm not going to prison.'

'You'll have to negotiate that with the PPU.'

Elena launched herself at Amelia, catching her off balance. They both landed heavily on the concrete floor. Elena punched Amelia in the face before she had the chance to block the blow. This didn't stop Amelia. She forced Elena back with her arm across her throat. Elena had almost toppled backwards, but she was strong – she managed to grab a fistful of Amelia's hair and used it as a lever to smash her head on the concrete.

Amelia spotted a shadow behind Elena and, before she could say anything, Elena was pulled back off Amelia. Before Amelia could even get up off the floor, Elena was face down with her hands in handcuffs. Carol just grinned at her.

'If you think I'm taking this lowlife into police protection, then you've got another think coming.'

Amelia wiped her bloody nose on her sleeve and felt the back of her head. There was an egg-sized lump already forming. 'Let's go into the house so I can get cleaned up before the girls see me.'

Carol held Elena's arm in a lock. 'I'm not changing my mind.'

Amelia opened the garage door. 'Tell Rodgers then. See what happens next.'

Chapter 36

Jake

It wasn't her job to check on Jake. It was possible that others had already done it. But then she realised that he hadn't made a big announcement that his marriage had ended, making it entirely possible that no one at WMROCU had his new address. She felt compelled to check.

Instead of entering her house, Amelia drove the few miles to Jake's flat. Before leaving the car, she flipped down the sun visor and checked herself in the mirror. If Jake was at home nursing his hurt pride, then she didn't want to turn up bloodied. In the glove compartment, she found a pack of tissues and, just as she'd wiped her children's faces when they were younger, she spat on one and used it to remove the blood from under her nose. The bridge of her nose throbbed and had begun to bruise but it wasn't noticeable if you weren't looking for it.

Amelia sighed and left the car. The outside of the flat looked as dull as ever. The lawn had been freshly mown and Amelia fought the urge to sneeze. Jake's flat was on the second floor, accessible by a set of stairs to the right of the entrance. There were no signs of police tape or the presence of white-suited officers, so either Jake was fine, or they hadn't found his body yet. As she stepped on the first stair, her head began to spin. She paused before continuing. It was probably just a delayed reaction from being punched.

When Amelia reached Jake's flat, she knocked as hard as any officer would. No one answered. What now? Maybe she should peer through the letterbox to see if there was a body lying prone across the hallway, or perhaps she should contact the local force to break in. But Amelia didn't need to do either of these things. The lock was your basic Yale and it wouldn't take a master thief to break in. Any local teenage burglar could manage it in a minute. It took her less than thirty seconds.

She recognised the smell immediately – the metallic smell that made lesser officers gag. She knew she should turn, leave the premises and phone it in but she felt compelled to see for herself. He could be in need of medical treatment. She knew though, deep in her gut. She knew he was dead and there was nothing she could do about it.

She found him lying sprawled on the bed, his naked body striped in red almost as though someone had sprayed him with paint. But they hadn't. They'd sliced him open like a piece of meat. Could Elena have done this? Or was it The Devil? Whoever it was must have been raging. This wasn't a calculated hit. It was butchery, not done by an expert but someone who wanted to kill… had good reason to. The force was unnecessary. One of these cuts would have been enough. Someone wanted revenge, pure and simple.

If she had murdered Jake, it would look like this, she soon realised. Not that she could have done it – it wasn't in her DNA.

Amelia exhaled. She hadn't noticed that since entering the bedroom, she hadn't moved or even taken a breath. It was time to report this. Then she could go home, knowing that there was nothing else she could do. Her family needed her now.

Chapter 37

Baby Shower

Three months later, Amelia sat at the large table in Poppy's Place surrounded by pastel-coloured parcels and balloons.

'Surprise!' yelled Siobhan, pulling a party popper.

'You've got to be bloody kidding me. A baby shower! When I had the other two, you were lucky if you got a few hand me downs from the last poor sod who'd gone off on maternity for a month.' Amelia prodded one of the parcels.

Carol raised a glass of something sparkly. 'And don't think you're doing that either. Take at least a few months. It'll all still be here when you get back.'

All except Chloe.

Amelia raised a glass to her without words.

'At least you can go off on maternity leave knowing that they're finally hunting The Devil.' Kesia still looked as concerned as she had the day Amelia went to visit her and Michal soon after she'd been rescued.

Amelia raised her glass again. 'Thanks to Elena, they've got enough dirt on him to send him down for good. But they've got to find him and his daughter first.'

'She came good in the end,' Carol begrudgingly raised her

glass, 'although it took a massive amount of wrangling with the CPS. I'm sure the whole thing put years on me.'

'Oh, well. You'll just have to find a young, handsome detective to take them back off again,' Amelia giggled.

'You did make sure she got the non-alcoholic version of the bubbly, didn't you?' Siobhan looked at Carol, who just smiled.

'Here's to us women.' They all raised their glasses for one last time.

Here's to Chloe.

* * *

Printed in Great Britain
by Amazon

41577652R00121